She exhaled and held him tighter.

"You being here makes it harder for me to get over you. I have to protect myself from you." She sniffed. His hands gently caressed her smooth back. "I know you need to be here and to be honest, I want you here. However, after you eliminate this threat you are going back to Atlanta. I'll still be in love with you and you will still be in denial. The fight will continue counselor." She could feel the heat emanating from his body. Placing her head more snuggly in the crook of his neck, she continued. "I have to set some rules."

"Rules?" He kissed her wet shoulder as his hands moved lower to her waist.

"Yes." She pulled his shirt from his pants to touch the heat she knew was beneath. "Rules just for you."

Printed in the United States of America
ISBN-13: 978-0-9801066-8-8
ISBN-10: 0-9801066-8-0
Library of Congress Control Number: 2013900501

This is a work of fiction. Names, characters, places and
incidents are with the product of the author's imagination or
are used fictitiously, and any resemblance to actual persons,
living or dead, business establishments, events, locales is
entirely coincidental.

SIRI ENTERPRISES
RICHMOND, VIRGINIA
www.sirient.com

Dedication

Cathy Atchison, a loving spirit whose undying commitment to giving the best of herself each day touches the life of many.

Acknowledgements

Thank you my Heavenly Father, My family, Raymond, Chris and Champaine and all those associate with Siri Enterprises, thank you for allowing me to be me. The woman who keep it real and drama free, Loretta R. Walls, Nikkea Smithers, Victoria Wells, Lafonde Harris, Rosaline Terry, Judith Wansley, Monica Jackson, Heather Jones-Marable, Angela Burrell, Zelda Holmes-Johnson and Shannon Pernell, thank you for the tears, laughter and hugs when I need them. Thank you to Deatri Bey-King and the Romance Slam Jam Organization. You inspire us to be the best we can in the literary field. Thank you for being there.

The following ladies are the inspiration for characters in one of my novels. They are introduced here, and you will see them again. They are: MsPrissy Parker (Karess Parker), Andrea Junee (Raven Junee), Cynthia Morgan-Medley (Genesis Morgan) and Loretta R. Walls (Rene Naverone). Thank you for the wonderful characters.

To the readers, it is your unyielding devotion to the written word that keep us, authors true to the game. Thank you and enjoy, **THE PENDLETON RULE**.

ALSO BY IRIS BOLLING

THE HEART SERIES

ONCE YOU'VE TOUCHED THE HEART

THE HEART OF HIM

LOOK INTO MY HEART

A HEART DIVIDED

A LOST HEART

THE HEART

NIGHT OF SEDUCTION SERIES

NIGHT OF SEDUCTION/HEAVEN'S GATE

THE PENDLETON RULE

GEMS & GENTS SERIES

TEACH ME

THE PENDLETON RULE

Prologue

*T*he same memory put Tyrone "Ty" Pendleton to sleep every night.

He took her hand and walked her over to the bed. Sitting on the edge of the bed, she stood between his legs. Gathering her waist in his hands, he pulled her close then kissed her navel. Reaching around, he cupped her rear end squeezing as if his life depended on them being there.

She slid her hands across his shoulders, down his muscle bound arms, around to his back, touching, feeling, and kneading. He reached into his nightstand and pulled out a condom, which she immediately took from him, "Allow me," she moaned as she bent down on her knees. She licked her lips, pleased with the sight that greeted her. Kissing his inner thigh on one leg, his member jumped at the feel of her breath near it. To be fair, she kissed the other thigh, sending surges of sensations through his body.

"Kiki." He dropped his head to touch hers.

"I know baby. I'm admiring." He moaned in response. She opened the package, held the latex in her hand, and took his member in her mouth.

Ty nearly leaped off the bed at her touch but she held onto his thighs. This was a new experience for her, but it was there, and so tempting, she just had to feel it on her tongue. He withdrew from her mouth, took the latex, and covered himself with the protection. Seizing her waist, he lifted her, kissed her, and entered her in one smooth motion. They both groaned at the touch, and began moving to a rhythm as old as time.

Two souls--becoming one with a need and hunger so deep they could not have stopped if their lives depended on it. Nothing could have quenched the passion of their two spirits as he drove deeper and deeper into her throne, searching and finding that glory that only he could expose and touch.

Holding on to the feeling of total ecstasy, she screamed out her orgasm. Her inner walls contracted around him, pulling everything he had to give, rhythmically squeezing his member from its base to the tip, demanding his release. He cursed when the release came, but reveled in the feel of it at the same time. It was too soon, he was not ready for it to end. Holding her, he turned onto his back bringing her to lie on top of him, never breaking their intimate contact.

They lay there holding, caressing, and kissing each other until he began to grow hard inside her again. Kissing his neck, his chest, his nipples, she slid down his body then sat up, and began slowly moving her body against him. The power and control of the position was what she loved. She controlled how deep he would go and she wanted him deep, as deep as her body would allow. Taking her waist in his *hands he raised his legs behind her as her body bucked wildly, attempting to fulfill its need. Her release came first. He pumped deeper and harder until he screamed her name.*

"Kiki," he sprang up in the bed, with sweat dripping from his aroused body. His morning had begun. Swiping his hand down his dark chocolate unshaven face, he exhaled, then threw the sheet aside. Sitting on the side of the bed, all he could do was shake his head knowing he had to endure yet another day without the woman who crept into his life, then left him shattered. The Luther Vandross song Creepin' came to mind as it had every morning. The one line, 'Why must it be, you always creep into my dream', was now his Achilles' heel. And as always, thoughts of the last day they were together followed.

"You want me to move to Atlanta to live with you?"

There was something in the way she asked that put his senses on alert. He pulled her body on top of his so he could see her eyes. The truth always resided in the eyes. "Yes. You could work from here. I'll help you get office space and get established here."

Their bodies were still trembling from the explosion that seemed to increase every time they made love.

Her eyes bore into his. "Then what Ty?" She caressed his chest, as her thighs tightened around his waist. "Will you eventually make an honest woman out of me?"

He closed his eyes. "Kiki," he rubbed her thighs, "I can't promise you that."

The caress stopped. "Then what are we doing?"

Opening his eyes, he was met with questioning ones. "We're enjoying being with each other, Kiki. Which is about all any human being can ask from another."

"I always thought that was love, Ty. The only and most precious thing that's worth having from another human, is

love." She stared at him. "See, let me show you how it's done." She kissed his eyes, his cheeks then his lips. Sitting back up, she smiled. "I love you, Tyrone Pendleton. I want to spend the rest of my life waking up just like this every morning."

"I want that too." He cupped her face, "That's why I asked you to move in with me."

"She held his hands to her face. "What about marriage, the house, white picket fence, two point three children?"

"That's not for me Kiki."

"What do you mean it's not for you?" She dropped her hands.

"That's life for Jason and Eric." He exhaled, "I'm a different breed." He dropped his hands to her thighs and continued to talk freely. "Jason writes the love songs Eric sings. I can't recite a love poem and don't want to. It only leads to pain."

She moved from the position of straddling him to sit on the bed beside him.

"What about the pleasure of love?"

He interrupted before she could finish. "The pleasure eventually turns into pain." He threw his legs over the side of the bed and stood. "Those two point three kids you talk about are usually not wanted and their parents end up leaving them behind. Believe me, I know." He picked up his shirt and slacks that had been thrown on the floor, folded them neatly and placed them across the arm of the chair next to the entrance to the bathroom. "I'm going to take a shower. Think about where you want to have breakfast," he said as he walked into the shower.

Ty turned off the shower, walked back into his bedroom to find it the same way he did that confusing day-empty.

Durham, North Carolina

"Once we go down this road there is no turning back until the deed is done." The person known as Rupid A. Mann sat in his vehicle outside the office of the man he had been hired to punish. His job was to right wrongs. Whose right or wrong depends on who was depositing the payment into his offshore accounts. "Be sure this is what you want."

"Complete this task the way I requested and your payment will be doubled."

"Let me reiterate, this type of revenge has a way of backfiring."

"My money, my way."

"As you wish. From this point on there will be no contact. Confirmation of the initial deposit into my account will set things in motion. Once the last task on the list is complete, you have twenty-four hours to submit the final payment. If the deposit is late, the penalty is death. Are we clear?" The sound on the disposable cell phone he bought for this job indicated a message had come through. Checking the screen he found a deposit of two hundred and fifty-thousand dollars had been deposited into his account.

"I don't like being threatened," the voice on the other end replied.

"Nature of the beast you unleashed." He replied then disconnected the call. It never ceased to amaze him how often people wanted to dictate how he did his job. They hired him to eliminate issues in their lives because he is the best in the business. If they could handle the situation themselves, he would be unemployed.

Parked in a rental car, several buildings down from his target's office, Rupid observed his surroundings. There was a clear view of the front entrance to the building. Surveillance of his target showed his normal path was a walk across the street to the parking deck where his vehicle was located on level three. The target would not reach his destination tonight.

The rain was relentlessly coming down in sheets as Rupid continued to survey the area. Yes, this first deed would be easy, he thought while adjusting his seat back to relax. His target worked late regularly and tonight was no different. It was a Thursday night around eight-twenty. The combination of the rain and the late hour rendered the streets practically deserted. Parked directly in front of him was a small vehicle, a mid-size sedan was in front of that, and a large white van was in front of the sedan, at the entrance into the parking deck. The van shielded him from the target's view, giving him the option of taking the man out before he reached the parking deck. If that didn't pan out, he would go with the original plan to take him once inside the deck. For now, he sat and waited.

An hour later, the door to the office he was watching opened and the target stepped out, locking the door behind him. Rupid watched as he ran across the street in a trench coat and hat, with a soft briefcase in his hand. Easing from the vehicle, Rupid walked briskly on the blind side of the van, ensuring that he would not be detected by the target. When he rounded the van the target was just at the entrance to the parking deck. He wasn't two steps from his target when he called out.

"Roy Kelly." The target turned just as he clicked the release to the four-inch jagged blade.

Roy Kelly stopped, but before he could respond the blade was shoved into his belly and twisted upwards. Roy Kelly's eyes widened with shock and pain.

"You're not going to die. You will only wish you had." The flash of confusion appeared in Roy's eyes. "Backstabbing a partner isn't cool Roy." He twisted the blade upward. "Karma is a bitch." He shrugged his shoulder and pulled the blade from Roy's body, turned, then disappeared as quickly as he had appeared.

Chapter One
Atlanta, Georgia

*I*t was two in the morning. Other CEO's with multi-million dollar businesses were in a comfortable bed cozied up with the wife, or mistress, or enjoying a peaceful rest by themselves. Not, Ty Pendleton. The Pendleton Agency clientele did not often allow restful nights. The clientele ranged from entertainers in the music and film industry to a few sports notables. To ensure his clients acquired lucrative endorsement deals, it was his job to keep their reputations clean. This proved to be a challenge from time to time. Tonight was one of those times.

"Where is he?" Ty asked, as he stepped out of his silver CL600 Mercedes Coupe.

"Security is holding him and his posse downstairs away from cameras," Tower Number One replied.

"How many?" Ty asked as he eased his long arms through his suit jacket, which he'd pulled from the back seat of the car.

"Eight," Tower One replied as he closed the car door. "You want me with you, Boss?"

"No, I can handle them," Ty replied scanning the area to assess the people standing around. The paparazzi had a special way of attempting to blend in. Spotting them ahead of time was the key to successfully avoiding them. "Ten o'clock, two and six."

Tower looked to his left, then to his right. "I see them. I'll move the ride to the secure exit."

"No, they're probably staked out there as well. Meet us at the tunnel entrance."

Tower One moved the car as Ty made his way across the street. ARC was one of the premiere nightclubs located in downtown Atlanta. Because of its elegant decor and unique style of entertainment, the patrons were members of the higher echelon of the economic ladder. Athletes, entertainers and socialites frequented the establishment regularly. Thus, the paparazzi practically lived there. Ty was recognized the moment he stepped onto the sidewalk. A line of party seekers were still waiting to get inside, when one of the bouncers opened the door to let him enter. "Mr. Pendleton, Naverone is waiting for you in Security A."

"Thank you, Clyde. You doing okay tonight?"

"Yes sir, thank you for asking."

"Take care man," Ty replied as he stepped into the lobby. Few knew the reason for the glass doors with chrome casing, but Ty knew inside the casing were metal detectors. The owners of ARC ran a clean establishment, with a first class security team that ensured minimal interruptions for the patrons that paid top dollars to party without drama. This call was a courtesy, from the head of the security team. While they prided themselves on drama free partying, they did not tolerate any behavior that could lead to a call to Atlanta's finest or a lawsuit for the club. To handle athletes and entertainers who earned more money than God, one had to use tact and at times coercion to get them to cooperate. This is where Ty came in. Unfortunately for his clients, Ty's level of tact was limited.

"Good evening Mr. Pendleton." The doormen dressed in black suits, white shirts and thin black ties spoke as they opened the door. Music from level one was bumping with the latest dance beats and the crowd's boisterous voices indicating their appreciation for the sounds. Ty turned to his left to take the stairwell, choosing not to walk through the crowd to take the elevator to the lower level. The basement of the five-story club was just as elegantly decorated as the upper levels. The stairwell was lined with framed pictures of celebrities that had visited the club and the owners. The carpet was so thick, you felt as if you were walking on a cloud. The offices carried the same chrome, glass doors as at the entrance, however, the inside was furnished in rich cherry wood with leather chairs.

Ty entered the third door on the right to find Naverone waiting for him. "We really have to stop meeting like this."

Naverone looked up to see Tyrone Pendleton standing in the doorway. At six-two, one hundred and ninety-five pounds, Ty was a dark chocolate, bow-legged, Armani suit wearing brother that made her inner lips moist just from watching him walk. She had experienced first hand that he knew exactly how to use that body to make a woman proud to be a woman. A year or two ago things were pretty good between them until another woman came into the picture. From that moment on, Ty was lost to her.

"It seems this is the only way I get to see you these days." Rene Naverone stood to reveal all five-six, one hundred thirty pounds, dressed in a black, form fitting, off the shoulder, shell dress that stopped mid-thigh, black knee high spiked boots, with her hair brushed in a ponytail that hung to the side across her shoulders. "This is getting old Mr. Pendleton."

"We're back to Mr. Pendleton now?"

"Your doing." She walked up to him, staring intently into his eyes. "You look tired. It's been over a year. Still not sleeping?"

Holding her stare, he acknowledged Rene Naverone was as beautiful as she was dangerous. The combination was sexy as hell. She just wasn't the natural haired, slim beauty that went by the name of Kiki Simmons. "I'm well."

"I can make you better."

Ty smiled. "I know." He softly kissed her lips.

She sighed, "Only a crazy woman would let all your dark chocolate go to waste." Stepping away from him, she opened the door. "Let's get your boy."

They walked across the hall. "It's quiet. They must have calmed down."

She shook her head. "We sound proofed the rooms." She swiped a card in the reader next to the opening, then pushed the door open. "I got tired of hearing the foul language."

When the door opened, the loud voices echoed through the hallway. The door closed behind them. Ty and Naverone stood at the entrance as they watched, eight supposedly grown men, sitting on a circular sectional leather sofa arguing over a game on the monitors. There was food and various bottles of alcohol on the table with glasses half full.

Ty looked at Naverone with a raised eyebrow. "Owners want them to feel comfortable while in the detaining room." Naverone replied as she pushed the control panel on the wall turning the game off.

"What the hell?" One of the men jumped up and yelled. "Bitch, turn that back on."

Before Ty knew it, Naverone had knocked the young man to the floor, had her spiked heel pressed to his throat and her Glock pointed in his face. "I got your bitch for you. Want to know what she feels like?"

"Damn Joe, man, she knocked your ass out." Jason Whitfield, the twenty-two year old newly acquired NBA player with a multi-million dollar endorsement deal pending, laughed. Thus the reason for Ty's presence.

"You got this?" He asked looking at Naverone, who was bent over the man known now as Joe.

Ty walked over to the sofa. "Let's go Jason."

Jason looked over his shoulder. "I ain't ready to go, man." He slouched back down on the sofa and picked up the controller. "Turn that switch back on, man."

Naverone was right, he thought. This is getting old. Ty unbuttoned his suit jacket, walked in front of Jason. "Get up and let's go now, or you can kiss the deal and me goodbye."

Jason stood up, towing over Ty who stood six-two. "You work for me, man. You don't tell me what to do. I tell you to jump and your only question should be how high."

Naverone stood, at the raised voice directed at Ty. "You got that?"

Ty nodded. "I'm good," he replied as he pulled out his phone. He pushed a button, then waited for the call to connect. He smiled when the person answered. "I apologize for the delay." He listened as the other person replied.

"Man, what the hell are you doing? I'm talking to you."

Ty put a finger up and silenced Jason. "Yes, that's him. Hold on." He pushed the speaker button and held the phone out for Jason.

"Who the hell is it?"

"It's your mother," the woman on the other end of the phone yelled. "What are you doing talking to Mr. Pendleton in that tone of voice? You apologize to him right now. You hear me, Jason?"

"Yes ma'am," a seething Jason stared at Ty. "I apologize Mr. Pendleton."

"I can't believe you're talking to him in that tone at his home. I know I taught you better than that. Do I have to wake your father up?"

"That's not necessary Mrs. Whitfield. We were playing a card game and things got a little heated," Ty glared at Jason. "We're good. I'll have Jason call you back in the morning. Have a good night." Ty hung up the phone.

"Man, he called your mother on you." One of the men in the room laughed.

Jason ignored his friends. "Man, you supposed to have my back."

Ty folded his arms across his chest. "Let's clarify our arrangement. I got mine, you trying to get yours. I don't need you or your little commission to live. You on the other hand need me to make this deal happen. Your ego is the last thing I'm concerned with. You want to let your friends interfere with a multi-million dollar deal that's going to change your economic status? Go ahead. I can walk away from this deal, can you?" Ty walked over to the door and held it open.

Jason hesitated as he stared at Ty. He threw the remote across the room then followed Ty out of the room.

"I'll send a car for them," Ty said to Naverone who had holstered her weapon.

"You taking the tunnel?"

"Yes." He kissed Naverone's temple. "Thank you for the call."

"Anytime." She watched as Ty walked away in his Armani suit. *The man looks good coming or going.* She shook her head, then turned back to the men in the room.

The view from the twenty-fifth floor office of Entertainment Agent, Tyrone Pendleton did not have the appeal that it once had. Standing in yet another Armani suit, Italian loafers, with only a few hours of sleep, it just didn't feel like home anymore. Granted, he knew this point in his life , when the business did not fulfill his needs, would eventually come around, but did not think he would feel so empty.

Thirty-five year-old Ty, as everyone called him, was a self-made man. Working hard since he was sixteen, he always put half of his paycheck into the bank, gave his adopted mother, Miriam Davies, something for allowing him to live with her and her two sons, Jason and Eric, and kept a little something in his pockets for himself. By the time he entered college, he was shocked to find that Miriam had invested every dime he had given her over the years. His graduation gift was a cashier's check large enough to cover his college tuition for undergrad and law school. Still, his work ethics never changed.

"Mr. Pendleton," Wendy, his secretary of five years' voice interrupted his somber review of his life. "Your mother is on line two."

8

"Thank you Wendy," Ty replied as he pushed the speaker button on the telephone sitting on top of his desk. "Yes, Mother, I have eaten. I even had vegetables," he said with a quirk of a smile.

"Don't try to out think me Tyrone Sylvester Pendleton," Miriam replied with a smile he could hear even with her being thousands of miles away.

"I would never attempt to do such a thing," he sat at his desk. "How is Paris?"

"Beautiful as always. Speaking of which, I met this beautiful model named Giselle. I told her all about my only single son and she seems very interested in knowing when you are coming for a visit. I'm sure she would love to show you parts of Paris I haven't experienced."

"I don't believe there is any part of Paris you haven't experienced and I have no idea how we ventured into the topic of women."

"You mentioned beautiful things..."

"No," he interrupted her. "I asked how was Paris. You said beautiful, then proceeded with the introduction of Giselle."

"So you remember her name."

Ty laughed at the futile attempt of his mother to continue down the road of trying to marry him off. "You are incorrigible Mother. Even so, it's good to hear from you."

"I felt you needed me."

It was uncanny how Miriam Davies always knew when he needed to hear her voice.

During his college years, while everyone else was pledging, playing ball, or just playing the field, Ty was working or studying. She would call and ask, "Are you eating well? What vegetables did you have?" Then she would always sneak in, "Did you meet anyone special yet?" As he grew older, she wasn't as subtle anymore. The questions were very direct. "When are you going to meet a nice girl and settle down?" He always wondered how could a woman, whose blood did not run through his veins, be so in tune with his needs? "I'm well Mother."

"That's your physical condition. How's your love life?"

"Nonexistent, and I'm fine with that."

"It's not healthy for a good looking, hot blooded, single man not to be dating regularly, especially a son of mine. You should be having sex nightly."

The statement caused him to sit up. "Mother, I am not discussing my sex life with you," he stated in that quiet no room for compromise tone.

"From what I've been told it would be a short conversation."

"Mother, I'm fine. I don't need my mother to find me companionship when I need it." He snapped. "I hope there is another reason for your call."

"I know you better get you some sex before you lose your life speaking to me in that manner."

"Mother, he sighed, "I didn't mean to snap. I'm working on three hours of sleep today."

"I know you didn't." He could hear that mother's got something to say voice and she's going to say it whether you want to hear it or not. "You are agitated because you are not getting any on a regular. I suggest you find Kiki and mend your broken heart. However, I understand that is not my business and I throw my hands up on the topic. You will not hear me say another word about the woman you should have married and gave me some grand babies."

"I thought you weren't going to say another word," he replied in a teasing manner.

"Well, it wasn't one word it was several. Now that I've had my say, that's not why I called."

Hearing the smile return to her voice, Ty sat back in his chair then swung around to look out the window. "I'm happy to hear that. What do you need?"

"Your mother is being awarded a lifetime music award. Since you are the only single son I have left, I would like for you to escort me." She hesitated. "We've all noticed you have been distancing yourself from the family, though I don't know why. So, before you say no, you should understand, this is not a request. I expect you to escort me. Now, I'm getting off the phone and lick my wounds."

"Mother," he hesitated. The last thing he ever wanted to do was hurt the woman that took him in when his own mother disappeared. "It will be my honor to have a beautiful woman on my arm. Let me know the day and time."

He thought he heard a sniffle. "I love you Tyrone. It's been too long since you've visited with the whole family. We miss you."

"I miss all of you too."

"We'll talk soon?"

"Definitely."

Ty could tell by the tone of her voice that he had hurt his mother's feelings when he snapped at her. He closed his eyes and said a short prayer asking for forgiveness. He was the successful man today because of her unyielding love. She was so determined to make him feel a part of her family that at times she sided with him even when she knew he was wrong. His brothers, Jason and Eric, didn't appreciate that at times and they fought, just like brothers. She never wanted him to feel she loved him any less than her biological boys. In return, he did everything he could to always make her proud of him.

While in law school he decided he wanted to be an agent. He was constantly giving advice to some of the athletes on campus about potential contracts or endorsement deals. Always insisting that whatever contract they signed included a financial planner, a publicist and insurance in case of injury. A few of those athletes remembered and never failed to give Ty his props for helping them. A few were waiting for him to finish law school and fully expected him to become a sports agent. He did become an agent, but his area of specialization was entertainment law. It was only logical, for he had a built in clientele. His adoptive mother was Miriam Davies, world renowned jazz singer and his adoptive brother was none other than Eric "Silk" Davies the Grammy award winning artist who broke sales records with his last CD, Heaven's Gate. Ty was proud to know some of those early deals he'd brokered for Eric paid off. He was determined to do anything within his power to repay the kindness of the Davies family. The same intensity he portrayed in handling Eric's career, he did for all his clients and each of them paid him handsomely for his deeds.

Ty stood back at the window as the memory of Kiki invaded his thoughts. Kiki Simmons was a beautiful, natural haired goddess who came into his life for a few months over a year ago. To this day, he did not know why she walked away. Not a day had gone by when she did not cross his mind. Looking out at the Atlanta skyline, the bright lights of the city just did not fill him with pride as it had at one time. The fireball, smart mouthed woman came in, disrupted his life, then walked out, just like his mother did. Even with her leaving, he could not help wondering what she was doing. He moved from the window as he realized nothing outside would ease the pain of his lonely existence. Sitting at the desk, he looked down at the contract he were reviewing, but, thoughts of Kiki continued to invade his mind. He wondered why thoughts of her were so strong today. Sitting back in his chair his eyes hit the spot in his office where she began to break through his sheltered existence.

"Mr. Pendleton."

"Yes, Wendy?"

"There is a Ms. Simmons here to see you. She does not have an appointment..."

Ty was at the door before she finished her statement, with a smile on his face. There she stood, all five feet eight inches of her slim, gorgeous body, with that sassy haircut. "Hi," she smiled. The grin on his face must have spoken volumes. She walked over, kissed him. "I'm glad to see you, too. Is this your office?" She asked as she walked by him through the door. He looked, shocked that she was there, and then turned back to Wendy.

"Hold all your calls," she offered.

"Yes," he said and closed the door behind him. Kiki had placed her purse on his desk and sat on the edge. He walked over, took her in his arms, and gave her a proper hello kiss. Every kiss they had shared since meeting had been like the first time. Slow, exploring and deep. "When did you get here? Your flight wasn't until four fifteen."

Still holding on to him she kissed his neck, loosened his tie, and replied, "I couldn't sleep after we talked last night, so around five this morning I gave up, threw an overnight bag into the car and hit interstate 95. And you know what happened?"

He was kissing her neck and savoring the feel of her body. "What?"

"It brought me to you."

He stopped and pulled away. "You drove," he thought for a moment, "ten hours to see me?"

"Yes." She pushed his jacket off his shoulders.

"Why didn't you call me? I would have sent the jet. I don't know where it is at the moment, but I would have found it."

"I wanted to surprise you," she said while pulling his shirt from his pants. She then threw her hands up. "Surprise!"

He began laughing as she threw her arms around his neck and they fell to the floor. She was kissing his neck, his chin, anywhere she could touch his skin and he was doing the same. Then he reached her lips and his body filled with need. He positioned his body over hers, placing the object of his desire snug within the juncture between her legs and they both moaned at the contact.

Every day since the night they met, they had talked until the early morning hours. They'd shared their wants, their needs, their desires. And now, they were together and the need to touch each other was overwhelming. He pushed her arms over her head, intertwined their fingers, and deepened the kiss. She moved in rhythm with his body, merging the point of his need with hers until their breathing was out of control. Lifting his head up for air, he puffed two times and returned to her lips. She began to giggle and so did he. "This brother is glad to see you." He smiled down at her and sobered. She had the most amazing eyes; he could see the world in them. "I want you, but not like this." She touched the side of his face. "I have this really nice condo with a really comfortable big bed that no one has ever been in but me. We never discussed it, but stay with me. If you want a hotel room, I'll get you one. But it'll be a waste of money and time. So you might as well just stay with me."

She reached under her into her back pocket, pulled something out and held it up. "I brought my toothbrush."

He laughed as he held out a hand to pull her up. "You are a crazy woman."

She put her hands in her back pockets and shrugged her shoulders. "I don't know any other way to be."

They stood there smiling at each other. "Let's get out of here." He grabbed his jacket off the floor and her purse off the desk. Walking out the door, he turned to Wendy.

She waved her hand. "All meetings have been cancelled for the weekend and all emergencies will be reassigned."

"Thank you." He smiled, took Kiki's hand, and walked towards the elevator. Kiki looked over her shoulder at the woman and mouthed, "Thank you."

"You forgot to shave this morning. Late night?" Wendy questioned as she walked into his office with a folder.

Thankful for the break in his visit to the past, Ty sat up. "Something like that," he replied with less than three hours sleep. "Jason Whitfield decided to have a little too much fun last night at ARC."

"The boy is only twenty. He's young and he's not like your older brother Jason." Ty gave her an incredulous look, as the telephone rang. Wendy, reached across the desk. "Everyone is not as focused as you were at twenty." She answered the call, "The Pendleton Agency, Tyrone Pendleton's office."

Ty opened Jason Whitfield's folder to review the contract one last time. His intent was to see the deal through then turn Jason over to another agent.

"Yes, he is available. Hold the line please." Wendy put the call on hold. "You have a call from Duke University Hospital. You are the emergency contact for Roy Kelly."

Closing the folder, Ty took the telephone then pressed the talk button. While listening to the call, he wrote a note for Wendy to call The Towers in.

There were two people, other than his brothers, that he trusted with his life, Tower Number One, Jake Turner, and Tower Number Two, Peace Newman. Both had been middle linebackers on his college football team and were drafted into the NFL on different teams. Jake Turner busted a knee in his third year and Peace Newman suffered a concussion in his fourth. The injuries ended their careers. Thanks to the deals Ty helped them sign, both were financially set. However, neither was ready to be sportscasters for any network and decided on a more lucrative, action filled position as bodyguards for the Ty Pendleton Agency. Their duties consisted of a variety of responsibilities, but were not limited to anything needed by their friend and the man they simply referred to as Boss.

The two men walked into the office just as Ty was standing to complete the call. "What's up Boss?"

Ty quickly stood kicking the chair back as he picked up the phone on his desk, walking with the cordless device as he talked. "That was the Durham Police. Roy has been stabbed."

"What?" Jake asked, as they followed behind Ty.

"Last night." He placed the phone in Wendy's hands as he purposefully walked by. "Have the jet ready to fly to Durham. I'll be out of the office until further notice." Wendy reached behind his desk and pushed the button to open the private elevator, as Ty continued to give orders.

16

"Send me the telephone number for The Brooks Agency in Virginia."

"Anyone in particular you want to speak with?"

"Nicolas Brooks."

"Regarding?"

"Jason Whitfield," he replied as the elevator doors closed.

Duke University Medical Center wasn't a small place by any means. It took Ty at least twenty minutes to finally find the wing where Roy's room was located. The police were still in the area outside the trauma center, as Ty and The Towers approached.

"Detective Jamison," Ty stated. The officers pointed towards two men in suits standing near the door with a cup of coffee each. "Detective Jamison?"

"I'm Jamison. This is my partner, Simpson."

Ty extended his hand to Jamison. "Tyrone Pendleton, we spoke earlier."

"Didn't expect you to get here so quickly."

"What can you tell me about Roy?"

"What's your relationship to Kelly?" Detective Simpson inquired.

Working off of three hours sleep did not afford Ty the amount of patience it sometimes took to deal with the police. "I'm his emergency contact."

Detective Simpson raised an eyebrow. "You care to expand on that?"

Ty glanced at Detective Simpson. "No." He turned back to Detective Jamison. "What do you know?"

"We suspect it was a robbery," Simpson testily replied.

Ty ignored Detective Simpson, again keeping his attention on Detective Jamison. "Facts, detective."

Jamison looked towards his partner and smirked. "The facts are simple Mr. Pendleton. Mr. Kelly was stabbed with a sharp object and left to bleed to death in an empty parking lot. Any idea who may be responsible?"

"None. Was any evidence found at the scene?"

"Not even a footprint. Which I found rather odd because it rained here last night."

"Any word on his condition?"

"Look," Detective Simpson spoke up again. "We've answered your questions. Now, you need to answer a few."

For the first time Ty took a moment to take a good look at the detective. He could see the man was young and eager, a little too much so. "No, I do not." Ty turned to Detective Jamison. "New partner?"

Jamison took a step towards the door of the hospital. "It shows."

Ty followed Detective Jamison inside. "They took Kelly into surgery upon arrival." They stopped at the door to the room. "The surgeon indicates rest is his best cure for the trauma his body experienced. He said something interesting."

"What would that be?"

"The surgeon said whoever did this knew exactly where and how to cut to injure, but not to kill."

Ty held the Detective's glare, understanding the unspoken message he was sending. He walked into the room and closed the door behind him.

Twenty minutes later Ty walked out of the room and stopped in front of the Towers. "Jake, have one of the nurses contact the Hospital Administrator. Peace, guard the room. No one in or out without my consent." He walked over to Detective Jamison. "May we speak in private?"

Detective Jamison threw his now cold cup of coffee into the trash. When Simpson attempted to walk with them, Ty stopped and turned to him. "Private."

"Now, look here Pendleton. I'm don't care who you might be in Atlanta. Here, I'm one of the lead detectives on this case. You have no authority here."

"Simpson," Detective Jamison spoke. "Have a seat. I'll get what we need."

Hesitantly, Simpson took a step back.

"He doesn't mean any disrespect. He's just a little eager to get his feet wet. What can you give me on Kelly?"

"Not much," Ty replied. "Roy handles security for clients of my agency that live in the North Carolina region."

"Could something have gone bad with a client?"

"No, I would have gotten wind of it one way or another."

"Did Kelly talk at all?"

"A man attacked him. Said something about backstabbing and Karma....." Ty paused. "Detective, I'm going to leave one of my men here to guard Roy while I check on a few things. I would appreciate any assistance you can offer."

"I'll do what I can. Sounds like payback of some type. Any one he may have wronged in someway?" Ty frowned. "Someone come to mind?"

Ty tilted his head before replying. "I'll check on a few things. I'll be in touch."

Ⓟ

The last person LaToya Wright expected to see while serving a fifteen month sentence was Tyrone Pendleton. Yet, there he was. Not quite her taste in a man, but he definitely had a certain swagger about him.

"Damn girl, you sure know how to pick eye candy of all races. Did you exchange Mr. Bucks for Mr. Fine?"

LaToya looked at the woman known as Bertha and smiled. "No, Mr. Fine can't afford me."

"He could afford me for one night." The woman gave Ty a once over. "Hell, I'll pay him."

LaToya laughed as the guard opened the door to the visitor's area. "You'll eventually want to kill him too. Believe me, I know."

The women walked into the open room with benches and tables placed around for friends and family to visit. A few guards were stationed around the room, two at the visitor's desk and one at the entrance to the courtyard. There were several visitors already in the room that were greeted with hugs and kisses from their loved ones. LaToya was met with angry, intense eyes.

As always, when she walked into a room, appreciative male eyes turned her way while her fellow inmates frowned in her direction. She was a beautiful woman. A year in prison had not altered the fact. She wore her khaki pants and shirt uniform as if it was the latest fashion on a runway model. Her hair was styled, nails manicured and skin glistening. Yes, she was well kept for an inmate. That was to be expected, after all, she was wealthy.

"Tyrone Pendleton," she shook her head. "You look well."

"This should be a private conversation."

The intense look in his eyes cautioned her. A serene smile appeared on her face. "There isn't an abundance of privacy here Ty," she quipped. "We are in prison." Ty's face remained impassive. LaToya looked around. "Huh, not a friendly visit," she sighed. "Okay, why don't we step out into the courtyard. It may give us a little privacy."

She walked to the entrance of the courtyard and waited while the guard checked the area then gave them both a once over. It was late October, at nine on a Saturday morning. The air was cool, in the low sixties. "It's going to be a nice day today. We might not hit the eighties." LaToya said as she took a seat at a picnic table. There was no response from Ty as he sat across from her. "Okay Ty, since you're not here for small talk. Why are you here?"

"To see how you are LaToya."

A small smile creased her lips as she pushed her shoulder length hair over her shoulder. "You couldn't careless how I am. But I welcome the company, so I'll play your game. I'm doing my time, with God's help. How are you?"

Ty grinned, "You've been saved?"

Seeing the skepticism, LaToya shook her head. "I can't blame you for being skeptic. I know what I've done in the past. To apologize for my past mistakes would not do you or anyone I've hurt any good. I accept it as mistakes and I look forward to righting the wrongs that were done."

"How you plan to right those wrongs is my concern."

"I guess I owe your family that reply. If you are concerned about me causing problems with Sierra, don't be. I was not a good mother to her and Jason was right to get custody. My only hope is that he will consider allowing me visitation rights at some point."

"You are concerned with your daughter?"

"I can't say it's always been the case, but yes, Sierra is my number one concern." With a somewhat confused look on her face, she tilted her head. "What else is there to be concerned with? I've moved on from Jason and Eric. I now realize that was a foolish crush I had on a superstar that I took too far. One day I hope they will forgive me for my actions."

"Who is your benefactor LaToya?"

The blatant question did not surprise LaToya, after all she was talking to Ty who never used small talk. "I don't have a benefactor, nor do I need one. Thanks to Jason, I have enough money to live comfortably."

"Who do you think you are talking to? This is Ty, not the parole board or a judge to determine if you have accepted and are ready to make amends for your sins. Comfortable was never enough for you. I'm curious, does he know why you are here?"

LaToya hesitated. There was no need to pretend there was no one in her life. Tyrone was the type of person who knew the answers to questions before he asked them. "Yes, he knows. He knows everything about me and he loves me anyway. That's the kind of commitment I need in my life. Really it's all any woman would need."

"What did you tell him?"

"I told him the truth."

"What was your truth?"

LaToya sat forward, entwined her fingers together, looked directly into Ty's eyes then spoke. "My truth is simple. I fell in love with a person that did not love me. In the process of trying to win him over I did some stupid things that landed me in prison. That part of my life is now over and I don't want any part of Eric or Jason Davies." She sat back. "I would at some point like to see my daughter again. However, I do understand if Jason decides not to grant that request." She glanced away for a moment, then looked back at Ty. "Look, that part of my life is over. I'm paying my debt to society for what I did. In less than thirty days, I'll walk out of here with a new start. The last thing I want is to have problems with you once I'm out. So are we good here Ty?"

Minutes ticked off the clock as she waited for Ty's reply. He stood and adjusted his suit jacket. Looking out into the courtyard he said, "I only allow a few people into my circle. Those few have my unyielding protection." He turned back to her. "Come after any of them and those thirty days will become a lifetime."

As he walked away, LaToya was seething on the inside. She hated his arrogance, as if nothing could ever touch him. She waited until he was outside the entrance then called out, "Hey Ty." She waited for him to turn towards her. "How's New York treating Kiki?"

It wasn't her asking about Kiki that concerned him. It was the smirk on her face as she turned away that sent chills down his spine.

Chapter Two

*T*he rain was putting a damper on her nightly run, but it was the only way she could burn off the frustration of that damn Ty Pendleton. It didn't matter if she was in New York or Virginia, that man, who was in Atlanta, would find his way under KiKi Simmons' skin and cause chaos all through the night. A year, an entire year had passed since the last time they'd kissed, touched, made love and still he lingered in her system.

"Why, Lord, why hast thou forsaken, me," she yelled as she ran the track in Central Park, punching in the air. The relentless rain didn't daunt the twenty-seven year old literary agent's quest. She was on a mission to keep that man from disturbing her sleep. The only way she could do that was to be bone tired by the time she reached the condo. With her black and pink tank top, matching black body hugging tights, Yankees baseball cap and black hoodie to protect her from the rain and forty degree October weather, she ran through Central Park, eleven o'clock at night, oblivious to her surroundings, only her mission in focus.

As she neared the end of the park her long sleek legs propelled her body one step at a time, challenging her thigh muscles until they screamed. She ignored the fact that her thighs and her heart ached, she ran steady and hard. Suddenly, a hand reached out and grabbed her hoodie from behind. She almost fell backwards, but her natural instincts kicked in as she pulled away then turned on her attacker, landing one of the punches she was swinging in the wind, right in his jaw. She jumped back as the man advanced on her. "You picked the wrong sister tonight. I'm itching to whip a man's azz." She karate kicked him in the chest then began bouncing with her fists up and ready for her attacker. The man jumped to his feet throwing a right hook her way. She bobbed low, throwing an uppercut into his gut. "Really…you better bring something better than that." She swung around, jumped and kicked him in the face before he had a chance to straighten from the uppercut. She went back to her defensive stance, bobbing and weaving as he fell to the ground. "Oh, don't stop now. I'm just getting warmed up," she yelled down at the man.

Another man ran towards the confrontation, positioning his body between hers and the attacker. "Hey, what the hell is going on?" A few park goers stopped to see the action.

Kiki continued with the bouncing stance. "Don't stop him. I got some more for him."

The man on the ground got up and ran off. The Good Samaritan was doing all he could not to laugh at the man high tailing it out of the park. Turning, he reached for her. "Are you all right?"

Kiki, still bouncing, rolled her shoulders, then tilted her head left then right. "Yeah I'm good. What, you want some too?"

The man held his hands up as if surrendering. "No," he shook his head, then started to laugh. "I just wanted to make sure you were okay."

Realizing the threat was over Kiki stopped bouncing and exhaled, mad because she didn't have another man to punch. "Damn." The man laughed harder. She stared at him for a moment, then let out a little chuckle.

The man continued to laugh. "I bet he'll think twice before he attacks anyone else in the park."

The man's laugh was contagious, Kiki couldn't help but join in. "I'm not the one tonight. I could whip him and a few more."

"Well, whoever you are, I think I'd like to stay on your good side. Whew." He straightened from laughing and extended his hand. "Ram Hunter."

Hesitantly, she extended her hand. "Kiki Simmons."

"You're not from here?" The frown on her face made him continue, "You have an accent."

"This is New York. Everybody has an accent."

"True. Well, Ms. Simmons, may I have the honor of walking you home?"

The rain hampered her ability to get a good look at her would be hero, but that really didn't matter, she knew it wasn't Ty. "Thank you for the offer, but I don't live far. I'll be fine." She exhaled and began walking towards the Central Park South exit near 59th Street. She turned back as she continued to walk. "Thanks for stopping."

"Anytime for a damsel in distress," he called out as she ran out of the park. She began a slow jog, as Ram Hunter watched from a distance.

Walking backwards, she teased by placing her hand over her heart, "My knight in shining armor." She smiled then jogged away.

Stepping into her condo, Kiki kicked her wet sneakers off and dropped the hoodie on the floor of the mudroom. Walking through the foyer, she stepped down into the sunken living room. She clicked the remote on the table to close the drapes, which hung at the windows and surrounded the room, eliminating the skyline and the lights of the city. The drapes were almost always open. Pushing another button the stereo system came on, filling the room with the smooth sounds of Rhythm and Blues singer, Silk Davies. Kiki had had the pleasure of meeting the man in person last year when his wife, Siri Austin, became her first client. She loved the couple, but hated each time they would invite her to one of their family gatherings. They were responsible for her meeting that damn Tyrone Pendleton. That alone was reason enough for her to want to kill both of them. However, it did not take away from the man's talent. Silk Davies could sing.

Kiki walked to the left, bypassing the kitchen, guest room and office, choosing to go directly to the shower stall, stripping out of her clothes along the way. A good shower, a few reads from potential clients and she should sleep soundly for the night.

The warmth and soothing beat coming from the multiple shower heads began to massage her muscles, clear her mind and briefly ease her soul from the moment she stepped in. She savored every minute of relief for her muscles were screaming.

After she rubbed baby oil over her chocolate brown body, she donned the only nightwear she owned, a Derek Jeter #2 jersey. She found her way to sleep with the man nightly, while others threw themselves at his feet. Yes, she was a Yankees fan and proud of it. That damn Tyrone Pendleton was an Atlanta Braves fan. They constantly argued over Chipper Jones and Derek Jeter. That was another reason she slept with the captain's jersey that Ty bought for her even though he did not like the man. It was sweet things like that that had made her fall irrevocably in love with the quiet, arrogant, nerd she passionately referred to as that damn Tyrone Pendleton.

Sitting on the bed, she watched ESPN as she finger twisted her natural hair. The Yankees were in a dead heat with the Baltimore Orioles for first place in the American League East Division. Every game counted. After checking the standings, she settled under the blue and white comforter, relieved to see her team won, frustrated to see, so did the other team. Still tied for the top spot with less than twenty games to go. Sighing, she pulled out the manuscript she had begun from the nightstand, turned the television off and continued reading. The job of a literary agent was at times, 24/7. Sometimes her clients would have an idea that they wanted to talk through with her and tended to forget that she had a life, or simply needed sleep. How her authors could be up all hours of the night writing was a mystery to her. However, she was making a very lucrative living from the work they produced. To be honest, she loved being a part of the process of delivering literary masterpieces to the world. In addition, reading their work at night helped her to fall asleep, as she prayed it would tonight.

An hour later, she was asleep with the manuscript lying open on her chest. Her cell phone chimed, startling her from her sleep. She jumped, knocking the pages to the floor as she reached for the phone. "Damn. Hello."

"Hey Rocket."

"T? Why in the hell are you waking me up at one in the morning?" She froze for a moment. "Has something happened to Ty? Is he all right? Is he hurt?"

"Slow down Rocket," Jake cautioned. "Boss is fine.

Angry now, Kiki yelled, "Then why in the hell are you calling me at one in the morning?"

"The Boss wanted to make sure you were all right."

Kiki sat back on the bed. "He knows how to use a phone, I've witnessed it myself."

Jake laughed. He had no idea why the Boss was letting this woman slip through his fingers. In his eyes, she was perfect for him. The Boss was quiet, soft spoken, always thought before he acted. Kiki, was loud, outspoken and rarely thought before she acted. Man, she had a mouth on her. The woman did not hold anything back. As different as they were, she and the Boss were explosive together. Anyone that wasn't deaf, dumb or blind could see it and feel it whenever the two of them were in the same room. "That's why I like you Rocket, you don't hold back."

Smiling, for she was happy to hear from him, she said, "I like you too, but my name is not Rocket."

"You are always going to be Rocket to me. Every time I see you shooting off that mouth of yours on somebody, I think of a rocket firecracker exploding."

"Not funny." She smiled. "So, seriously, what's up? Why the late night call?"

Jake hesitated. "Boss has a feeling something's up."

"You know what he can do with his feelings," she huffed.

"Seriously, Rocket. The man that worked with us on the LaToya Wright sting was stabbed Thursday night. He just wanted someone to touch base with you."

"LaToya Wright. The woman that tried to blackmail Eric?"

"One in the same."

"I thought she was in prison."

"She is, however, something about the way Roy was hurt made Boss think of her. Roy has been very low key. Moved to North Carolina after the sting. Been doing the right thing, you know. I don't have to tell you how revengeful the woman can be. You were there, you know. Just like you know the Boss is usually not too far off beat."

"If he was that concerned, he could have called himself."

"When was the last time you answered a call from his number?"

"He is a very resourceful man. He could have found a way."

"He did. That's why I'm calling."

"Well, as you can tell, I'm fine. Besides, LaToya Wright does not want a piece of me. She'll think TeKaya was a lamb compared to the azz whipping I'll give her. She doesn't want to mess with me."

Jake laughed. "Pshhh...there goes the Rocket, taking off again."

She laughed. "I appreciate your concern. You know I can take care of myself."

"Boss's concerned."

"Yeah, well, he has yet to prove that. Where is he anyway?"

"I'm not sure. He left here about a few hours ago."

"Without you? Where is Tower 2?"

"We're in North Carolina with Roy. Boss don't want Roy left alone until he knows for sure what's happening."

"Then who has his back, T?" she asked in a voice laced with concern.

"Boss can take care of himself, you know that."

There was a knock on her door. Kiki looked at the clock on the nightstand. "What the hell is this--Grand Central Station?" She mumbled as she walked to the door.

"What's going on?" Jake asked.

"Someone's knocking at my door. I have security that's supposed to call up when I have a visitor. I'm going to have a few choice words for him in the morning."

"Don't open the door," Jake ordered.

"The hell I'm not. My neighbors will be calling NYPD if I don't answer the door. It's probably my client that lives in the building with the next great manuscript. I'm coming damn it," she yelled when the person knocked again.

Kiki heard Jake yell, "Hold on Rocket," but it was too late. She swung the door open and was immediately hit with a bolt of electricity. The phone dropped to the floor with Jake yelling through the line. Her body was scooped up into a bag similar to a potato sack, with a drawstring, with her bare feet dangling from the bottom. Her body was picked up and thrown over a broad shoulder as if it was nothing more than a gym bag.

The chime signifying the elevator had arrived must have startled the man. He looked back over his shoulder to see a man step off the elevator. Recognition hit him immediately. What in the hell was Tyrone Pendleton doing in New York? He turned and walked purposefully towards the exit at the end of the hallway.

Ty had just stepped off the elevator when he saw a male figure with a sack over his shoulder. For a moment he dismissed the scene, thinking, New York, you might see anything. It was the sparkle from the toe ring on the foot hanging from the bag that caught his attention. He looked at the pink toe the ring was on and an instant dread filled his body. That foot dangling with the pink painted toenails and toe ring belonged to Kiki--his Kiki.

"What the....." He took off running towards the man. Ty ran past the open door he knew belong to Kiki's condo. A neighbor opened her door and peeked out. "Call the police," Ty yelled as he ran to the stairwell. They were on the twentieth floor of the building. There was a breezeway on the thirteenth floor that led to the garage. His gut told him if the man made it to the garage Kiki would be lost to him forever. That he could not allow.

The man was a floor down by the time Ty reached the stairwell and looked over the railing. "If you value your life, you will drop her now." By the tone of his voice, he was not posing a threat, it was clearly a promise. Ty jumped across the railing, reducing the number of stairs that separated him from the man. His lined trench coat swung wide behind him as he jumped three or more steps at a time. He was now at the top of the steps with the man on the bottom. Ty jumped over the railing again, this time blocking the man's escape to the next landing. The man was definitely in shape. He was holding Kiki over a shoulder with one hand, as he pointed the object in his other hand at Ty.

Ty ducked the blast of electricity meant to stun him. "What the hell?" He in turn tackled the man, leading with his shoulder and grabbing the man's legs just beneath his butt. Pushing the man backwards, he pulled his legs from under him. The man fell backwards, dropping Kiki and the device in his hand on the landing. The man kicked Ty down the stairs before jumping to his feet. Ty was stunned for a moment as blood seeped from his nose, and his back screamed from the slam against the cement stairs. A second later, he saw the man's body propelling through the air towards him. He reached up just as the man was about to collide with his chest and pushed his body away, down the next flight of steps. Both men were slow getting up, however, the man made it to his feet first. He took a good look at Ty as Ty did the same. The man was dressed in all black, with a matching skull cap that covered his face showing only his eyes. The look in the man's eyes let Ty know he had not seen the last of him as he ran off.

Ty crawled up the steps to reach the bag. He pulled the string apart and pulled Kiki's still body from the sack. "Aww hell. What did he do to you babe? Open your eyes Kiki." There was no response. He frantically searched her body, trying to determine what her injury may be, but nothing was evident except a bump on her head, from where the man dropped her. He pulled out his cell and pushed 1. Tower 1 picked up immediately.

"Boss, where are you? Something's happening with Kiki."

"I'm here with her. Somebody tried to grab her."

"I called the police when I heard the scuffle. What in the hell is going on?"

"I don't know," Ty said bewildered. "I'm sending the jet back. Get here."

"You got it Boss."

Ty picked up Kiki's body and carried her back upstairs. As he reached the hallway, two police officers turned on him with guns drawn. The neighbors and the building security were standing in the hallway near the elevator.

"Put the woman down," one officer demanded. Ty ignored them and walked into the apartment. "Sir, put the woman down or I'll shoot."

"He's the one that told me to call the police," the neighbor explained.

The officer ignored the woman.

Ty turned with an incredulous look on his face. Was there something in the stars that indicated he had to deal with stupid cops? He gently placed Kiki on the white sofa in her living room. Taking his coat off, he covered her body, then held his hands up. In as calm a voice as he could muster, he stated. "I have identification in my left jacket pocket and a gun in my back pocket." At the mention of a gun the officers became alert and fidgety.

"What are you doing with a gun?"

"It's my constitutional right to bear arms. I have a permit to carry a weapon. My name is Tyrone Pendleton. I'm an attorney from Atlanta," he stated while one officer frisked him and pulled the gun. The other officer held his weapon aimed directly at his head. Ty nodded towards Kiki. "She needs an ambulance."

"What did you do to her?"

"I brought her back into her apartment."

The officer checked his identification then looked at Ty. "I know you." He lowered his weapon a little, not much. "Aren't you an agent or something?"

"I am." Ty nodded, frustrated with the situation and worried about Kiki.

"What in the hell are you doing here?"

"I came here to check on her. When I arrived, a man was carrying her over his shoulder. I chased him down the stairwell. We scuffled, he dropped her then ran off."

The other officer was now bending to examine Kiki. "Don't...touch her," Ty snarled through clenched teeth. "She is not properly dressed." He knew from experience that Kiki rarely wore anything underneath the God-awful blue and white Yankees jersey. "If you want to be useful, the bag and the instrument used are in the stairwell, somewhere between the seventh and eighth floor." He looked to the officer he believed to be ranked. "I have been cooperative and patient. If you hold me in this manner another minute, this city is going to see a lawsuit the likes of which you will never forget."

The officer scrutinized Ty then nodded his head towards Kiki. "Go ahead."

Ty went to Kiki, picked up her limp body and held her until the Emergency Medical Technicians arrived.

Chapter Three
Manhattan, New York

*T*y met her a little over a year ago at his brother, Jason Davies', engagement dinner. Their affair had been brief, but Lord, did it leave a mark on him. Since that time, he had not looked at nor desired another woman. Only Kiki. However, he was not ready for the forever after she wanted, nor did he believe in it, at least, not for him. Both of his brothers, Jason and Eric, were very happy with their spouses, and that sort of thing worked for others. It just was not in the cards for him.

He sat with his long legs stretched out and crossed at the ankles as he continued to watch for any movement from the still body of the woman who had rocked his world for a few months, then walked out of his life. Women had a way of doing that. He shook the thought from his mind. It wasn't all on her. The physical attraction overwhelmed them so much that they had not taken the time to get to know each other. If they had, the misunderstanding as to what each of them was expecting from their relationship would not have happened. Her walking away did not diminish how deeply he cared for her and probably always would. The one thing he did learn about her was that she was very close to her family. Even though she was now working and living in New York with her stepmother and father, he knew she would want her mother there. He took the time to call her brother, Garland Simmons, whom he had met the same night he met Kiki, and told him what had happened. He had his jet stop in Virginia on the way from North Carolina to pick up her mother and bring her to New York.

As an agent, Tyrone Pendleton had clients all over the world. He was a man of means and connections wherever he was. By the time they reached the hospital, the officers at the scene had called in the incident. Someone recognized his name and the brass of the New York Police Department was there to grant whatever he needed. The first thing being around the clock security until his people were in place.

He glanced at his watch. It was now 2:45 in the morning. After meeting with LaToya, there was something about the situation that sent his senses into alert mode. His instincts told him to check on Kiki personally. He had no idea if she would even open the door to him. He bribed the security officer with tickets to any sports event he desired to gain access without the customary call to the resident. He was glad he'd followed those instincts. Those instincts were now urging him to contact both his brothers. For if, what he suspected, was happening, their wives could be in danger as well. He pulled out his phone to make the call when a small commotion outside the room caught his attention.

"You can't stop him from entering the room. He's her father." A slim blonde woman was explaining to the officer as Ty stepped out of the room.

"Who in the hell are you and where is my daughter?" A brown skinned man, standing a little taller than Ty with gray at his temples frowned angrily at him.

Ty looked at the officer.

"He says he's her father."

Ty turned to the man with his hand extended. "Mr. Simmons, my name is Tyrone Pendleton. I'm a friend of your daughter's."

"A friend--he's a damn friend," the man said sarcastically to the blonde woman, then turned back to the officer. "He's allowed to be in there with my daughter and I'm not."

The woman stepped between Ty and the man. "Hello Ty. I'm Maxine Long. We met at Siri Austin's book signing last year." She looked up at her very angry husband. "Kenneth, this is Kiki's...." She looked back at Ty, then back to her husband, "friend from Atlanta. Ty, this is my husband and Kiki's father, Kenneth Simmons."

"I regret we are meeting under these circumstances Mr. Simmons."

Still angry, Kenneth huffed, "You want to tell me why you have carte blanche around here and I can't see my daughter." He sneered at the officers that were detaining him.

Exhibiting the patience he was known for, Ty explained the situation. "Someone attempted to kidnap your daughter tonight. I intend to see that does not happen again and that the guilty party pays for even considering touching her.

Until I have a better understanding of the situation, no one will have open access to her--no one." The look on Ty's face should have been enough to warn Kenneth, however, it wasn't.

Taking a step closer to the man standing between him and his daughter, Kenneth angrily glared at him. "You and what army are going to try to stop me?"

Ty stepped closer to Kenneth and spoke calmly and quietly. "Mr. Simmons. I prefer that your daughter does not wake to see me whipping your ass. So please, step the hell back."

"Maxine, get your husband before that young man kills him." The mellow voice belonged to a slim, dark skinned woman, about five feet six inches in height, with short boy cut hair, a touch of gray and black mixed throughout, her hands on her hips and three men standing behind her. Jake walked over and stood next to Ty.

"Kenny step back please." The woman literally pushed the blonde out of the way. Hesitantly, Kenneth stepped back. The woman stepped between the two and looked up. She sighed with a smile, "You must be Tyrone."

Ty hesitantly looked away from Kenneth down to the woman smiling up at him. "Yes, ma'am I am."

She patted his chest. "Now, I understand," she sighed. "Where's my daughter?"

"She's right inside." Ty looked over his shoulder.

"I'm going in to see Kendra. When I come out I want to know what you think is going on." She looked over her shoulder at Kenneth. "Kenny, you're coming in with me. One cross word and I will have Jake escort you out. Do we understand each other?"

Jake, who was a good six four, two hundred and fifty pounds, folded his arms across his chest and posed as if ready for battle.

"Don't talk to me like that Issy. She is my daughter too."

"You are lucky I'm talking to you at all, and I know she is your daughter. However, something serious is happening here and I need you to understand, that whatever it is, this is not about you and your ego."

"I don't have an ego. This boy was keeping me from my daughter."

"Kenneth stay calm," Maxine cautioned.

Isadore sent a look her way so intense, Maxine simply took a step back and bumped into Garland.

"I see you remember that slap," he whispered then cleared his throat when his mother sent him a warning look, then turned back to her ex-husband.

"He doesn't look like a boy to me. He looks like a man who just saved our daughter's life. Keep that in mind." She sighed. "Now, are you coming Kenny?"

"His name is Kenneth," Maxine mumbled.

"He's good old Kenny to me," Isadore stated as she took a step towards Maxine. Kenneth grabbed her by the arm. Isadore looked at him as if he had lost his mind. He wisely released her arm. She walked towards the hospital room door with Kenneth behind her, never taking her eyes from Maxine. "Garland introduce Tyrone to your brothers," she ordered as she slowly looked away from Maxine and stepped inside the room.

Tyrone looked at the men who were intently staring at him. He understood their frowns, for he still had a few unanswered questions himself.

Jake nudged him. "They're cool Boss. Like us, they just want to know what the hell is going on."

Garland, with his low cut hair, jeans, an Atlanta Braves t-shirt, and a black jacket, walked over extending his hand. "Thank you for the call Ty. This is my brother, Martin and the bald guy over there with the chip on his shoulder is Wayne."

Ty shook both Garland and Martin's hands and just nodded at Wayne.

"What's going on Ty? Your man here wouldn't tell us much of anything other than Kiki's condition."

"I don't have any facts at this time Garland. I wish I did."

"Is that Kiki's blood on your shirt?" Martin asked

Ty looked down, noticing the blood for the first time. "No." Ty turned to Jake.

"It's just a little crooked Boss." Jake put the overnight bag that he carried on the floor. "What'd he do, drop kick you?" He asked as he pushed Ty's nose back into place.

Ty flinched as the group looked on, grimacing.

"Damn man." Martin frowned. "Don't that hurt?"

"It's good," Ty replied. "Will you see if I can get a couple of aspirin," he said to Jake.

Jake walked to the nurse's station, as Ty took a seat, holding his head back.

A shadow appeared over him. "You fought for my sister?"

Opening one eye, he looked into the eyes of Wayne Simmons. He was big, thick, and looked mean. However, none of that mattered. Ty had dealt with men Wayne's size all his life. "I did."

"Looks like he kicked your ass."

"I got the girl." He wasn't sure, but Ty thought he saw the man's lips curl upward for a moment. He held his head back again.

Wayne pushed his head up from the back. "Hold your head up."

Damn, he was about as gentle as a grizzly, Ty thought.

Jake returned with an icepack and aspirin.

Ty threw the aspirin into his mouth, then swallowed a cup of water. "That's my bag?"

"Yeah Boss," Jake replied.

Standing, Ty grabbed the bag, took a look into the room. Kiki was lying so still on the bed. He could clearly see the worried look on her mother's face. "Jake, stay at this door. No one other than the family we know goes in. He pointed to a nurse at the station. "She is cleared. Dr. Rosenthal is cleared. Those are the only two that go in that room. Understood?"

"You got it Boss."

Ty spotted the two officers who were assisting him at the nurse's station. He walked over and shook their hands. "Thank you."

"Chief stated we are to have two officers assigned to you during your stay. Just let us know what you need."

"I appreciate that. What's your name?"

"Officer Ronnie Banks and this is my partner, Joel Kaminsky."

"Thank you for your help," he replied as he walked away. He could feel the eyes of the people in the waiting area staring at his back. He knew they all wanted answers and so did he. At the moment, ensuring Kiki's safety was the priority. He would have to work on his bedside manners later.

Ty washed up and changed his clothes. He looked at his watch wondering if he should wake Jason. It was now 4:15 in the morning. Dressed in a gray Armani suit, white collared shirt, gray and black striped tie and Italian leather shoes, he leaned against the vanity in the bathroom to take a deep breath. He needed a moment to compose himself. The sight of Kiki slung over the man's shoulder in a sack, of all things, scared the living hell out of him. The thought of anything happening to her shook him to the core.

Seeing her again stirred the memories of the times that they were together. It was one of the happiest times of his life. It was only about six weeks total, but with the drama that was going on, Kiki was the spark of light that helped him deal with the situation. He wished he could have stopped her from walking away. He offered all that he could at the time. He knew it wasn't enough, but, he couldn't afford to give anymore. The sacrifice was too great.

He turned and washed his hands as he reached a decision. He would take every precaution he could to keep her safe. However, self-preservation had to take priority. There was no way he could deal with her walking away from him again. He shook his head at the thought. He just couldn't go through it again. The mother he loved walked away and never looked back. He was twelve years old. It nearly destroyed him. There was no way he could give Kiki that kind of power over him. She had captured his body and soul last year. He threw the paper towel he had used to dry his hands into the trash. He would make sure she was safe, then he had to step back, to protect his own heart.

(P)

The moment she went from unconsciousness to sleep he knew, for he had not moved since he changed clothes. Her breathing changed to a steady rhythm. Now all there was to do was wait. His attempt to send everyone to the condo to get some rest was futile. Only Maxine left. All of Kiki's brothers were bunked down outside in the corridor leading to the private room in a restricted area of the hospital. Her parents sat on the other side of the bed asleep. Ty sat in the chair next to the door where Jake stood on guard. The nurse had come through about an hour earlier to check her vitals and now he sat watching over her, waiting for the moment she opened her eyes. He needed to know for certain that she was all right. Once he looked into her eyes, he would know. The eyes tell all, as a very wise woman once told him.

His gut told him LaToya was behind this. With her being in prison, she had an unbreakable alibi. The question became who is handling this for her and how does he get his hands on the person. After talking to Roy, he was certain this was the act of that vengeful woman. What she did not realize, was that she'd just signed her own death warrant. His cell phone buzzed. It was close to six o'clock Sunday morning, he thought. Hell, the days seemed to be merging into each other. Usually a call at this time of the morning meant one of his clients had an issue. He pulled the device from the pocket of his suit jacket, which was hanging on the back of his chair and answered the call.

Okay, this time she knew she wasn't dreaming. That was Ty's voice she heard. She turned towards his voice but did not open her eyes. What would he be doing in New York? And why in the hell was he running down the stairs in her building of all places? Was that her father snoring? It was all too confusing. She decided now was not the time to wake up so she allowed the darkness to take over again.

"Kill her."

Screech, hold up. Who is Ty killing? Her eyes opened. It took a moment for her to focus, to figure out where she was. Then her eyes settled on his. Through the puppy dog brown eyes that stared back at her she saw anger, fear, relief, and then there was the one that made her smile, love.

Never taking her eyes from his, she watched as he stood and walked over to her. He bent down until his lips were a mere breath away. He rubbed his thumb across her brow as he intently stared into her eyes. She knew he needed to see for himself that she was all right. God help her. As much as she hated him, she loved him, in that moment, and her eyes revealed that to him. He gently kissed her lips, as he continued to smooth her temple. The gentle caress let her know that the man loved her too. The next kiss was deep, scorching, and sincere. It let her know he would protect her with his life. Kicking off his shoes, he climbed into bed beside her then gathered her into his arms. He closed his eyes and breathed a deep sigh of relief.

She placed her head on his shoulder and wrapped her arm around his waist then closed her eyes. Before they fell asleep she asked, "LaToya?"

"Yes."

"You cannot kill her."

He kissed her temple, pulled her closer and replied, "Yes I can," then promptly joined her in slumber.

Isadore watched under lowered eyelids with a smile. She basked in the knowledge that the man that her daughter loved, was also in love with her. Now all she had to figure out who this LaToya woman was.

Chapter Four

*W*hat seemed like a few minutes, but was actually a few hours later, Ty was awakened by loud whispers in the room. It took him a moment to focus on the three people at the foot of the bed. He turned towards the door to see Jake staring incredulously at the so called adults making a scene in the hospital room. What happened next made Ty want to laugh. Isadore walked over to Jake, said something then walked out of the room. Jake walked inside, picked up Kenneth and physically carried him from the room. Maxine stood in the spot as if she was rooted to the floor until Isadore pulled the door open and gave her a 'don't make me come get you' look. Then she followed them out of the room.

Ty looked down at Kiki, who was watching the adults in her life making a scene outside the room.

"Welcome to my life," she sighed.

He kissed her temple and pulled her a little closer for he knew the truce was going to end soon. "How are you feeling?"

"I have a monster headache and my shoulder feels like the marshmallow man over an open flame."

The smile touched his lips before he could stop it. She always had an interesting way of explaining her feelings. "The doctor indicated you will feel some discomfort for another day, but the burn will take a little longer to heal."

"What happened?"

Ty explained the events after his arrival and told her about his visit with LaToya. "What I have to do is find who she has on the outside working for her."

"Follow the money," Kiki said. "The woman is all about the dollar bills."

"My concern is what's next. I interrupted the plan last night. Will he come after you again? Why did he try to take you instead of attacking you in the condo?"

"Whew, two attacks in one night. I swear a girl can only take so much."

Ty sat up and looked down at her. "Two? Something else happened?"

"It was nothing. Some fool tried to mug me in the park while I was jogging."

"Did the police catch him?"

"I didn't call the police. I kicked his azz myself."

Ty got out of the bed and stood over her. "You did what?" He asked in a dangerously calm voice.

"You know me Ty, I can take care of myself," Kiki sat up in the bed.

"Like you did last night?"

"Don't yell at me Ty."

"I don't yell."

48

"Yes you do. Oh, your voice doesn't rise, but your tone certainly changes. And then you have that damn condescending look that makes people want to crawl under a table. You yell with your eyes. Just like you are doing now."

"What happened?" He refused to allow her to divert from the topic.

"I told you what happened. A man jumped me in the park. I kicked his azz. End of story."

He stood there glaring at her. The last thing he ever wanted to do was allow anyone to harm her. But at that moment he wanted to do something, anything, to get her to understand that she was not as tough as she thought she was. She cannot walk around fighting with men that are out to hurt her.

"Don't." She threw the hospital sheet off her and stood a little too quickly. Her head throbbed and nausea took hold, causing her to sit back down on the bed.

That only fueled his anger more. Ty grabbed his suit jacket off the chair and shoved his arms inside. "Do not leave this hospital room until I return."

She crawled back under the covers. "That's going to be easy since I can't stand yet. But that's the only reason I'm staying. Certainly not because you said so. When I can stand, I'm going home."

Her voice sounded so weak he almost wanted to console her. But at some point Kiki had to learn she can't fight the world alone. "We'll see about that." He pulled the door open.

"Where are you going Ty?" Her back was to him and her voice was not as boisterous as before.

Ty closed his eyes, trying to keep the anger contained. "To handle business."

"If you kill her, then I will have to visit you in jail."

Ty walked out of the room, past the family to the nurse's station. He spoke with the nurse then walked over to Jake. "Get me a record of every person that has had contact with LaToya Wright since her conviction date."

"Is she involved in this?" Jake asked.

"My gut says yes."

"How do we prove it? She's been behind bars for over a year."

Ty hesitated. "Follow the money," he said. "Have Rosa Sanchez review LaToya's bank records from the day we made the initial deposit from Jason. I want to know where every dime went." He waited a split second then said, "Have her to check on any cellmates and their visitors as well. I want to know every person she has had contact with since the day she was arrested."

He walked over to Isadore. "Mrs. Simmons."

"I'm Mrs. Simmons," Maxine stated.

Isadore put her hands on her hips and glared at Maxine. "You don't really want to go there, do you Ms. Long?"

"Issy," Kenneth cautioned.

"Kenny?" Isadore raised an eyebrow. Kenneth and Maxine walked off.

Jake chuckled. "I'm scared of you."

Isadore exhaled and looked at Ty. "What do you need Tyrone?"

"Mrs. Simmons, I have to leave to handle some things. Kiki is still experiencing some discomfort. I've asked the nurse to give her something for the pain. But what she really needs is rest."

"I can handle that." She touched Ty's arm and began walking away from the others. "Can you tell me what's happening here? Why is someone after my daughter?"

"Anything that I tell you now would be pure speculation. I'd like to have the facts before I say. There are others, who I think may come to harm if I don't warn them. That's why I have to leave. I won't be gone for long. But I need something more from you."

"Name it."

"We don't know each other. Kiki happens to be her own worst enemy. She's not as tough as she thinks she is. When I return I want to take her back to Atlanta to keep her safe."

"You want me to convince her to go?"

"Yes."

"Before I agree, I want to know details."

"Understandable."

"I'll handle her here, while you warn the others involved. Then I expect to hear details Tyrone."

"Fair enough." He hesitated. "I don't like your ex-husband."

Isadore smiled. "I don't like him very much either. So we have two things in common. Neither of us likes Kenneth very much and we both love Kendra." She walked away.

Ty was about to say he did not mention the word love, but Isadora was already walking back into the room.

The thirty minute drive from the hospital to the private airstrip in New Jersey gave Ty time to think. Now the thoughts were no longer probable, but actual. LaToya was behind the hit on Roy and the attempted kidnapping of Kiki. All he had to do was prove it. His gut never steered him wrong. The moment he saw Roy's condition, he knew this was revenge. The person did not want him dead, they wanted Roy to suffer and be alive to remember what happened to him. Kiki wasn't attacked, she was taken. Only a woman would think that way. A man would kill the person and call it a day.

Since the con went down on LaToya, Roy had been clean. He moved to North Carolina and was handling cases with integrity. In fact, as Ty had offered, some of his business with his North Carolina clients was now being handled by Roy's agency. The Towers, who covered Roy during the con, had formed a good relationship with the one-time enemy. Roy was doing well and Ty was happy to help the man find his way. Roy was now considered a part of his family. Seeing him with the tubes attached to him caused Ty to think who could have done such a thing. LaToya Wright was the first person that came to mind. Ty's heart skipped a beat at the thought. She went after Roy and Kiki. Who would be her next target, Jason, Eric, TeKaya, or Siri?

He pulled out his cell and pushed a button. "Jason. I need to meet with you and Eric. I should be there in a little over an hour." He disconnected the call. He loved his brothers, but wasn't sure he had the patience to deal with the dueling personalities.

"Welcome back Mr. Pendleton." Trent, his third year pilot spoke. "We've refueled. The flight plan has been filed. We're ready to take off at your command.

"Thank you Trent."

"Mr. Pendleton, Rosa Sanchez is waiting for you on the plane."

Ty nodded, but in his mind he was on how he was going to break this news to his brothers. "Mr. Pendleton she asked about the flight plans."

That caught his attention. Ty stopped to listen. Trent rarely detained him with chatter. "What's your concern Trent?"

Trent hesitated. "Mr. Pendleton, I'm uncomfortable with the questions she asked. I figure if you wanted her to know where you were going and why, you would tell her. I understand her position in the front office, and don't want to cause issues for her or myself, you know what I'm saying?"

Ty nodded with a smile. "You're right. Don't worry about it. I'll take care of it." With a pat on his back Trent walked off towards the plane. Ty pulled out his phone to call his secretary. "Wendy, anything happening I need to know about?"

"You don't pay me enough money. That's about all I can think of at the moment."

That brought a chuckle from him. "Hell, I know that. Is there any reason for Rosa Sanchez to be on my plane?"

"None, other than the fact that she has the hots for you."

"Not funny."

"I wasn't laughing," Wendy replied.

"Anything from Jason Whitfield over the weekend?"

"Nothing that came to my attention. Do you want me to handle Rosa?"

"No. I'll handle it." He disconnected the call as he boarded the plane.

"Mr. Pendleton, it's good to see you. I have a few documents that need your signature. Also, I have those financial records you requested." Rosa pushed her waist length hair over her shoulders as she stood and approached him. "At first sight, things look normal. However," she stood next to him pointing to the figures on the computer.

"If you look closer, there are questionable movements a few months after Ms. Wright was incarcerated."

Ty looked at the spreadsheet on the computer where she was pointing. "Can we determine where those funds were disbursed?"

She looked up at him. "The court order issued at the time of Mr. Davies' payment only allows us access to her bank account. We cannot access or be given the account number to the person on the receiving end. I'm sorry sir."

"Do we have a name?"

"Yes sir, we do. However, there is something a little more interesting. About six months ago, regular deposits have been made into the account almost doubling the original balance."

"Where are the deposits coming from?"

She looked up at him with a sparkle in her eye. "An offshore account in The Cayman Islands."

"Find out who that account belongs to."

"Yes, sir," Rosa smiled brightly at the thought of pleasing him. "Do you need anything else? T1 indicated you would need an overnight bag so I stopped by your condo to pack one. I didn't know where or how long you would be away, so I wasn't sure what to pack."

The question given in a statement form was clearly her way of seeking information. Not inclined to answer the unasked question, Ty took a seat. "I'm sure whatever you packed will suffice. I'll need the information on that account as soon as possible."

"Yes sir." Clearly the enthusiasm from earlier was gone as the woman gathered her purse. "Mr. Pendleton, I flew in with Trent thinking I could be helpful in someway."

Rosa Sanchez was an exotic beauty, with eyes so expressive you could read right through them. She was the complete opposite of Kiki, willing to do whatever you wanted without any back talk. All he had to do was say what, when and where. There were two problems. One, she was his employee. He never got involved with an employee. Two, she wasn't tall, slim, sassy, smart-mouthed Kiki Simmons. "I need you in Atlanta working on identifying that account. Thank you for the offer."

"Of course. I'll take a commercial flight back to Atlanta." She began gathering her things.

"You don't have to do that Rosa. You can work from the plane until Trent returns to Atlanta.

"Thank you Sir," A smile graced her face as she walked back to the seat she was occupying. "Mr. Pendleton, one more thing. You have been going non-stop for a few days now. Try to get some rest on the flight."

"I'll do that. Thank you Rosa."

"You're welcome, sir."

Ty pushed the button on the console next to him. "Take her up Trent." Laying his head back he took Rosa's advice, closed his eyes and tried to get some rest before he had to tackle the next battle.

"Hello Tyrone. How are you?"

The cheerful smile of TeKaya Davies greeted him at the door. Seeing her always generated a smile regardless of the seriousness of the visit. This time she was eight months pregnant and more radiant than ever. "I will never understand why you married Jason. He doesn't appreciate your smile the way I do."

"You're right my brother," Jason said as he joined them in the foyer. "I appreciate all the other attributes my wife has. Why are you putting your life in danger by hitting on my wife?"

"I should have known you weren't far away from her."

"I can't man, she keeps tripping over her feet," Jason laughed.

"That's not funny Jason. You made me this way."

"And I love all of you, big belly and all."

"Uncle Ty." His five-year old niece Sierra ran and jumped into his arms.

"Hello Sierra." He caught her in the air and swung her around. "How's my favorite niece?"

"Oh, Heaven is not going to like that," TeKaya warned.

"She's my favorite baby niece. Sierra is my favorite big girl niece."

"Un huh. Nice clean up." TeKaya laughed.

Ty heard the laughter, as they neared the kitchen. Seeing his eighteen month old niece Heaven, walking gingerly towards him in bare feet, with her arms up, made him smile. He reached down and picked her up with the other arm.

"You look good holding them." His brother Eric smiled. "You need to have some of your own."

Looking around the room at the happy couples, made him regret the reason he was there. At the same time it reinforced his determination to keep them this way.

"It's easy to do Ty." Jason walked over to the stove where he was preparing lunch for everyone. "All you have to do is stop being so stubborn and make Kiki your wife."

"I don't recall asking your advice on my love life."

"What love life? Your life is the agency. I don't give a damn if you ask my advice or not, you're going to get it.

You need that woman in your life, period. The only time you took a moment to enjoy life was when Kiki was with you. That's all I have to say about the matter."

"Wait for it." Eric held up his hand.

"When the right woman comes into your life, you've got to grab her and tell her you love her and want to spend the rest of your miserable life with her. That's what I did with TeKaya. You need to do the same thing."

"I thought you were finished with the matter." Ty replied.

"Deal with it my brother, I've had to," Eric laughed.

Siri walked over, kissed Ty on the cheek, as she took Heaven from his arm. "Hello Ty. How are you?"

"Hello Siri." He placed Sierra back on the floor. "Would you ask Gabby to take the children? I need to talk to all of you."

The seriousness of his tone caused everyone to take pause for a moment. TeKaya looked at Jason as Siri stole a glance at Eric.

"Gabby," TeKaya called out.

Gabby, the fifty something year old housekeeper, came into the room. "Tyrone." She hugged him. "How are you son? It seems like it's been forever since we've seen you."

"Hello Gabby. It has been awhile," Ty replied.

"Gabby would you take the children in the other room while we talk?" Jason asked.

"Sure, come on pumpkin eaters," she teased as she took Heaven from Siri's arm and held her hand down to Sierra.

Eric was the first to speak. "What's up Ty?"

Jason asked in a concerned voice, "What's going on?"

"Roy Kelly was stabbed night before last."

"The investigator?" Jason asked.

"And?" Eric coolly replied.

"Eric, the man helped us get LaToya out of our lives. Show a little sympathy here."

"Why should I? He was the one that took the video of my wife and I while we were in the privacy of our home. Then he sold that video, which cost my wife her job and public humiliation. Why should I have any sympathy for Roy Kelly?"

Siri walked over and placed her hand on her husband's shoulder. "He redeemed himself," she said.

"We would not have been able to salvage the situation without his help," Jason added.

"We wouldn't have had the situation if it wasn't for him."

"Excuse me," Ty interrupted his brothers. "There's more."

"What?" TeKaya rubbed her protruding stomach, as she stood closer to Jason.

"Someone attempted to kidnap Kiki last night."

Eric stood, taking Siri's hand in his. Jason's arm surrounded TeKaya's waist, pulling her closer to him. "Attempted?" Jason asked. "Where is she?"

"In the hospital in New York. Her family and the Tower One are with her."

"What happened Ty?" Eric asked.

"Short version, when I received the call on Roy we flew in to see him. He was able to tell me what the attacker said while he was on the ground nearly bleeding to death."

"What?" TeKaya asked.

"Karma. The moment Roy said that, only one person came to mind."

"LaToya," Eric hissed. He closed his eyes and shook his head before looking up at Jason.

"LaToya. I left Roy and flew back to Atlanta to pay her a visit."

"What did she say?" Jason asked.

"She's been saved. Her only concern is with her daughter."

TeKaya inhaled. "She cannot have Sierra." She turned to look up at Jason. "She cannot have her back Jason."

"I know babe. Let's listen to all Ty has to tell us."

"She's not getting my baby girl, I don't care what Ty has to say."

Ty had to smile. TeKaya was just as spicy as Kiki. He shook the thought from his head. "After the visit with LaToya, my gut told me to check on Kiki. I flew to New York. When I arrived a guy had her in a sack slung over his shoulder and was heading down the stairwell. A chase ensued, I got Kiki back then took her to the hospital." After a brief moment of hesitation, he replied, "I think LaToya is behind both incidents."

"We should have killed her," Eric sighed.

"We don't kill people Eric," Jason replied.

"Maybe we should start thinking about it big brother."

"Eric," Jason began.

"No, Jason." Eric cut him off. "It wasn't TK that suffered at LaToya's antics, it was Siri. She had nothing to do with the situation, but she was the one that paid the price. I understand and accept your position on LaToya. She is your daughter's mother. Okay, but this woman is dangerous. She plotted against me for years. Years, Jason. That's crazy man. I say handle crazy with crazy."

"Eric you are letting your emotions control your actions again," Jason cautioned. "Calm down."

"You calm down Jason. Ty, kill her."

"I'm with Eric on this one," TeKaya stated.

"TK," Siri cautioned. "Ty is not going to kill LaToya."

This is where Ty sat back and allowed the two brothers, and now their wives to have their say, then he would step in and tell them how to fix the situation.

"Why the hell not? She's after Kiki now," Eric stated. "Hell, I'm surprised he hasn't already killed her."

Everyone in the room stopped talking and turned to him.

There was silence for a moment. "No," Ty replied to the unasked question.

"If you did, it would certainly take care of the problem," TeKaya suggested.

Ty looked at his brothers. "Why do your wives think I kill people? What have you been telling them?"

"The truth," Eric and Jason replied in unison, then looked at each other and laughed. "People that mess with us usually disappear," Jason stated.

"I handle people. I don't kill them. Even if they push in that direction as LaToya is doing."

"So what are you going to do?" TeKaya asked.

"I've called your security team together. They will be with you until we have the situation under control."

"What about Kiki?" Siri asked.

"I'll be with Kiki. Nothing is going to happen to her or to any of you."

A sigh of relief resonated around the room.

"Is it okay if I call her?" A concerned Siri asked.

While TeKaya was sassy and feisty, her sister Siri was the quiet, thoughtful one. He loved both of them and wished he could find a woman with a little of both of them. Kiki popped right into his mind. "I'm flying back to New York after the meeting with security."

"We want to be a part of that meeting," Jason suggested just as the doorbell chimed.

"I thought you might." Ty turned to let the head of security in.

Jason and Eric looked at each other then at their wives. "Neither of you will be out of our sight until this is over," Jason demanded.

Chapter Five

"*W*hat in the hell do you mean I can't leave? The tests came back negative. There are no side affects other than the burn mark on my shoulder. Why do I have to stay here?" Kiki asked, furious that the doctor would not release her from the hospital.

"Ms. Simmons, the doctor will explain everything," the nurse stated for the third time.

"Kendra, watch your tone. It's not the nurse's fault that the doctor did not sign the release papers."

"I know Mom. But I want to go home." Kiki sat back on the bed.

"I'm sure Mr. Pendleton will explain everything when he gets here," the nurse stated with a smile, thinking that would ease her patient's anxiety.

"Mr. Pendleton? What does Mr. Pendleton have to do with this?"

"Well, he's the one that spoke to the Doctor early this morning," the nurse replied as she took a step back realizing she may have said the wrong thing.

"Did he tell the Doctor to keep me here?"

"Kendra," Isadore cautioned.

"Did he?" Kiki asked again. "Why would he do that? He doesn't have the right to speak for me. Where is the Doctor? You call him right now and tell him he will release me or I'm walking out the door."

"No, you're not." All eyes went to the doorway where Ty stood looking like he just walked off the cover of GQ magazine. "Would you excuse us?" He smiled as he spoke to the nurse. "Mrs. Simmons would you give Kendra and I a moment alone?"

Issy stared at her daughter, but she already knew she was leaving the room. "Of course."

"Mom."

"I'll be right outside," she said to Ty. As she walked out the door, she looked back at her daughter and smiled. Ty closed the door.

"Did you tell the Doctor to keep me here?"

"Yes."

"Why in the hell would you do that? You know I do not like hospitals. The tests came back clear, there is no lingering effect from the electric shock. Besides, you have no right to control where I go or don't go."

"How are you?"

"What do you mean how am I? I'm fine as you can see."

"Yes, you are."

"Ohhh," she stepped back shaking her head, "don't do that." She turned away from him.

"Kiki, someone tried to kidnap you. If you think for one moment I would let you out of my sight you don't know me very well."

"Now that I can agree with. I don't know you Tyrone. I don't know why you were at my condo last night. I don't know why you are here now. So we finally have something we can agree on."

"I need you to stay with me in Atlanta for a while."

"I don't stay with men I don't know."

"You're going to stay with me."

"No, I'm not." She stood, folded her arms across her chest and stared him down.

He wondered if she thought he did not see her grimace when she folded her arms. God, she was a stubborn woman. "You are under the impression that this is a negotiation Kiki, but it's not. You can leave here with me willingly or I can carry you back to Atlanta. The choice is yours."

"Let me tell you something Tyrone Pendleton." She unfolded her arms and used them to animate her words. "You can't come here telling me what I am going to do. I have a job, a career here."

"Not with that again."

"Yes, that again Ty. I'm not going to give up my life and or career to live with you in Atlanta or anywhere else. You can take that caveman mentality and go straight back to your precious Atlanta. I don't need you. I can take care of myself."

"Can you?" He asked so quietly she barely heard him. "Last night a man shot a bolt of electricity through your body, put you in a bag and was carrying you out of the building. You needed me then and I was there. I will always be there."

God, she hated him. She had never been afraid of much. However, the fact that someone took her out of her home scared her to death. She felt safe when he held her while she slept this morning. He never raised his voice but his words cut through her armor a little. "I don't want to need you Ty," she said in a whisper. "You aren't here the way I need you to be."

"I'm here in every way that I can be."

"It's not enough."

He took a step towards her. She stepped back and sat on the side of the bed. Thinking straight when he was around was difficult. Just being in the same room with him turns her brain into mush. When he touched her it was total surrender. Even after a year her body still could not resist his touch. "I don't know what happened last night. All I can do is thank you for being there. But you have to understand, I can't go to Atlanta with you. I want to go home."

Seeing the desperation in her eyes cut him. This was a strong woman, who could handle most situations. He hated that something like this was happening to her. It demonstrated weakness, and that was always difficult for her to show. "Compromise. I can take you home, but I'm staying with you."

"Like hell you are!" She shouted as she jumped up. "You can't stay at my place."

"Then you'll be coming to Atlanta," he replied as calmly as he could with the vein in his neck throbbing at full speed.

"I am NOT, let me say it again, I am NOT going to Atlanta."

"Atlanta or New York I don't give a damn!" He yelled then caught himself. He closed his eyes and exhaled. When he opened them he could see the surprise in her eyes at him raising his voice. He reached out, placing his hand under her chin and looked into her eyes. "Someone tried to cause you harm. I can't let that happen. Will it be Atlanta or New York?"

The look in his eyes was so intense she knew he meant exactly what he said. If he had to, he would carry her back to Atlanta. "New York," she whispered.

He gently kissed her lips. "Thank you."

Outside, Issy watched as her daughter and Tyrone argued. At one point, she took a step towards the door but was stopped.

"They're going to be okay." Jake smiled reassuringly.

"You think so?" She looked back towards the room.

"Yes, I do. They have been having this argument for over a year."

Issy turned back to him. "What are they arguing about?"

"It's not my place to say. But I will tell you it's stupid as hell."

Issy looked at the bear of a man and smiled. "Really?"

"Oh yeah," Jake replied as he retook his seat outside the room. "One day I'll tell you about it over a few bottles of Merlot."

Issy raised an eyebrow. "A few bottles?"

"Oh yeah."

The door to the room opened and Ty walked out. "We'll be staying in New York for a while."

"Tyrone, how serious is this threat against my child?"

"Mrs. Simmons."

"Issy."

"Issy, I can't say. What I can tell you is as long as I'm breathing nothing is going to happen to Kendra."

"I appreciate that. But, I still want to know what's happening with my daughter."

"As soon as I have all the facts, I'll share them with you. Right now I better give the Doctor the okay to release that wildcat of a daughter of yours before she actually does kill me. Excuse me."

Issy watched as Ty walked to the nurse's station, then looked back at Kiki in the room. "He's in love with her and fighting it."

Jake nodded his head. "She's in love with him and doesn't want to be."

The two began laughing. Issy went and sat next to Jake. "Who's out to hurt my child?"

Jake looked to the side where she was now sitting. "That was smooth the way you did that."

"I have three grown sons. I have to work things out of them all the time. You're no different."

"There's a huge difference."

"What's the difference?"

"I'm not one of your sons." He held her gaze for a moment then smiled as he stood. "I'm going to pull the car around. I'm sure Rocket is more than ready to leave this place."

"Rocket?"

"Yeah, those firecrackers that shoot off like a rocket going in twenty different directions, and you know if you're not careful they will burn you, but you are still fascinated by them?"

"Yes, I know what you're talking about."

"That's your daughter."

Issy laughed and she nodded her head in agreement. "You know her well."

"I do. After this morning, watching you handle the unpleasant situation with your ex-husband, I know where she gets it from."

Issy pulled back and gave him one of those mother looks. "Where?"

Jake glared at her, laughed then walked away.

It was after six o'clock Sunday night before they left the hospital. Kiki was so exhausted,she fell asleep on the ride home. Ty carried her inside, undressed her, then tucked her in bed. He walked into the kitchen to find Issy, Wayne and Jake sitting at the table.

"Is she still sleeping?" Issy asked as she pushed a cup of coffee in front of the chair they left for Ty.

He nodded. "Yes."

"Kendra mentioned something to me about some kind of sting operation you had her involved in last year," Wayne stated. "Is this situation connected to that?"

"I believe so."

"Was it the situation with Silk Davies?" Issy asked.

"Yes."

"That was a sad situation. I felt bad for Siri." She shook her head. "She's such a lovely person."

"It takes nerve to come into a person's home the way he did," Wayne stated.

"It does," Ty nodded agreement as he drank his coffee.

"Not much of a conversationalist are you?" Wayne asked.

"Not when I feel as if I'm being interrogated."

"You feel right, you are being interrogated. You pulled my sister into a sting operation and now her life is in danger. You're lucky interrogating is all I'm doing right about now."

"Wayne," Issy cautioned. "Tyrone kept Kendra from harm's way."

"He should have, he placed her there."

"That's not quite true," Jake interceded. Ty gave him a look that indicated not to say anything more. Jake ignored him. "Rocket has a way of placing herself in situations as the need arises. She saw where she could help in the extortion case and she was instrumental in putting the guilty party away."

"Now that person is seeking revenge?" Issy asked.

Jake nodded and looked at Ty for him to continue the story.

"Yes," Ty replied.

"Do you care to elaborate on that?" Wayne asked.

"Don't answer." Issy began to laugh.

"No," Ty replied.

"I knew it. You are as exasperating as Kendra." She continued laughing as she walked over to the kitchen counter. "It must be something they teach you in law school." She shrugged her shoulders. "Anyone hungry?"

"I am, for information." Wayne continued to stare at Ty. "We are her family, while I'm not sure what you are to her."

"I am," Issy said as she opened the refrigerator. "Well, I'll be. That girl does listen to me sometimes." She pulled out salmon and vegetables.

Jake walked over. "Ty had me stock the fridge this morning." He pulled out a few steaks, green peppers and onions, then walked over to the center island.

Ty and Wayne were the only two remaining at the table, staring each other down.

"Don't you think we have a right to know what's happening? We are her family."

"Say it again. I don't think I heard you the first few times," Ty stated as he placed his coffee cup back on the table, then stared up at Wayne.

"I could beat it out of you."

"You could try."

Jake and Issy now stood at the island watching the battle that was sure to take place.

"Nobody is going to beat anybody in my house," Kiki stated as she walked into the kitchen. Ty stood to pull her chair out. She looked around. "Where's Garland and Martin?"

Wayne replied as he continued to stare at Ty. "Garland had to get back to the restaurant. Martin went to handle things at the office while I stayed here to make sure you are protected."

Kiki sat, placing her face in her hands. "I'm fine Wayne. The only thing wrong with me at the moment is that I have a monster headache."

"That's to be expected," Ty said as he stood, walked over to the cabinet next to the refrigerator and pulled out a bottle of aspirin. He pulled a bottle of water from the refrigerator and placed it on the table in front of her, then gave her the aspirin.

After taking the pills, she closed her eyes and took a moment to let the tablets flow down her throat. When she looked up all eyes in the room were on her. "I'm not dead people."

"People in this room and some that are not here care about you," Ty replied as he took his seat.

"Do they?" She stared at Ty.

Holding her stare, he replied, "Yes, they do."

She held his stare a few seconds longer, then turned to her brother. "He's a lawyer. He's not going to reveal any details about the sting until I give him permission to." She turned back to Ty. "You can tell them."

Ty nodded as he sat forward. "A year ago LaToya Wright attempted to blackmail Eric Davies. What the public does not know is that she had been paid millions by Jason Davies the week before. The family was going to continue to be extorted by her one way or another if she wasn't stopped. We set up a sting operation with the local authorities. Ms. Wright insisted someone other than myself had to handle the transaction. Kiki stepped in to carried the plan to fruition."

"LaToya said it wasn't over when they carried her out," Kiki added. "I guess she was right. Wright is right," she said and began laughing. "You get it," she said as she looked around the room. No one saw the humor in her joke. "Oh come on, loosen up people. We don't even know if kinky LaToya is behind this."

"You have men shooting you with a bolt of electricity and throwing you over their shoulder regularly?" Ty asked in a seriously low voice.

"Maybe," Kiki gave the sassy reply.

"It ends now."

"You can't tell me what to do." Kiki raised her voice. "Why do you care one way or another?"

"Because I care," he replied in his quiet way.

Jake and Issy turned away from the soon to be argument and began to prepare the food. Wayne sat at the end of the table not believing what he was seeing.

"Why in the hell are you here? Why are you insisting on interrupting my life?" Kiki yelled in disgust.

Ty shook his head. "I'm not here to interrupt your life Kendra." He sat up. "I'm here to keep you safe."

She hated it when he used her given name. He only did it when he wanted to drive a point home. "You're the one that is creating a danger zone for me. I don't give a damn about some unknown person."

"How am I doing that Kiki?"

"You're driving me crazy just by being here."

"Both of you are driving me crazy," Wayne yelled. "What is wrong with you?" He asked Kiki. "I don't know this man but he clearly cares something about you. Hell, at the very least he saved your behind from that unknown assailant. Why are you trying to send him away?"

"She has her reasons." He glared at Wayne. He and Kiki may have their differences, but that was between them. No one else could criticize her in front of him. He sat up then took Kiki's hand in his. "You can yell, kick and scream. I'm not leaving until I know this person has been apprehended and we can determine his reasons for attempting to take you from your home."

Jake nudged Issy's shoulder. She looked up and he tilted his head towards the actions at the table behind them. She looked back and saw the two dueling lovers holding hands. Looking back at Jake, they smiled then turned back to the food.

Kiki relished the feel of his powerful hands. She momentarily closed her eyes, allowing his strength and confidence to ease her fears. Yes, she was afraid. There, she admitted it to herself. "What are we going to do?" She asked as she slowly pulled her hand from his.

"Do what I do best, eliminate irritants." Ty sat back.

"Why are you so sure this is LaToya?"

"The hit on Roy," he shook his head, "It was brutal."

"Yeah but according to you this Roy Kelly had been involved in dirty dealings before."

"Not since the sting. He's been living right, building his agency, keeping a very low profile. Tower 1 and 2 have been keeping a close eye on him. We have a few clients in the area he has been handling for us. There was no reason for him to go back to sleazy cases."

"Roy was clean," Jake stated as he placed a platter of steaks with sautéed' green peppers and onions in the center of the table.

"Who is Roy and what does he have to do with what happened to Kiki," Wayne asked as his mother placed a platter of salmon, and another platter with steamed vegetables on the table.

Kiki started to stand, but Ty touched her hand to stop her. He stood, walked over to the cabinet, pulled out plates, then silverware from the drawer. "Roy was the investigator who took the pictures that LaToya used to blackmail Eric." He walked back over and began setting the table.

"How did he come to work for you?" Issy asked as she placed glasses on the table.

"I made him an offer he couldn't refuse." Ty grinned. Wayne and Issy looked at each other.

"I came in after Roy." Kiki added, then asked, "What was the offer?"

"I paid him fifty-thousand to help us take LaToya down. I also placed the Towers as his guards."

Kiki laughed. "That would have been enough to scare Mother Teresa."

Jake took a seat at the table.

"Who are the Towers?" Wayne asked.

"Jake and Peace," Issy answered.

Kiki and Ty glared at her. "What?"

Kiki and Ty glared at each other then turned to Jake, who ignored them and began filling his plate.

"I also promised to send work his way if he stayed clean," Ty continued as he slowly turned his glare from Jake.

"Ah, so that's why you are so certain Roy had cleaned up his game," Kiki stated as she accepted the plate Ty had prepared for her.

"Why would a promise of work from you guarantee he stayed straight? Someone could offer him more money," Wayne suggested as he prepared his plate.

Kiki laughed as Ty replied. "We gave him a hundred grand from the sting. Work from my office will total at least 2.5 million in his pockets from the clients in North Carolina." Wayne froze while transferring food from the platter to his plate. Issy looked up and stared at Ty. "Monthly." Wayne dropped his fork. "That alone will give him a comfortable life."

A stunned Wayne and Issy stared at Ty. "If this Roy was making that amount of money, what do you make?" Issy asked.

Ty prepared his plate, bowed his head and said grace. "I'm comfortable."

Kiki shook her head. "You have no idea what that means coming from him, Mom."

"Okay, so what made you think it was this LaToya Wright person who is involved?" Issy asked.

"The person that attacked Roy did not intend to kill him. They wanted him to feel it. To suffer," Ty explained. "A man would have simply killed him. Only a woman would seek that kind of revenge."

"So you went to see her, didn't you?" Kiki asked.

Ty glanced at her with a grin. "I did."

"And, did she confess?" Kiki asked.

"No, not her style. She's found God."

"Ha ha," Kiki laughed.

"What's wrong with finding God?" Issy asked.

"LaToya Wright is Lucifer's daughter," Jake offered.

"You got that right," Kiki replied with a yawn.

"You okay?" Ty inquired. "You need to rest. Your body has been through a trauma."

"I want to know what she had to say," Kiki ignored his question.

"She has a new man in her life."

"How? She's been in jail for the last year."

"That's what I'm going to find out." His phone rang and a picture of Rosa Sanchez appeared.

Kiki looked over. "Who is she?"

Ty looked at the phone. "An employee."

"You carry pictures of your employees now?"

"I have to take this." Ty picked up the phone and walked out of the room.

Kiki looked at Jake.

"Don't," he said as he stood and walked over to the sink with his plate.

"Why?"

"Because he's my boss, my friend and you know better," Jake replied.

Kiki stared at Jake's back. "Make sure there's a battle before you start the fight Kendra," Issy said to her daughter. "Make sure there's a battle." She leaned across the table and patted her daughter's hand, then walked with her empty plate over to the sink.

Ty walked back into the room and for a moment everyone held their breath. He looked at Kiki. "She's an employee and you know better."

Jake looked over his shoulder. "Told you."

Kiki got up and walked out of the room. Ty closed his eyes and exhaled, then looked up. "Excuse us."

Issy looked up at Jake. "I don't know you, but I trust what you'll tell me. Is he in love with my daughter?"

"Yes," Jake replied.

"Is he involved with another woman?"

"No."

"Then who was the woman on the phone?" Wayne asked.

"His employee," Jake said over his shoulder. "Let's be clear. My loyalty lies with him and any extension of him. That includes Kiki."

Ty knew the moment he opened the door to her bedroom he was in trouble. Kiki was pulling her blouse over her head as he walked in. She threw the blouse in his face and walked into the adjoining bathroom.

Ty folded the blouse and placed it neatly on the chair in the corner of her room. Looking around he had to smile. It was exactly as he imagined her bedroom would be. Most people would think she would have a punked out bedroom because of the spiked hairdo, the funky style of dress and that sassy mouth of hers, but he knew better. The cherry wood high poster bed with the royal blue comforter set, pillows piled neatly on the bed before he had pushed them aside earlier. The drapes matched the comforter and the fabric on the Queen Anne chair near the door. It was a taste of Virginia in the middle of Manhattan. Standing in the bathroom doorway, he watched as she brushed her teeth in her black lace bra and jeans.

"Rosa Sanchez is an employee. You know me well enough to know I don't do my employees."

"Who you do is not my business." She rinsed out her mouth and placed the toothbrush on the side of the sink. Ty walked over, picked up the toothbrush, rinsed it and placed it in the holder. He turned just as she stripped out of her bra and jeans then stepped into the shower. The effect of her naked behind gave him an instant hard on. "Damn," was all he whispered, then sat in the Queen Anne chair, laid his head back to try to get his libido under control. Emotions were high and all he wanted to do was hold her until her fears and anger subsided.

The water turning off indicated she had finished with her shower. He held his head up,."It's going to be a long night." He stood, walked back into the bathroom, pulled a towel from the warmer and waited. The moment she pulled the shower curtain back his body yearned for her. His eyes traveled down her long sleek neck, across her shoulders, then to the bruise above her left breast. His heart sank. He stepped over with every intention of wrapping her in the towel. Instead his lips kissed the bruised area. "I'm so sorry this happened."

Kiki knew it was hurting him to see her hurt. All she wanted to do was comfort him. "It's all right." She caressed the back of his head. "You got here in time."

He kissed her neck, then stepped back to wrap her in the towel. "I will never let anyone hurt you. You know that." He looked into her eyes.

It was on the tip of her tongue to say you hurt me everyday you stay away. But she knew he needed her reassurance at that moment, not her mouth. "I know." She kissed the top of his head. "I know." She wrapped her arms around him as he did her. "It all happened so fast." He felt the first drop of a tear touch his neck. He held her tighter. "You know I'm a fighter."

His lips curled up for a second. "I know you are."

She exhaled and held him tighter. "You being here makes it harder for me to get over you. I have to protect myself from you." She sniffed. His hands gently caressed her smooth back. "I know you need to be here and to be honest, I want you here. But after you eliminate this threat you are going back to Atlanta. I'll still be in love with you and you will still be in denial. The fight will continue counselor." She could feel the heat emanating from his body. Placing her head more snuggly in the crook of his neck, she continued. "I have to set some rules."

"Rules?" He kissed her wet shoulder as his hands moved lower to her waist.

"Yes." She pulled his shirt from his pants to touch the heat she knew was beneath. "Rules just for you." The towel and his clothes were all that separated them from what they both desired. It had been over a year since they had touched each other, kissed each other, caressed each other. Neither was sure if the wetness between them was caused from her wet body or the heat that was engulfing them. Her hands traveled up his spine, causing his desire to rise more than it already had. She then turned her face to his neck and kissed the vein that was pumping furiously from her touch.

"Rules," he stated as his hands roamed over the globes of her behind, bringing the junction of her heat in direct contact with the bulge inside his pants that was growing by the second. He heard her sharp intake of breath from the contact. "What are your terms?" He asked as he kissed her temple.

She raised one leg to get closer to the heat penetrating through the cloth barriers, hooking it right over his buttocks. He lifted her from the floor as her other leg completed the circle. He kicked off his shoes and stepped into the shower stall. Pressing her against the back wall, he allowed the towel to fall then captured one of her protruding chocolate tipped buds between his lips. First he sucked gently, allowing the joy of touching her to invade his being. It felt so good as the suckling intensified.

"No kissing," she moaned as his tongue circled her nipple.

He released the bud. "You mean like this?" His lips fiercely captured hers with a power, that rendered her speechless and completely incapable of moving when it ended. He reached between them, unbuckled his belt, unzipped his pants allowing them to fall into the stall, then pressed more intimately against her core. "Can I do this?" He kissed the area between her breasts, then ran his tongue up to her throat, suckling right under her chin.

The heat was building and there was no way she was going to ignore it. Hell, she missed it, wanted it, craved it. With the heel of her foot, she began to push his briefs down over his butt. The bulge in the front was blocking the path. Ty reached down and smoothly removed the material that was blocking them. The moment the briefs dropped, Ty lifted her body by the waist and entered her in one powerful thrust. They both stilled, stared at each other, allowing their eyes to reveal what they were feeling inside. His hands tightened around her waist as he began to move within her. She pulled his head down until their lips met in the sweetest kiss. Their tongues moved rhythmically against each other, their bodies following in turn. His thrusts inside of her deepened as did the kiss. The rhythm increased. The urge to go deeper was consuming him. His body, moving faster, harder, until they could no longer concentrate on the kiss. His head dropped to the crook of her neck as her hands tightened on his buttocks, pulling him deeper and deeper into her. His body, continuously merging with hers to reach that peak that they both had to have. His thickness touching everything in her and yet she wanted more. She wanted everything he had to give. She squeezed her thighs together, taking all of him as deep as she could, until the moment he slammed into her and they both screamed their release. He didn't stop even then. His hands moved to her face, cupping it and kissing her as he continued to move within her, savoring the heat from the juices her body was releasing. She anxiously squeezed all the fluid of life from him as the muscles in their bodies contracted with joy.

They remained entangled with each other, their chests heaving, arms not willing to release the other. Ty reached over, turned the shower on, then moved their bodies under the water. The coolness of the flooding water eased the pounding of their hearts.

"Your clothes are wet," she whispered in that voice that always sent chills down his back.

"Not as wet as you are," he replied, kissing her cheek.

"I'm always wet when you are around." She brushed her lips against his.

He inhaled the scent of her hair that was now slicked back and wet from the shower and the scent of their lovemaking, the essence of them. "Why did you leave me Kiki?"

She eased one leg back to the floor of the stall. With one hand braced against the shower wall and the other securely around her waist, he remained lodged within her. He just wasn't ready to let her go.

"You aren't able to give me what I need."

"Tell me, what you need." He eased out, then pushed back in hitting her from a different angle. "Tell me."

She ran her hand across his powerful back. "I need you Ty. All of you, heart, body and soul." She kissed the side of his neck, his earlobe, his cheek, then rested her cheek against his.

The regret in his voice was clear as he withdrew from her. "Kiki."

She eased her other leg down, and exhaled. "I'll let you shower." She stepped out, taking the wet clothes with her.

The once heated shower was now cold as Ty took a moment to get his senses back under control. It didn't matter that they'd just made love, he wanted her again. He just didn't think he would ever get enough of her. Therein lie his problem.

When he stepped out of the shower, there was another towel on the warmer. He dried off, then walked into the bedroom where he found a pair of slacks and a dress shirt neatly lying across the chair, but there was no sign of Kiki. After dressing, he walked down the long hallway leading to the great room where he found Wayne and Jake.

"You appear to be in more trouble than you were before," Wayne stated as he took a drink.

"Where's Kiki?" The concern was clear in his voice.

"In the guest room with Issy," Jake replied.

The relief was clear on his face.

"I think it's safe to say they are discussing you," Jake added as he gave Ty a glass of bourbon.

Ty took the drink, gulping it down in one swallow. "Any word from Peace?" It took Jake a moment to reply. Normally, that glass would last the night with Ty.

"Not yet," Jake replied.

"We need to find the outside person to link LaToya to what's happening."

"Any leads on how we can find that person?" Wayne inquired.

Ty shook his head as he placed his feet on the table and crossed them at the ankles. My resources did locate her new source of income. An account in the Cayman Islands is making direct deposits into her bank account. The information I received tonight shows a total of two-hundred and fifty-thousand had recently been received into the account and then immediately deposited into another."

"Who does the account belong to?" Wayne asked.

"That's the information we cannot access," Ty stated. "The Cayman banks will not release account information."

"So she hired someone to hurt those involved in the sting beginning with your friend Roy," Wayne summarized. "So who else was involved in the sting?"

"Kiki, Eric, and the Chief of Police," Ty stated. "Barry Goldman."

"We should check on him." Jake stood to make a call.

"What happened with you and my sister?" Wayne asked when Jake walked out of the room. "You two clearly care about each other. So, what happened?"

"Boss," Jake rushed back into the room, "Chief Goldman had a heart attack on the same day Roy was stabbed."

"Coincidence?" Wayne asked.

"I don't believe in coincidences." Ty stated.

Chapter Six

*T*he next morning Ty was sitting at the island drinking a cup of coffee when he heard the heels clicking against the wood floor step into the hallway. He was still a little miffed about her mother taking his place in her bed, which meant he had to either share the spare room with Wayne or sleep on the couch. He chose the couch. Jake took the night shift patrolling the hallway.

All of that became a second thought as Kiki walked in dressed in a short black skirt and red blazer with a black tee underneath. The heels were at least three inches high, which just made her legs seem longer than they already were. Her hair was held back by a band that created a short afro puff on top of her head, hoop earrings and little to no makeup completed her look.

"Good morning," he said as she walked into the kitchen.

"Good morning."

"You're dressed for work."

"That's good Sherlock." She grabbed a container of yogurt from the refrigerator, then walked towards the closet next to the door.

He leaned against the wall as she pulled a coat from the closet. "You can't go to work today."

She glanced at him, then continued putting her coat on. "Watch me." She grabbed her purse, then turned and opened the door.

"Morning Rocket." Jake smiled.

She turned and looked at Ty. "Really Ty? Why?"

The disappointment was clear on her face. It was something he would just have to suffer through. He took her hand pulling her back inside and closed the door. "Kiki," he hesitated.

She just shook her head, then dropped her head on his chest. "Just tell me. Whatever has happened now, just tell me."

He took the purse form her hand, then took her coat off and hung it back in the closet. Taking her hand he walked into the family room, he sat her on the sofa, while he sat on the end of the chaise lounge. Rubbing his thumb across her knuckles, he began. "The police Chief that assisted us with the sting on LaToya, Barry Goldman, had a heart attack the same day Roy was assaulted. We asked the doctors to run his blood work, again. They found a drug that induced the heart attack." He hesitated for a moment as he contemplated how much he would tell her.

"Don't hold back. Tell me everything you know."

"My sources indicate, whoever is doing this is well trained in torture. He wasn't able to complete what he had planned for you. If he is the professional my source believes him to be, he will be back to finish the job."

Kiki pulled her hand from his as she sat back. "My life hasn't been the same since the day I met you." She sighed, then stood. "I'll call work to let them know I will be out indefinitely."

Ty watched as she walked into her room. The thought that he was the reason she was in this predicament grated on his nerves. His cell phone chimed. "What do you have for me Peace?"

"Boss, for the first few months, the only visitor Wright had was her mother. Her cellmate had no visitors in ten years. However, the visitor's log shows a Roberto Garrison that was visiting an inmate by the name of Bertha Michaels. About six months ago, each time Garrison visited Bertha it appeared on the list under Tina Wright. It's a long shot Boss. But, it's all we got."

"Send me those names. Let's see what we can do with the information." Ty disconnected the call. When he received the names, he forwarded them to Rosa Sanchez to do a money trail. He placed his phone on the tabletop then walked over to the balcony.

It was cold in New York. The temperature was in the high forties here while in Atlanta it was in the seventies, in October. The last time he saw his bed was Thursday night. His normally organized life had been spinning out of control for the last 72 hours. That was unacceptable to him. He controlled life, life did not control him. It was time to get a grip on what was happening, then turn the tables on LaToya. He opened the balcony door, then stepped outside. There were times when you had to think like the opposition. This was one of those times. The cold air hit him immediately, waking his senses, putting them on alert.

He leaned against the bannister looking out over Central Park to the right, then the high-rise condos across the street. The contrast made him smile, a little of the suburbs on one side and the metropolitan area on the other. Looking over the park he stared off at nothing in particular. If he really wanted to eliminate someone where would he go to hire someone? Seconds ticked away, then he suddenly bolted upright. He walked back into the condo to get his phone. He dialed a number.

"I have a security question."

"Good morning to you too."

"Good morning. How would you find a professional assassin?"

"Hang up this phone. I'll call you back."

Ty hung up the telephone and waited. He answered as soon as the phone chimed. "How would I find an assassin?"

"First things first. Conversations of this nature only take place on a secure line. Cell phones are not secure. Talk to me. Why would you need an assassin?"

Ty explained the situation to Naverone. When he finished, she exhaled. "In this situation I would look for who is active then eliminate from there."

"Can you initiate a search?"

"Possibly."

"I need a definite."

"Give me a day." The call was disconnected.

"You really think an assassin is out to kill me?"

Ty turned around to see Kiki standing behind him. She had changed into a pair of jeans and a Yankees jersey.

Looking into her eyes he could not lie. "It's best to be prepared for all possibilities."

"My life is being altered and I don't like that. You fix things. I've seen you do it. Fix this. In the meantime, I'm sending my mother and brother home. I don't want any other person in the line of fire when this maniac comes after me again."

"Maniac or not, he's not getting near you again if I can help it."

Their eyes held for a moment. If she wasn't careful he would have her under his spell again. Kiki pulled away. "We have to talk about those rules."

"Rules in a relationship insinuate there is a lack of trust between the two parties involved."

"We're not in a relationship Tyrone. If you are going to stay here, and it appears that you are, we have to set some limits."

"Limits?"

"Ty, we can't keep our hands off each other. And I can't take having sex with you knowing when this is all over you are going to walk out of my life."

"I don't have to. You walked away, not me."

"You want me to live with you without a commitment. I can't do that."

"Why buy the milk if you have the cow for free?" Issy stated as she walked out of the bedroom. "I like you Ty," she said as she placed her overnight bag by the door. "But my daughter deserves as much love as she gives."

"Yeah, and from the sound of things, she gives good love." Wayne grinned.

"That's not funny Wayne," Kiki replied from the kitchen.

"It's as funny as your *Wright is right*."

"This is not a family discussion," Ty declared. "Kendra and I will decide where our relationship will go." He grabbed his jacket off the back of the stool. "I've requested a car to take you to the airport. My pilot will fly you back to Virginia. Jake is going to ensure you get home safely." He walked towards the door.

"I believe that's our cue to leave, Wayne."

"Mom," Kiki gave an angry eye to Ty, "Ty didn't mean it the way it came out. You are welcome to stay here as long as you want. It's just not safe right now."

"It's a touchy subject with us at the moment Mrs. Simmons. I did not mean it in a harsh way."

"I know you didn't Ty." She kissed his cheek. "You're a good man. A little lost, but a good man nonetheless. I think you are the perfect man for Kendra."

"Arugh," Kiki grabbed her keys off the table next to the front door. "Let's walk you down to the car before you cause more problems for me." She turned to Ty. "On the way we can discuss The Pendleton Rules."

Wayne and Issy looked at each other and shrugged.

"Rule number one," Kiki said as they walked out of the door. "There will be no sex."

Jake, who was standing in the hallway when they walked out, laughed. Ty stopped, looked over his shoulder and gave him a warning look.

"Rule number two, you will not interfere in my personal life." Kiki continued talking oblivious to the humor she was supplying to her audience. "That means dates or meetings or whatever is on my personal schedule."

"Do you have many of those?" Ty asked as they stepped into the elevator, that had several occupants.

"What?" she asked as the doors closed.

"Dates."

"No," she rolled her eyes, "but that's not the point. The point is you will not interfere if I do have any." He nodded as the elevator stopped on the eighteenth floor. "Rule number three, You will stay in the guest room, you will not sleep in my bed." Several people in the elevator turned to look at the couple. "That's right, Kendra," Issy offered her daughter a little support. "He doesn't have to buy the cow if he's already getting the milk for free."

Jake looked at Ty. He shrugged his shoulder. "She said it earlier and I don't understand the statement now any more than I did before."

"You will," Wayne laughed.

Ty smiled and continued to listen attentively.

"Rule number four..."

"Are there many of these?"

"Many of what?"

"Rules."

"No, just two more."

The elevator stopped on the tenth floor and one of Kiki's neighbors boarded. "Good morning Kiki." Sandy smiled as she looked Ty up and down. "Good morning."

"Good morning," Ty replied and smiled.

Kiki rolled her eyes. "Rule number four. You will not disrespect me by bringing other women into my home," she looked over her shoulder at Sandy," or by having sex in the state of New York."

Jake and Wayne did not hold back. They laughed as Ty continued to keep his composure. "Is it possible for us to finish this in private?" Ty asked as the elevator stopped again, allowing passengers to board.

"Yes, Kendra." Wayne said, "This is better discussed in private."

Kiki frowned at him. "There's just one more. Rule number five." She put five fingers up to his face. "NO SEX."

The people in the elevator turned and looked at the two of them. Sandy looked over her shoulder at Ty and smiled.

"You're repeating yourself counselor. If I remember correctly, that was number one."

"It's intentional. In light of your actions last night, I thought it bore repeating. I know you have a difficult time understanding the concept of rules."

As they stepped off the elevator into the lobby, Ty received a few sympathetic glances from the men. Sandy gave Ty her card. "If I can help with rule number five, just call."

Kiki took the card, tore it in half and gave it back to Sandy. "He won't be needing that. He is celibate. Is that our car?" She pointed to the black sedan waiting at the curb with the door open.

Jake was literally bent over laughing. When he stood he sobered at the look he received from Ty. Jake cleared his throat as he opened the back door for Issy, then got into the passenger seat. "At least I can have sex before leaving the state."

"You could always drive to Jersey," Wayne teased.

Ty leaned into the back window that Issy had rolled down. "Take care of my daughter."

"I will," he promised her then stood with Kiki and watched the vehicle pull off. He turned to walk back into the building. "Celibate? Since when?"

"Since nine p.m. yesterday."

"How convenient for you."

"I thought so." Kiki smiled up at him. "I mean what I say Tyrone. Those rules are going to be enforced."

"I believe you."

She unlocked the door, looking at him over her shoulder. "You are taking this too calmly. I need you to understand, I'm serious."

Taking her by the shoulders he turned her to face him. "I'm not going to lie to you. Every morning I wake up wanting to make love to you. I want you now. But you know what I want more?"

Kiki shook her head, reeling from his words. "No."

"I want you safe. If that means I have to keep my libido in check, so be it. It's a small sacrifice to ensure I get to see your beautiful face another day." He dropped his hands "The Pendleton Rules are in effect."

How was she supposed to keep her heart safe from him when he was constantly saying things like that? "Okay," she sighed as she turned away. "There is no reason we should not be able to cohabitate under one roof. We are adults, after all."

"I agree."

She walked behind the island. "What would you like for breakfast?" she asked from the kitchen.

"Surprise me."

The scope was being adjusted as the couple in the condo across the street came into view. The distance was not an issue. He had taken a man out from twelve hundred yards out. If he had his way, he would have taken Pendleton out while he stood on the balcony. It's fortunate for Pendleton that he was not next on the list. However, if he interfered in his plans again he would be the next casualty in this game.

Chapter Seven

*I*t had been less than forty-eight hours and it seemed like the last year had evaporated. They sat at the table eating breakfast, talking as if they had talked every day for the last year.

Ty had set his computer up on the table near the window. Her condo was a corner unit with a south view of Central Park from the front window and another set of condos from the west view. It could be distracting if he was not a dedicated worker. After a few days away from the office, he had several contracts that he needed to review, in addition to clients he needed to get back with. He was in the midst of a conference call on the computer with his secretary, Wendy, when Kiki called out.

"Breakfast is served."

Wendy looked up from the papers on the desk she was working from to grin at Ty. "We're having breakfast?" she asked with a little shake of her head.

"Yes Wendy," Kiki replied from the kitchen. "If you were here with us you would be feasting on omelets, bacon, apples, bagels, juice and coffee." She placed two plates at the breakfast bar, then turned back to the counter top.

"Wendy," Ty cautioned. "Nick Brooks, you were saying?"

"Oh yes boss." She cleared her throat. "We have his office and cell number to reach him. Would you like for me to make initial contact?"

"No, forward the information to me. I'll make contact."

"Coffee's up," Kiki announced.

Ty looked over his shoulder and smiled at the domestic sight of her in the kitchen. When he turned back, Wendy was grinning. "What?"

She smiled, leaned forward as if to whisper. "You must be in heaven right now." She sat back.

"Not sure what you mean." He clicked the document she had just placed on the monitor. "This is the report from Naverone on Jason Whitfield. Secure it, in case we need it in the future."

"Don't tell me it doesn't feel great to be around her again. I can see it in your demeanor. You haven't had that relaxed look in over a year." She waved her hand at him. "Oh, don't deny it. I can see you blushing through the computer."

Ty never looked up. "You are not above being replaced." He clicked another document. "When did this document come in?"

Wendy looked at the document he was in from her computer. "It came in this morning. Are you going to bring her back home?"

"No he's not," Kiki replied over his shoulder. "Hey Wendy."

"How's it going Kiki? We miss you around here." She smirked at Ty.

"The unemployment line is a cold place," he mumbled.

"Pay him no mind Wendy. He can't function without you." She patted Ty on the shoulder. "Time for breakfast." She bent over to see Wendy eye to eye. "He'll finish this up later." She winked as she disconnected the conference call.

He sat forward. "Kiki, I'm working."

She put her hands on her hips and frowned. "When was the last time you saw me in a kitchen cooking?"

"I've never seen you in a kitchen cooking."

"My point exactly." She pulled his chair back, and took his hand. "Breakfast."

Ty took a seat on a stool at the breakfast bar, bowed his head and said grace. Kiki sat next to him. "Did I hear Wendy mention Nicolas Brooks, from Brooks Sports Agency?"

"Yes. You know him?" Ty asked as he tasted the omelet. "Mmmm."

"Good?" She smiled.

"Better than good." He smiled at her. "Hidden talents."

"Have you met my mother?" She smiled. "Between chapters of whatever book she was writing, we were all being taught to hold our own in the kitchen."

"I never knew that."

"There's a lot you don't know about me." They held eyes for a few seconds, then she turned away. "I know you are doing a full investigation on Brooks. My question is why. You don't need more clients. You have the cream of the crop in the entertainment world."

Ty smiled at her while biting into a bagel with jelly instead of cream cheese. "Jarrett Bryson, Jason Whitfield and Justin Hylton."

Kiki almost choked on her coffee. "You're representing Jarrett Bryson now? How in the hell did that happen?"

"Their agent asked me to take them over as clients when he found out he had cancer. I promised him I would take care of them."

"Wow, I mean wow! Hylton and Bryson are so well established. What are you going to do with Whitfield? He's a wild card."

"Tell me about it," Ty replied as they continued to eat.

"He's young Ty." She sipped her coffee. "You have this strict code of professionalism that he is too young too understand."

"What are you talking about, I'm a great boss."

"I know you are. But we're talking about a kid that just came into millions after living with parents that could barely pay for his college books. He's away from the parents, the coaches, with women coming at him from every direction. He's going to need your touch Ty."

"You think I have a nice touch." He ate a slice of bacon as he eyed her at an angle.

"I know you do." Again she was the one to break the stare. "He could benefit from working with you. I've worked with you before and enjoyed every minute of it."

He sobered a little. "This is how I repay you. With someone trying to take your life."

"That's not on you. Hell, I loved seeing you at work. That brain of yours should be donated to science. You couldn't have stopped me from being a part of that if you had tried." Kiki smiled as she sipped on her coffee. "Your plan was flawless. How often do you have to do things like that for your clients?"

Shrugging his shoulders, he sat back. "It depends on the situation and client. All of my clients aren't as easy to control as Eric."

"Eric was easy?" She laughed. "If I remember correctly, didn't he want you to kill LaToya? You two were fighting because you refused to do as he asked."

Ty nodded his head with a grin. "Yesterday he asked me if I had killed LaToya for harming you. They all did."

"Siri too?"

"Siri too."

"Well, I can't blame her. LaToya did ruin her life."

He stood, taking her now empty plate and his. "I'll see her in hell before I'll allow her to ruin yours. That's for sure."

Kiki watched as he walked into the kitchen. "Watch it, Pendleton," she grinned. "I'm going to start thinking you care."

He placed the plates on the counter top then walked back over to the table to pick up the glasses. He stopped next to her and looked down into her beautiful brown eyes. "I do care, very much."

She held his gaze that filled her with warmth and longing. "You are going to make me break my own rules, aren't you?"

The ends of his lips curved into a smile. "No, I happen to think your rules are helpful." He walked off into the kitchen.

"How so?"

He turned and leaned against the sink. "Think about when we were together before. Did we ever sit down and talk like we have in the last hour?"

"That first night we talked for hours."

"Not like this."

"I know." She stood. "We didn't have death hanging over our heads then." She put her hands in her back pocket and dropped her head. "I thought we had forever in front of us." Standing there for a moment, she looked up at him. "I have a manuscript to review." She walked out of the room just as there was a knock at the door.

Kiki froze and turned to Ty. It was the same thing that happened the night she was taken. There was no call from the front desk.

"Go into your room," Ty said as he pulled his gun from the back of his pants.

"I'm not going to run to my room." They then heard a key enter the lock.

Ty looked questioningly at her. She shrugged her shoulders indicating she had no idea who was about to enter the condo. Ty pushed her against the wall in the hallway leading to the bedroom, while holding the gun aimed at the door. He reached in his pocket for his cell phone only to find it was not there. He glanced over to the table where he was working to see the phone lying there next to the computer. He would have to cross the foyer, giving the person entering direct access to him, but more it would mean walking away from Kiki, leaving her exposed as well. That was out of the question. They heard the lock turn. He felt as Kiki walked away. Good, she's going into the bedroom, he thought.

Wrong. Kiki came back out with a baseball bat and ran to the other side of the foyer, standing ready to swing. "I called security."

His attempt to catch her before she sailed by him was futile. "Kendra!" He ran and jumped in front of her just as the front door opened. Ty raised the gun and was about to fire when he heard a female voice call out.

"Kiki, you in here?"

Kiki looked around Ty's shoulder, then quickly pushed his arms down.

"What the hell are you doing here and when did you get a key to my condo?"

Ty put the gun back in the back of his pants as he watched a young woman in her early twenties look up and frown when she saw Kiki. The frown turned into a bright smile when those eyes met his.

"Well, I guess I don't have to ask where you have been for the last few days. Can't say I blame you," she spoke never taking her eyes off Ty.

"Why are you here?" Kiki put the bat on the floor against the wall.

The woman placed the folders in her hands on the table next to the door. "Aren't you going to introduce us?" She continued to smile up at Ty.

Kiki looked up at her, then at Ty. "No."

Ty almost laughed, but he had become accustomed to Kiki's bluntness. "Ty Pendleton," he held out his hand.

The woman extended her hand. "Laura Simmons."

"Any relation?"

"Unfortunately." Kiki stepped in between them and held out her hand. "Key."

"No," Laura said as she walked by both of them into the condo.

"What in the hell are you doing here?"

"Your father sent me."

Kiki grabbed her by the arm and directed her back towards the door. "Why?"

"He said as long as he is paying you, you will work." She folded her arms "So what's going on with you?"

"You don't need to know. Now leave."

"I'm not ready to leave." She walked around Kiki. "So who are you?" She grinned up at Ty. "More to the point who are you to her?" She nodded her head towards Kiki without looking at her.

"Not your business." Kiki got in the young girl's face. "Do I have to show you the way out?"

The two women stared each other down. For a minute Ty thought he was going to have to step in, but the woman stepped back and laughed. "You know, you can be a real bitch at times."

Kiki reached around and opened the door. "I've been called worse."

Laura looked over her shoulder as she walked out of the door. "You should be more selective of the women you let into your life Mr. Pendleton."

Kiki slammed the door behind her, then walked over to the kitchen and picked up the telephone. "Hello. This is Kendra Simmons in 812. I need the locks on my doors changed immediately." Ty frowned as he listened to her. "No, not tomorrow, within the hour. Thank you." She hung up the telephone.

"You will not take precautions against someone that attacked you, but you will against this girl?"

"That girl is.....evil," Kiki said, unable to come up with a better word to describe the woman.

"Who is she?" Ty wanted to grin but didn't dare. The look on Kiki's face indicated she was serious.

"The result of my father's sperm swimming in unmatrimonial territory."

The response puzzled Ty for a moment, then realization hit him. His gaze swung to the door Laura had just walked out of. "She's your sister?"

"Half....sister," she snapped as she picked up the folder and walked out of the room.

Ty was still a little thrown. Laura was a curly haired brunette, with skin so fair he thought she was Caucasian. "Talk about people passing," he mumbled then followed Kiki into a room off the family room. It turned out to be her office.

As he stood in the doorway watching her throw a mini tantrum, he had to smile. The office looked like her, wild and untamed. Compared to his home office, it was small, or maybe it was all the books and piles of unopened mail that made the office seem small and cluttered. There was a window that looked out onto the traffic below, a L-shaped desk, with the usual, telephone, computer, books, more books, and a round pencil holder with an assortment of red pencils inside. Two chairs were in front of the desk, with unopened mail piled in one and her purse and coat now thrown over the other. The wall to his right was covered with bookshelves, and loaded with more books. Behind him was a small refrigerator with a coffee pot and microwave on top. He had no doubt it was organized clutter, but clutter nonetheless.

"I don't want to talk about it Pendleton," Kiki exclaimed from behind the desk. "Besides I have work to do and you need to get back to your conference call with Wendy.

Ty smiled, then looked around. "I really don't like your back to that window."

Kiki looked over her shoulder. "Do you have any idea how many people in New York would kill to have this view? This was my father's way of compensating me for not being on the top floor in the office."

"Your father has issues with you being here?"

"Whew, that's an understatement. I remind him of his past life. One that he wishes to forget."

"Why not work at Battle with your brothers?"

"Maxine may be a home wrecker, but she is a damn good editor and can spot talent from reading a page of a manuscript. If I want to be at the top of my game, I need to learn from her. Besides, I have two of their five top grossing writers signed to exclusive contracts right now. My father will let me go, but he is not going to let them go anywhere."

"Your father was the one that broke the commitment he made to your mother, not Maxine."

"That's the same thing my mother said. She's the forgiving type. Me, I hold both of them responsible for breaking my mother's heart." She huffed and slammed her hand on the pages of the manuscript she had opened. "Can we talk about something else?" When she saw he was not moving, she turned away from him. "So, how are we going to do this? You're going to stand there and watch me all day?"

"As much as I would like to do just that, I do have an agency to run." He pulled a pile of mail from a chair and looked around. There was nowhere to put the mail, so he placed it on the floor next to him. "Tell me about your sister."

Kiki got up quickly from her desk. Ty caught her by the waist to slow her down. "What do you want to know Ty, that I'm going to kill that child one day?"

"Operative word, child." Ty rubbed his thumb across his brow. "If I could, I would hold you and kiss the anger away. But the Pendleton Rules are in affect." She looked down at him and a smile formed before she could stop it.

"I'm going to workout." She slowly pulled away from him. "I will not kill her today. I make no promises about tomorrow."

Ty stood in the hallway and watched as she walked into her room. Once he heard the treadmill start, he looked back into the office.

Over an hour later Kiki returned to her office refreshed and ready to tackle a manuscript. The sight shocked her. "What have you done to my office?" She looked around horrified. Twirling around in the room with her hands swinging, she nervously asked, "Where are my TBR pile, my NWH pile and my ML pile? Ty, you--you destroyed my system!"

Ty held up his finger indicating to hold on. She started to protest, but he threw her a look warning against it. He listened a minute longer, then interrupted the caller on the other end of his cell phone, "Jarrett, I understand your concern. However, I don't think 132 million for five years is a bad deal. I'll look at the marketing aspects and call you with my findings." He disconnected the call then looked up at Kiki. "What is TBR?"

"To be read. Books my assistant deems worthy of taking a look at."

On the shelf, neatly arranged in the order she'd had them on the desk, were the piles of manuscripts he thought were important because of where they were located on the desk. On the computer he typed TO BE READ on a label, printed it, peeled it off the paper and placed it on the tray the manuscripts were in. "Your To Be Read pile."

"Okay, where's my maybe later pile?"

He typed MAYBE LATER, printed it and placed the peeled label on the next tray. "Maybe later."

He saw the beginning of a smile forming on her lips. "No way in hell."

He smiled and typed, NO WAY IN HELL, peeled the label and placed that on the next tray. "Anything else?"

She stood admiring the space she now had in her office. The books were on the shelves in alphabetical order, her note cards were on the bulletin board in neat columns and the top of her desk, which she was sure she had not seen for over a year, was clear, clean and had the nerve to have a vase with roses in it. She put her hands on her hips and just smiled at him.

"I couldn't think the way it was." The thought that he had made her smile warmed his heart. "How was your workout?"

The man was going to make her break her own rules. To think he took the time to organize her office. He is so thoughtful and caring, it's hard not to love him. The man saved her life, stayed at the hospital with her, held her when she was afraid, and now he was organizing her office. Everything he did or said were signs that he cared. She shook her head, then sat down in the now empty chair and looked around. "You are the neatest man I have ever known."

"Is that a bad thing?"

"No." She crossed her legs and grinned at him. "Was that Jarrett Bryson on the phone?"

"Yes."

"A measly 132 mil. He is so worth more than that." He nodded, but did not respond. "I know client-attorney privilege."

"Again." She smiled. "Yeah. That pesky ethical gene of yours."

"You still representing Siri?"

"Hell yeah. That girl's a gold mine. I'm not letting her go anywhere."

"Smart girl. So," he sat back in the chair, "what's the deal with you and your sister?"

"Half-sister," Kiki corrected.

"Okay," he grinned. "Half-sister."

"First daughter, baby daughter drama. My Dad has been a bad father all the way around."

"The man that I met loves you very much. He was ready to take me out to get to you."

"Daddy does what is expected of him. He was expected to be upset about his daughter being kidnapped, so he was. Now if it had been his baby girl, then you may have experienced some real concern."

"How old is your sister?"

"Half-sister," Kiki stared up at him. "Twenty."

"I didn't know Kenneth and Maxine had been married that long."

"They haven't. That happened when he was still married to my mother. Yes sir, that bundle of joy is what caused my parent's divorce."

"Doesn't seem like the type of thing Issy would condone."

"It wasn't," Kiki said almost in a whisper. "Maxine was screwing around with my Dad for years before my Mother found out." She pulled her feet up in the chair under her. "My Mom didn't find out about the affair until the witch was three. To tell you the truth, I think my Dad is still in love with my Mom."

"Every little girl wants to believe that."

"No, it's more than that." She shrugged her shoulder. "I mean it's in the way he looks at her when he doesn't think anyone is looking. He doesn't look at Maxine that way."

"Something must have been right, he's still with her."

"She may be married to him now, but I don't think he truly loves her. He still hasn't forgiven her."

"Forgiven her for what?"

"The way my mother found out about them."

"What happened?"

"Whew, rough story."

"I'm here to help you through it." He smiled as he sat ready to listen.

"My Mom had just finished her third novel and Crimson was having this huge release event at their main offices here. The place was packed. Hundreds had showed up to stand in line to get her autograph. All of us were dressed to impress." She smiled remembering the day. "Wayne fussed all day because I didn't want to wear my Yankees jersey." She sighed. "Anyway, my Mom had proudly introduced us to the crowd. Then she introduced Daddy. He came up and kissed her, smiling at the cameras that were snapping pictures left and right. Suddenly, this little girl came running up to the stage, calling, "Daddy, Daddy." To everyone's surprise she was extending her arms up to my father. I was ten at the time and didn't really know better. Of course, the mouth I have now was developing then. I pushed the little girl away saying, That's my Daddy, not yours." Kiki sighed.

"She fell on her butt and really started crying then. My Dad smacked my hand. "Don't do that again," he said as he reached down and picked her up. There must have been something in the way the little girl rested her head on my Daddy's shoulder. The look on my Mother's face was nothing but disbelief. When Maxine came up to claim the child, the look on my Mother's face was devastation. She knew the moment she saw the three of them together." Kiki looked up at him. "You know what my Mother did then?" Kiki smirked. "She turned to Maxine and told her to let the child stay with her father. She took my hand, then turned to Wayne and told him to take us back to the room. Therein began the battle of the Simmons girls. It was clear early on, whose baby girl won the battle."

"Did you ever talk to your father about your dislike for your little sister?"

Kiki sat there as if thinking back, then she shrugged her shoulders. "This is the first time I've ever talked to anyone about it."

The realization that she trusted him with something so personal touched him. He was now beginning to see the real Kiki, not just the woman she let the world see. "Did your father ever call you baby girl?"

The telephone rang. Kiki stood and answered the telephone on the desk. "Hello."

"Ms. Simmons, we sent the locksmith up," the security from the front desk replied.

"Thank you." She walked out of the office and stopped in the hallway. "The day after Laura was born, he started calling me Kiki. I remember because it was my seventh birthday."

There was a knock on the door. "That's the locksmith," Kiki stated as she walked towards the door.

"No." Ty stood then walked out of the office past her. "You stay back."

106

"Ty, it's just the locksmith."

He turned back towards her as he continued on towards the door. "Stay back."

Kiki frowned at him but stayed in the hallway as Ty opened the door.

The man at the door blinked for a brief second as Ty stared him down. "May I help you?" Ty asked.

"I'm here to change locks for," the man looked down at the paper in his hand, "Ms. Simmons."

Kiki came to the door and smirked at Ty. "Don't mind him. Come on in."

"Wildcat," the man smiled.

Kiki's brows tightened. "Excuse me?"

Ty closed the door behind him as he watched the two.

"Ram Hunter, Central Park, a few nights ago."

Kiki's face softened with recognition. "My knight in shining armor." She smiled.

Boldly he gave Kiki the once over. "You look no worse for the wear. Take anyone out lately?"

Kiki laughed. "No." She looked over at Ty. "I'm behaving these days. Save any damsels in distress lately?"

"Just you."

"Excuse me," Ty interjected with a rise of his eyebrow. "Your purpose for being here?"

The man never looked at Ty, he kept his eyes on Kiki. "The lock. Someone bothering you?"

Ty stood between the two of them. "You're here to change the lock on the door, which is there." He pointed behind him. "The door."

The man, who stood as tall as Ty and was just a bit thicker, flinched. "I'll take care of it, Mr.?"

"You don't need to know." Ty replied.

Kiki looked around Ty. "You two want to pull down your pants and get the pissing contest started or can I get the lock on my door changed?"

The man laughed as he walked back to the door. "I gave you the right name. Is he your husband?" He asked as he bent to take a look at the door.

Kiki looked at Ty, who was standing with his arms folded across his chest with the meanest look she had ever seen on him. "No, he's my protector. I'm not married."

The man looked over his shoulder. "How in the hell did the men in New York let a natural beauty like you slip through their hands?"

Ty rolled his eyes, grabbed Kiki by the wrist and pulled her away from the door.

"I've been asking the same question Ram," Kiki laughed as she was being pulled away. "Hey, he's kind of cute and he wasn't intimidated by you and your power suit."

"He's here to change the locks Kendra." Ty removed his suit jacket, then sat back at the table where his computer was set up. "What's with the wildcat name anyway?"

Kiki walked around and stood in front of him. "Tyrone Pendleton, you're jealous?"

"I have no reason to be jealous." Ty raised his eyebrow. "The man is here to change the locks."

"True, however, he thinks I'm a natural beauty," she teased.

"I'm sure many men do." He all but dismissed the conversation.

"It doesn't bother you that the man finds me attractive?"

"No."

"And if he asked me out you wouldn't have a problem with that?"

"As you said, you are not married. You're free to date anyone you choose."

She held his cold glare. "Okay," she nodded her head.

"Hey Boss, Kiki," Jake spoke as he walked towards them. "What's up with the door?"

"You want to go out with the guy?"

Kiki shook her head. "You're as bad as my father. No, I don't want to go out with anyone, but I want you to care one way or another."

Jake watched as Kiki stomped out of the room. He looked at Ty. "What did you do now?"

Ty shook his head. "We were having a good day until the locksmith showed up." He exhaled. "Give me something man. Any leads on LaToya's visitor?"

"Nothing. Whoever she has on the outside is damn good, Boss. There's no trail of him."

Ty shook his head. "There's something T. There is always something."

Jake grinned at his friend. "Rocket taking you through the ringer?"

"You have no idea," Ty sighed. "We've gone from the rules this morning, to a few laughs with Wendy, then a few tears from the past and then the locksmith. Is he finished with the door?"

"The locksmith?" Jake grinned. "He was still working when I came in."

Ty stood. "I need to go for a walk."

"Wrap up, it's cold out, Boss." Jake called out as Ty pulled a coat from the closet.

"Aren't you finished with that door yet?" He asked the locksmith.

"Putting the finishing touches on as we speak." The locksmith opened the door. "You leaving?"

Ty glared at the man, then walked out of the door. He looked back over his shoulder to see the man's back turned to him. There was something about the man he did not like. Of course, the fact that he looked at Kiki as if he could swallow her up like a snake would choke down a rodent had nothing to do with it.

Ram Hunter had finished the lock fifteen minutes ago, but he wanted another opportunity to see the wildcat before he left. He walked to the end of the foyer and saw the big guy sitting at the breakfast bar. "I have the new keys for Ms. Simmons. Do you know where I can find her?"

"You can leave them with me," T replied, standing and advancing on the man.

"Can't do that. Can only put them in her hands. What she does with them after that is up to her."

"Rocket," Jake called out, slowly taking his eyes off the man.

"What?" Kiki asked as she stepped out of her office.

Ram looked down the long hallway, then he held the keys up. "I have your new keys."

"Oh." She smiled as she walked towards him. "Thank you," she said as she took the keys.

"You're welcome," Ram smiled holding her gaze. "Look, do you mind if I call you? I'd like to see you again. I don't like leaving things up to fate."

"Maybe we could have dinner or go dancing," Kiki replied in a loud voice.

Jake's brows knitted together, wondering why she was talking so loud.

"I'd like that. Tomorrow good for you?"

"Tomorrow," she boomed again. "Why don't you give me a call and I'll see if I can free up some time."

"I'll do that," Ram replied, but continued to just stand there. Jake opened the door. "I think that's my cue. I'll call you tomorrow."

Jake closed the door as soon as the locksmith walked out then turned to Kiki. "What are you doing?"

"Nothing," she smirked, then looked toward the table where Ty had set up to work.

"He's gone," Jake announced.

"Gone?" Kiki frowned. "Damn."

"You trying to make the boss jealous by agreeing to go out with the locksmith?" He laughed. "He's not even around to hear the exchange and there is no way in hell he's going to let you just walk out with some guy. Especially not now."

"Oh shut up Jake," she smirked at him. "Where did he go anyway?"

"Out for a walk."

Kiki looked at her watch. It was after six. "Fine." She turned and stomped back into her office.

Kiki emerged from the office a few hours later to find Ty still had not returned. Jake was not in the family room, out in the great room or in the kitchen. She knocked on the guest bedroom door, no reply. "Well, where is everyone?" She was used to living by herself, but for the last four days Ty had been around. It dawned on her that she may have gone a little overboard trying to make Ty jealous. After all, the man was there to protect her. She walked through the dining area and spotted Jake sitting out on the balcony on his cell phone. She smiled. The relaxed look and the slick smile indicated he was probably talking to a woman. Good for him, she thought. As she walked from the livingroom, the house phone buzzed. She answered it quickly thinking Ty may not have been able to get by security.

"Simmons."

"Ms. Simmons, there's a Rosa Sanchez here. She stated she is here to see a Tyrone Pendleton that is staying with you. Is he available?"

A frown creased Kiki's forehead. "No. But, you can send her up."

She walked out onto the balcony. "Who is Rosa Sanchez?"

Jake, who was still talking on his cell phone, looked up at her and saw the frown on her face. "Issy, I'll call you back."

"You're talking to my mother?"

"I was. What's this about Rosa?"

"Who is she?"

"An employee. We told you this yesterday."

"Who is she to Ty?"

"An employee," he said again.

"Does she know that?"

"What's with you Rocket? This morning you lay down these rules on the man. He accepts them only because he wants to make sure you," he said again pointing at her, "you are safe. What more do you want from the man?"

"I want him to love me damn it," she exclaimed then walked back into the condo.

"The man does love you," Jake mumbled to himself as he watched her walk towards the door. He opened the door to find Rosa Sanchez with a garment bag and a briefcase standing there. "Rosa." he took the garment bag and the briefcase.

Gorgeous was not sufficient in describing the woman standing in the foyer. Then she had the nerve to be dressed in Michael Kors. She knew because she had been eyeing that exact same double-breasted coat for months, hoping to be able to afford it one day. Hell, she needed to work for Tyrone.

"Good evening. You must be Kiki."

Kiki didn't mean to, but the action happened before she could stop it. She brushed her hand over her hair and prayed every strand was in place. "I am."

The woman smiled and Kiki just about cursed. This is the woman that is around Ty all day. Hell, she didn't stand a chance. She had no problems with her looks, however standing in the same room as this woman would intimidate anyone.

"I'm Rosa Sanchez. I work with Ty, umm, Mr. Pendleton."

Jake heard the slip of the tongue and wondered, what the hell, as he hung the garment bag in the closet and the briefcase on the table near the door.

"He's working on a situation that I've received some pertinent information on and I really need to speak with him. Do you happen to know where he is?"

Kiki stepped aside. "No I don't. Jake?"

Jake shook his head. "I'll try to reach him." He looked at the two women and knew this was not going to be good.

"You have a nice place Kiki," Rosa commented looking around.

"Thank you," Kiki said, feeling a little self-conscious about her looks with the woman in the room. "May I take your coat?"

Rosa turned back towards her, interrupting her scanning of the room. "Yes, thank you." She unbuttoned her coat and handed it to Kiki. "I saw the weather was cold here. I stopped by the condo to pick up his coat before flying out."

Kiki's mouth fell open. Damn if she didn't have on a MK red crepe dress, thick gold belt around her waist, black four inch MK patent leather pumps with a gold zipper on the back of the heel. If she did not know the cost of the coat, she would have dropped it on the floor where she stood. "You have a key to Mr. Pendleton's condo?"

"Of course."

Jake rolled his eyes upward as he pulled his cell phone out to call Ty.

As the woman turned from her, Kiki could have sworn she caught a smirk on the woman's face. She glared at Jake.

He did not want any part of what was about to go down. He opened the door and stepped out into the hallway.

Kiki turned from the now closed door and walked behind the woman. "What exactly do you do for," she hesitated, "Mr. Pendleton?" she asked as she hung the coat in the closet.

Stepping down the two steps leading into the great room area, Rosa swirled back and replied. "Whatever he needs." She walked through the room. "Wow, that's quite a view. How do you afford a place like this in New York?"

"How do you afford a twenty-thousand dollar work outfit?" Kiki asked with her arms folded across her chest.

Rosa turned back to Kiki, smugly. "Touché, please forgive me. I was thinking out loud."

"Why are you here Ms. Sanchez?" Kiki's hospitality was beginning to waver.

"I have something he needs."

"Really?" Kiki asked with snicker. "What would that be?"

Rosa leaned forward a little and grinned. "For his eyes only." She straightened, then flipped her hair across her shoulder. "Any idea when he will return?"

"No, I don't," Kiki testily replied. "Is the information concerning me?"

"I couldn't say. Who exactly are you Kiki?" Rosa now stood with her arms folded, glaring.

"Oh that's cute." Kiki turned to keep from punching the wench. "Look Ms. Sanchez, I don't know who you are and I really don't give a damn. I have to give it to you though, you're a bold bitch to walk up in my home and play the inquisitive other woman." She heard the balcony door open as she turned back to Rosa. "Here's a little advice," she walked over until she was nose to nose with Rosa Sanchez, "if you are going to make a play for him come direct. He never liked weak women."

"I have no idea what you are talking about Kiki."

"It's Ms. Simmons to you. You are a paid servant of the agency, nothing more."

"What's going on here?"

The women turned to find Ty standing on the last step from the foyer. "Hello Rosa. What are you doing here?" Ty asked as he walked towards them.

"Mr. Pendleton."

"Oh, it's Mr. Pendleton now."

Rosa sent a side look Kiki's way. "I have a name."

He picked up his steps. "Talk to me Rosa."

"The name on the Cayman Island account was a dummy corporation," she said quickly as she walked to get her briefcase.

"Did you track down the owners?"

"I did." She walked back, placed the open file on the coffee table as Ty took a seat on the sofa. "There are ten names on the account that was incorporated here in New York. I paid a visit to the State Corporation Committee and these are the names I came up with. Any of them look familiar to you?" She smiled triumphantly.

Ty looked at the names then smiled up at her. "Roberto Garrison. Tell me you've tracked him down."

She placed her hand on his shoulder, then sat on the sofa next to him. "Of course." She looked up at Kiki, then turned to another document in the folder. "Six months ago he purchased a place in Marietta, twenty minutes from the facility where Ms Wright is housed."

"What else do you have?"

"Don't you think that is enough?" Ty looked at her side ways. She blushed. "Oh all right." She smiled, "You know me too well. How about his financial records," she placed another document on the table. "Flight schedule for each trip between New York and Atlanta, and," she dropped another document on the table, "car rental receipts with GPS reports of trips from his place in Marietta, to Atlanta to guess who's address? Oh, you'll never guess, so I'll tell you. Tina Wright." She stood, put her hands on her hips and laughed. "How you like me now?"

Kiki watched the scene from the kitchen. The woman had Ty captivated and she knew it. From the moment he walked back into the condo, he hadn't so much as looked her way. She walked out of the room. Sitting there watching the woman squirm her way into Ty's space was not something she wanted to do.

Tonight completed his meetings with Rosa. Afterwards he knew he had to speak on her actions. He could not allow the fact that she had stepped out of the professional realm to go without speaking on it. When he walked her to the door, he took her coat out of the closet and began helping her into it.

"Rosa," he began as she put her coat on then turned to him. "You are a valued employee. It is for that reason that you are being placed on a 90 day paid suspension." The shock was clear on her face.

"Why?"

"I want you to take the time to look for another position or to contemplate your actions. Accept the fact that the only place you have in my life is employee to employer. There is one more thing, before you decide to return to the agency. Know this, if you ever disrespect Kendra Simmons again you will be among the ranks of the unemployed." He opened the door for her. "Trent will be at the airport to return you to Atlanta. Give your coworkers any excuse that you choose for your absence. Only Wendy and I will know the circumstances of the suspension." He held her look of disbelief. Her young eyes clearly not understanding his reasons for his actions. "You crossed the line into my personal life. That is not acceptable. Think on it Rosa, make your decision. We'll see you in 90 days."

He was an expert at masking his thoughts. It took all his resolve not to react to the scene he walked in on. Any other man would have been proud to have two beautiful women sparring over him. To him it was a show of blatant disrespect of his personal space on Rosa's part. She was young and learning. It was imperative to her continued association with the agency that she understood the consequences of crossing the professional line. Not only where he was concerned, but as it pertained to his clientele as well. As for Kiki, she had every right to lash out at Rosa, this is her home and no one should be allowed to disrespect her here. However, that did not give her the right to belittle his employees. Words can cut deep. In some cases, it can have a severe impact on a person's emotional security.

Granted, Kiki had no way of knowing that Rosa had been a victim of forced prostitution. Calling her a paid servant could open emotional scars that everyone around Rosa had been trying to mend. At some point, Kiki had to understand that mouth of hers could kill.

Ty pulled out his cell phone to call Wendy as Jake walked in.

"Wendy, call Rosa. She's been placed on administrative leave with pay for 90 days. I'll allow her to explain. Take every step possible to assure she is emotionally well."

"Had to put her in her place, hmm?"

"Something like that."

"I knew it was coming," Wendy sighed. "She's a good girl, very loyal to you. Her emotions are just misplaced."

"You maybe right, Wendy. Just make sure she comes back to us."

"Will do boss."

Ty disconnected his call and looked at Jake who was sitting at the island with a beer, grinning.

"Don't say it," Ty said as he removed his suit jacket, placed it neatly on the back of the bar stool, then took a seat.

Jake reached into the refrigerator, pulled out a beer and sat it in front of his friend. "Rosa brought your coat all the way from Atlanta so you wouldn't get cold."

Ty opened the beer, took a deep swallow then sat the bottle on the island. He looked up at Jake and both of them burst out in laughter. It took them a moment to settle down. All Ty could do was shake his head. "Man, what in the hell is happening?"

Jake smiled. "God has taken over your life, my brother. You are no longer in the driver's seat."

"What exactly is that supposed to mean?"

"Simple man. You've been standing at the intersection of Heart's Desire and Mind Control." He laughed. "God pushed you down the right road. All you can do now is go along for the ride." He took a drink of his beer. "I suggest you take the night, accept the fact that you love Rocket, then figure out how you are going to get out of the thunderstorm before a lightning bolt cracks the two of you apart." He topped off his beer. "Life is short my brother. Handle your business. I'm going to check on security, then go back to the hotel. Calling it a night."

Ty picked up his beer and took a seat in the chair near the window. It was after midnight. The New York skyline was alive, yet calming. Kicking off his shoes, he placed his feet on the ottoman, crossing them at the ankles. He loosened his tie, laid his head back and exhaled, thinking, Jake may have a strange way of describing the state of his life, but the description hit home. He was at a crossroad and he had to make a decision. The last year was miserable without Kiki. The events of just that almost fatal day, forget about the kidnapping, forget about the hospital stay, forget about someone trying to physically take her from his life, but the emotions of that day clearly indicated he was in love with this woman. Fight it as he may, the facts were there. From the time the locksmith came in, the jealousy erupted. He could not stand there as the man stood there boldly admiring Kiki--his Kiki. That's why he had to leave. He had to take a walk to keep from losing his cool. To increase his discomfort, he remembered the rules. She felt she had to set rules. There shouldn't be any rules or limits when it comes to love. Every rule she set had to do with the physical. That's the only thing that existed between them, at least in his estimation. None of it had to do with the heart. That's what he had to change. He had to make her love him as much as he loved her. He turned his head towards the window and chuckled, there he admitted it. He loves that woman. Everything about her, from the afro puffs on her head, the big hoop earrings, and he loved-- loved that sassy mouth. He was in love with Kendra Isadore Simmons. He could feel his heart opening and accepting the fact each time the thought entered his mind. The reality frightened him, but not as much as the thought of him losing her.

He reached over to the table and picked up the folder Rosa left with him. Then he pulled his laptop from his briefcase. The first goal was to get her out of this situation. Then he would tell her he wanted her in his life in every way. Was he ready for the big house, white picket fence, two point two children and a dog? He didn't know, but he did know he did not want to live that life without her.

The situation had to be approached the same way he handled everything in his life, methodically. On the computer he keyed in these words, motive, who and why. He read over his notes from Peace, and the information from Rosa. Roberto Garrison's name appeared from both sources. He keyed in Garrison's name on the internet. After locating who he thought was the right Garrison, he soaked up every tidbit he could about the man. The information he found was superficial. He needed a more in-depth details on the man and the dummy corporation. People formed dummy corporations to cover up or hide assets. Which is it with Garrison, he wondered? And what was the real connection between him and LaToya? There were still too many unanswered questions. He needed to hear from Peace or Naverone. His cell phone chimed. "Pendleton," he answered.

"Boss, I am sitting outside the home of Tina Wright minding my own business when this, Mercedes-Benz SL-Class pulls up. Now you know how I like cars, so I snap a picture and run the plates. Take one guess who owns it?" Peace smiled knowing the information was going to please his boss.

"Who?"

"Roberto Garrison. Now why do you think he is at LaToya's mother's house at two in the morning?"

Chapter 8

*P*eace sat outside a restaurant watching Roberto Garrison and Tina Wright having what he assumed was breakfast. He had taken several photos of the couple, then sent them to Wendy at the office to have them identified. When he received confirmation that the man with Tina was indeed Roberto Garrison, he decided to keep an eye on them. It was the only lead he had come up with in this game LaToya was playing. The problem for him now, was he originally thought that Roberto could have been LaToya's man. However, the events of last night may have proved him wrong, unless this was a very kinky family where the daughter and mother shared their beds with the same man. He wasn't mad at that, but damn. About twenty minutes into the surveillance, the couple was joined by another man. At first Peace didn't think too much of it, but then it seemed a heated discussion was taking place. Peace quickly snapped a picture of the man. It was only a side view, but maybe it was enough to identify him.

Kiki awoke to the manuscript she was reading spread out on the bed, some on her chest and still more pages on the floor. After the visit from Ms. Prissy, Kiki took a shower to wash away the memory of the beauty smiling in Ty's face, then lost herself in the manuscript she had received earlier that day. For most of the night she thought Ty would at least come in to talk about the woman, but he never did. She placed her arm over her forehead. *He's right in the condo and he was still causing her sleepless nights.* Walking on the treadmill did not release the tension like walking in the park did. She needed to get out of the condo. She just had to before Ty's presence drove her crazy. The generic tune played on her cell phone, indicating the caller was not anyone close to her. "Hello."

"Good morning Wildcat. Is it too early to call?"

The name made her smile despite how low she was feeling. "Hello Ram. No, I'm awake. How are you this morning?"

"That depends on you Wildcat."

"How so?" Kiki said as she sat up in the bed.

"Before I tell you how, I have a question."

Kiki was stacking the pages together. "Okay, shoot."

"The man that was at your condo yesterday, is he your man?"

Kiki hesitated as she thought about the question. "No, he's not." She threw the covers back, then stood to pick up the pages off the floor.

"He seemed rather intense."

She stood up with pages in her hand and thought about that. "Yep, that's the word to describe him."

"I picked up on a vibe between you two. Am I wrong?"

"No, there was something, but it ended a year ago. He's here to help with a situation." She saw no reason to share the events of the week with a stranger.

"If that's the case, have dinner with me tonight." Kiki hesitated. "Look, I'm not asking for forever. I really would like a chance to get to know you without a mugger and an ex interrupting what could be a pretty nice evening."

She thought about her conversation with Ty. All she wanted to see was that he cared one way or another about a man hitting on her. "Just dinner?"

"Just dinner."

Kiki knew Ty was not going to let her out the door alone. "I have a security detail on me. Would that bother you?"

"Security, no. Why, if you don't mind me asking?"

"Long story."

"Should make for interesting dinner conversation."

Kiki smiled. "What time?"

"Seven."

"See you at seven." She disconnected the call. For a moment, she wondered if she was doing the right thing. Then the picture of Rosa Sanchez smiling up at Ty entered her mind. "Let's try the shoe on the other foot."

After a shower and a debate on what to put on. The controversy wasn't lost on her. She knew exactly why she was having a hard time picking out something to wear. The woman from last night had her self-conscious about her appearance with Ty around. On the norm, she didn't care what others thought about her attire, she wore what made her feel good. "The hell with it." She pulled out a pair of leggings, a large Yankees jersey, a thick black belt to match the leggings and a pair of short two-inch heel black boots. She left her hair in the twists, added a pair of dangling earrings, a bracelet and called it a day.

Walking out the room, she stopped at the guest bedroom to listen. Nothing. He must still be sleep. She glanced at her watch, seven-thirty. "Hmm," she mumbled. He was usually up by now. She walked down the hallway. When she reached the kitchen she pulled the refrigerator door open, then stopped and looked back over her shoulder. Ty was stretched out, still in his suit from the night before. There were two things wrong with that picture. First, she'd never seen him fall asleep in his clothes and second, she'd never seen him in the same suit two days in a row. She tip-toed over and he was sound asleep. The sight made her smile. The man was just too damn good looking, with his rich dark brown skin, that strong square chin and those delicious thick lips. She was getting wet between her legs just looking at him. She shook the feeling away. Taking off her shoes, she walked back into the bedroom and pulled a throw from the closet. While placing the throw over him, she wanted to kiss those lips, but that would be counter productive. She took a big step agreeing to go out with another man. The more she stared down at him, the more she knew that was a mistake. No man could replace Tyrone Pendleton. Where in the hell did that put her? Next to the chair was a folder with papers half out. Reaching down, to pick them up, she recognized the name written on the outside. Roberto Garrison. That was the name the stringy longhaired bitch mentioned last night. She'd walked out before she heard all the details. Now she wondered if this was the man after her. She sat at the table where his laptop was and began to read the file. Nothing about the man was familiar. Why would someone that she had no dealings with want to hurt her? She accidentally hit a button on the keyboard of the computer, at least that was what she would tell him if he woke up. To her surprise there was a picture of him and her at dinner the first time she visited him in Atlanta. She looked over at him and sighed. Why did he make loving him so easy, yet so hard? Back to the computer. She needed to know more about this situation. Damn, it was locked. She knew from experience that he changed his password every thirty days. Looking at the computer, then at him, then back at the computer, she smiled and keyed in her name, then frowned. Okay, they have been separated for about a year. She keyed in her name and the number twelve. Nothing. She tried her name and thirteen, nothing. Her name and fourteen, it opened. She almost giggled out loud. The reality of what she keyed in touched her. The man had her picture up on his personal computer. Her name was his password and probably had been for the last fourteen months. Everything he did proved he loved her, yet he refused to accept it. The thought almost brought tears to her eyes. "Stop it." She sighed then read the notes he had written.

A call was coming through on his computer. She started to log off, but the thought of the itty, bity titty girl calling to wake him up stopped her. She clicked the message. It wasn't the face of Rosa. It was Jason Whitfield.

"Where's Ty?" the young man asked.

"Good morning." Kiki smiled.

"Where's Ty?"

"Okay, let's try this again. Good morning."

The boy rolled his eyes upward. "Look I got a situation. I need to speak to Ty."

Kiki raised an eyebrow and waited.

"Good morning, damn. May I speak to Ty please?"

Kiki smiled. "That is so much better. However, he's asleep."

"Look I got to talk to him now."

She could sense the urgency in the boy's face. "What's wrong Jason?"

"Look I don't know you. I need to speak with Ty. Is he around?"

"Yes, but as I stated, he's asleep. I'm an attorney, what you tell me is confidential. What's the problem and I'll see if I can help."

The boy was clearly conflicted. "I'll show you." He opened the door, walked in another room and scanned it around, then turned the phone back to his face.

"You have some friends over?"

"No." He closed the door. "That's just it. I don't know these people. My boy isn't even here."

"Is that your room?"

"Yeah, I think so."

"You think so? Jason were you drinking, 'cause I know you damn well better not be doing any drugs."

"No, I don't do drugs. It'd messes up my game. I was out drinking last night."

"Drinking messes up your game too. Who are the people?"

"That's just it, I don't know."

"Where did they come from?"

"I don't know that either. I woke up this morning and they were here," he whispered into the phone. "I think there's a few grams of coke on the table."

That's not good, Kiki stood up. "Jason, get your wallet and walk out of the room."

"Why?"

"Just do it. Now."

She watched as Jason gathered the few things and walked towards the door. "Wait. Wait. Put your hat and shades on before you leave the room. Leave your phone on, put it in your pocket. Hunch over so you won't seem so tall."

"Like this."

"Like you're sneaking out of the house." He bent over. "All right, now leave the room." She watched as the boy stepped inside the elevator. "Okay, when you get to the lobby, walk out of the side door."

She picked up Ty's phone. "Damn, password protected too. Hold on." She ran into her bedroom then came back with her cell phone. She called Jake, and explained the situation.

"Okay Jason. Where are you?"

Jason told her. "55th Street."

"You're in New York?"

"I told my boys I wanted to see Times Square. So we hired a private plane and flew out. Then my boy ditched me."

"Did you give your boy cash?

"Just some spending money."

"Don't talk anymore. Just go out the side door and keep walking straight until I tell you to stop."

Kiki saw the irritated look on Jason's face. "How tall are you?"

"What?" the angry voice replied.

"How tall are you? I ask because I want to know how high of a chair I will need to whip your ass when we meet."

He frowned at the phone in his hand. "What?"

"Is that as far as your vocabulary goes? You should have stayed in school. You're not ready for this. I'm not going to give you the stats on how many players would kiss the ground Mr. Pendleton walks on to be in your shoes. Oh, and by the way, make this the last time you call him Ty. His name is Mr. Pendleton until you earn the respect to call him Ty."

Jason looked at the telephone as if he was about to hang it up. "Hang it up and I swear I will have every gang banger I know in this city to meet you around the next corner. But don't worry, I'll just have them hold you there. I reserve the right to teach you a lesson all by myself. Keep walking and listen."

"When I was in high school I played point guard, my friend played center. I was good, she was great. Ten major colleges were constantly at our games scouting her. You would recognize the name if I told you, but her name isn't important, her story is. In addition to the boys trying to get into our panties, we always had people wanting to hang out with us. We were close and knew the dangers in the street so we kind of stayed to ourselves. Our coach and parents had schooled us well. On the night she made her final choice to commit to the University of Connecticut, we went out to celebrate. We were on our way home when two of our schoolmates asked for a ride home. We knew them, didn't really hang out with them, but what the hell, we gave them a ride. My house was first, so my friend dropped me off. Now, I wasn't there, so the rest of this story is what she told me. They were riding and jamming to the tunes, you know how it goes. The rider in the back seat spotted someone they had a beef with. She rolled down the window, pulled out a gun and sprayed the group of people with bullets. Two people died, three were injured. Needless to say, my friend was scared shitless. The rider in the back pointed the gun at her and told her to keep driving, so she did. Now, mind you, my friend did not know the people that were shot and was only an acquaintance of the riders. The DA charged her with complicity to commit murder, because she did not stop at the scene. Her family obtained an attorney and got her cleared, but in the meantime, her reputation was ruined and she lost her chance at a full ride scholarship. That changed her life irrevocably. I tell you this story to make you aware of the danger you put yourself in every time you hang out with your buds, who hang out with other buds, that just want to party. Those riders, they didn't have much to lose, my friend did. The people in your hotel room, they don't have anything to lose if the drugs were found. You have a life ahead of you. Your parents sacrificed everything, even put a second mortgage on their house to keep you in sneakers to foster your talent. You owe them. That's right, you owe them to do the right thing, make good decisions. Instead of hanging out, you should be working out. Improving your game so when your virgin ass hits the court, the veterans won't screw you too bad." She wiped a tear from her cheek. "I don't know you Jason, only your rep as a player with a bright future. Don't let a few moments of pleasure with people you don't even know destroy that."

Jason had stopped walking as he listened to the story. "The pressure is hell," the boy cried. "It's like I don't even want to be here. At home it was easy. I had my parents, my girl and my boys. Here I don't have anybody."

"You have Mr. Pendleton and now you have me. I can't be your girl even though I'm all of that and some more."

Jason wiped his face and smiled. "All of that, huh?"

"And some more," she teased. "Look, I moved to New York by myself because..." she hesitated, remembering Ty was in the room. "Well, I can't tell you why. But, I'm here and it does get very lonely. There are times when I cry myself to sleep, I'm so lonely. When it overwhelms me, I call home. I talk to my Mom, or my brothers. You can do the same."

"I can't call home to my parents, I'm twenty years old."

"I'm twenty-seven and I call to talk to my Mom all the time."

A car pulled up. "Jason, get in the car," Jake opened the door.

Jason did as he was instructed.

"Well, you're good now. I'll turn you over to Mr. Pendleton."

Kiki stood to wake Ty up.

"Hold on shorty," Jason called out.

"First you need to understand I'm not anybody's shorty. I have a BA in English Lit and a Law degree. If you want to get my attention, you need to step to me correct."

"Hold up, hold up. I didn't mean any disrespect, it's just you talk my language. Ty, I mean Mr. Pendleton is cool, it's just, you know." He hesitated. "The man is so straight laced. I've never seen him in a pair of jeans, you know, just chilling. How is someone in my generation going to trust somebody that don't own a pair of jeans?" Kiki laughed. "I bet you have a pair of jeans, don't you?"

"Several, however, Mr. Pendleton owns an agency. He has to meet constantly with owners, music execs and the like. He can't very well expect men wearing twenty-thousand dollar suits to take him seriously if he's wearing jeans. Listen, you want the best representing you. Your agent was the top in his game, do you think for one minute he would turn you over to just anyone? No, he wouldn't. He turned you over to the best in the business. Now, Mr. Pendleton did not represent sports figures. However, he respected your agent and knew he wanted the best for you so he took you and a few others on. Trust Mr. Pendleton. He will guide your career and one day you may be man enough to walk in a pair of his shoes."

Jason sat back in the car and sighed.

"You know what I think you should do?" Kiki said.

"What?"

"I think you should call your Mom."

Jason smiled. "I think I'll do that."

"I'm signing off."

"Hey, what's your name?"

"Kendra."

"Hey Kendra."

"I'm still kicking your ass, but it's nice meeting you too. Take care."

Kiki disconnected the call and stood to find Ty standing behind her with his hands in his pockets. "Good save."

"Jason is on his way here. You need to get someone over to the hotel to clear out that room."

Ty nodded. "I'll take care of it."

They stood there in silence for a moment. "About last night," they both started.

"Ladies first," Ty conceded.

"I know you're here to protect me and I appreciate it. But you broke the rules. You brought a female to my home."

"I did not ask her to come."

She put her hand up to stop him. "She felt she could, because you were here. I need you to leave. Let Jake or

Peace stay here until we figure things out. I don't care which one. But I need you to go."

"I can't do that, Kendra."

Kiki closed her eyes and exhaled. "Do you have any idea how disrespectful it was to have a woman in my home, openly flirting with you? To add insult to injury, the moment you laid eyes on the woman, you completely ignored the fact that I was even in the room. You never acknowledged my presence. Your attention was on the brainiac bombshell."

"She had information on the situation."

"It's not even about her Ty, not really. How do you think I felt standing there watching her fawn all over you and you smiling up in her face? You know the situation between us. You know how I feel about you. Yet you had no problem allowing the woman to display the relationship between the two of you."

"I don't have a relationship with her. She's an employee. Nothing more."

"Really, an employee. Tell me, does she always come to work with a screw me dress on, along with the heels. Oh, not to mention she has a key to your condo." She put her fingers up in quotations. "She had to pick up your coat to keep you from being cold. You have no idea how that heifer made me feel last night. But you will."

Jake walked through the door with Jason Whitfield behind him. The tension in the room was immediately felt. "Should we go back out?" Jake asked.

"There's never a good time around here."

Kiki rolled her eyes at Ty. She extended her hand. "Hello Jason. You're lucky. I need to save that azz whipping for somebody else." She walked out of the room.

Jake looked at Ty. "Didn't I tell you to handle that last night?"

Ty shook his head at Jake, then looked at Jason. "What are you doing in New York?"

"You really should go talk to her," Jason said to Ty.

"You're giving me advice?"

"Look, you may know business, but I know women," Jason stated as he walked further into the condo. "That woman is fine, but pissed." He stretched out on the sofa.

Ty ignored the young man's warning. "Is the hotel room registered in your name?"

"Man, I can wait, seriously. You need to handle your business. But, I got to say," he grinned, "I have a new found respect for you man. That's not the type of sister I thought you would have."

"The hotel room, Jason."

"Yes."

Ty turned to Jake. "Take some backup. Get the hotel room cleared out." He turned back to Jason. He could tell this was going to be a long day.

The shower in the guest room was on. Kiki was sure it was Ty, which meant Jason was probably in the living room alone. Regardless of what's happening, her mother always taught her how to be a good hostess. Putting the manuscript away, she walked down the hallway, and stopped at the family room to find Madden on the big screen with Jason handling the controller.

"It's a good thing you play basketball. Your football game is weak."

Jason looked over his shoulder. "Sounds like wolf tickets to me."

Kiki walked over, slid one leg over the back of the couch, then the other. She picked up the second controller, and hit the reset button. "Pick your team. I hope you are ready for that butt whipping."

"Bring your best game shorty." Jason smiled.

"I can see now I have to teach you how to respect your elders."

Jason laughed. "Hey you are not that much older than I am. Show me what you got."

Ty emerged from the shower. His cell phone was buzzing with messages. There was a message from Wendy. He pushed a button to return the call.

"What do you have Wendy?"

"Peace sent in two sets of photos. We identified Tina Wright and Roberto Garrison, however, we have not been able to identify the third person in the photo. It just wasn't enough of a profile."

"Send it to Rene Naverone. She has access to more sophisticated equipment. Ask her to contact me directly with her findings."

"Will do. Also, Trent should be landing to pick up Mr. Whitfield around four. The coach excused the missed meeting but insists on a firm date on when he will be joining the team. Have you placed the call to Nicolas Brooks?"

"No, I'm trying to settle the kid down before passing him to another agent."

"Makes sense. One more thing, Rosa is off the grid. After I spoke with her last night, I got the feeling she was more devastated than any of us know."

"I can't focus on that right now." The shouts from the family room roared.

"Sounds like you're having fun."

"Hold on." Ty stepped out into the hallway.

"Whoa," he heard Jason holler. "That was sweet."

The scene in the family room was crazy. Kiki and Jason were in the room playing a game of Madden and it looked as if Kiki's team was beating Jason's.

She jumped up from the sofa. "Take it like a man," she shouted with laughter. As she looked up and saw him, the light in her eyes disappeared and the laughter ended.

Ty's heart sank. He wondered if she would ever be that carefree around him again. He wanted to be the recipient of those shining eyes and her joyous laughter.

Jason looked around. "Hey Mr. Pendleton. You know, this is the third game she has won. I could get used to having her around."

"Is that so?" Ty said a little more cooler than he meant.

"It's nice to be wanted." Kiki turned her back on Ty then sat back down and continued with the game.

"You need me?" Jason asked.

"No, continue with your game," he said then walked away.

"I'm back Wendy."

"It appears Kiki and Jason are getting along well."

"Let it go Wendy."

"Yes sir. Who do you want me to put on the Wright case now that Rosa is out?"

"No one. I'm going to handle it myself. Anything else major?"

"Nothing we can't handle here. How long will you be away?"

"I have no idea Wendy. Something is going to have to break soon. We can't go on like this."

"You take as much time as you need. I'll hold things down here."

The laughter coming from the other room distracted him, so he decided to work from the living room. Pulling up his computer, the first task at hand was to get Jason the hell out of the house. Kiki was paying a little too much attention to the boy. He keyed in the conference call number and waited for Nicolas Brooks to answer.

"Nicolas Brooks."

"Hello Mr. Brooks, I'm about to make your day."

"How's that Mr. Pendleton."

"What would you think of Brooks Sports Agency taking on a new client?"

"You have a name in mind?"

"Jason Whitfield."

Nicolas sat up. "You have my attention."

The two talked for a few hours about the league contract, the endorsement deals in place, in addition to those contracts he had already secured. They then discussed the personal issues surrounding Jason. Two hours later they had reached a compromise. Now all Ty had to do was convince Jason this was the right move for him.

Jake returned to fill Ty in on the happenings from the hotel. The sound of laughter reached them in the living room. "I need you to get him back to Atlanta. Stay on him until I can settle things here with Kiki."

"I'll put someone on him. I'm not leaving you to deal with this alone, Boss."

"This kid is special, Jake. As much as he is getting on my last nerve, I don't want him to fall through the cracks. I want this kid to make it. I need someone I trust watching over him until the negotiations are complete."

"What about Naverone?"

"She's working with me on this situation with Kiki."

"You like having woman problems, don't you?"

"It's business with Naverone, you know that."

"It was business with Rosa. How did that work for you?"

Ty ran his hand down his face when he heard them laughing again. "You get him to Atlanta. I'll see what Naverone can do."

"You got it Boss." Jake walked down the hallway and returned with Jason and Kiki in tow.

"Jason, Jake is going to take you back to Atlanta."

"Cool." Jason walked over to Ty. "Mr. Pendleton, I owe you an apology. I didn't realize how the things I was doing was causing your job to be harder. I know you are working to get me the best contract you can. I appreciate it." Jason extended his hand. "No more antics."

"Cool," Ty replied and shook the young man's hand.

Jason looked back at Kiki who was leaning against the door. He smiled, then walked over and hugged her. "Thanks for the talk. I hope you have fun on your date tonight."

"Date. What date?" Ty asked.

Jake hung his head and blew air slowly out as he took Jason by the arm and slowly moved him out of the line of fire.

"I didn't tell you? My bad. I have a date tonight."

"With who?"

"That's not your business."

"Yes, it is."

"Oops, did I say something wrong?" Jason asked Jake.

138

Jake gave him a questioning look. "What do you think?"

"It really isn't," Kiki smirked, "but if you must know I'm going out with Ram."

"The locksmith?" Ty asked.

"Yes."

"You'll have to cancel it. Jake is leaving and will not return until tomorrow. Unless you want me to accompany you?"

"Call someone else," Kiki demanded.

"I don't trust anyone else."

"Look," Jason interjected. "Mr. Pendleton, Jake can take me to the airport then return here to go with Kendra on her date. Really, I'm cool. Kendra and I had a long talk. I know what I need to do now. You don't have to worry about the small stuff with me. I'm good."

The anger seeping through Ty's body was clear to all except Jason. He didn't know that when that vein in the middle of Ty's head began to throb, that was him reaching his limit.

"I think that's a perfect solution." Kiki smiled. "I'm going to get ready for my date." She kissed Jason on the cheek. "Take care Jason," she said before she left the room.

Jake looked at Ty shaking his head. "You're in trouble now."

Jason walked over to Ty. "Man, I don't know the deal, but I do know she is all in with you. Let her go out with this dude. When she comes home, you make sure she never wants to step out on you again. You've got the upper hand. You're in, he's trying to get in. Use it." Jason walked back towards the door. "I can't wait to see how this turns out," he laughed.

Ty looked at Jake. "Drop him at the airport."

"You sure Boss?"

Ty looked at Jason, who gave him that it's on you look. "I'm sure."

Ty looked up to see Kiki walk from her bedroom. The sight paralyzed his body and mind. The dress was lavender in color. The length was nonexistent in his opinion. The heels were too damn high. They made her legs seem to go on forever. Any man would drool at just the thought of having them wrapped around him. He knew the game and damn if it wasn't working. To keep his composure and her knowing the affect she was having on him, he turned his back to her as he spoke. "You're really going out tonight?"

"That's the plan," she replied as she stopped at the mirror on the wall next to the door. That was not the reaction she anticipated, she thought as she reached into her purse, for what she didn't know. All she knew was she wanted to stand there long enough for him to get a good look at what he was throwing to another man. With her back to him, she looked at his reflection in the mirror. Hell, he wasn't even looking her way. His cool demeanor was aggravating every blood vessel in her body, bringing them to a boiling point. Taking a quick once over, she doubted herself for a moment, but only one before she said, "Oh hell no," and shook the thought away.

"Did you say something?" he asked.

Looking up into the mirror, she saw his back was still to her and he appeared to be reading something. Probably a contract for one of his clients. That was one thing she admired about him, the man was a workaholic just like her.

However, she thought as she snatched a tube of lipstick from her purse, that was no reason to ignore her. She reached behind her back and unzipped the dress, which had an oval shaped opening around the shoulder blades and a choker collar. "I asked if you would zip me, please."

Watching his actions in the mirror as she pretended to put lipstick on, she poked her butt out a little to ensure he had a good look. He looked over his shoulder and it seemed more of an aggravation, than a sexual enticement. For a moment, she wondered if he was going to comply or just stand there staring at her.

Fire, that's what she was playing with. Until now, he had kept his hands to himself as her rules required. Why he agreed to put himself through this hell, he'd never know. That was a lie. He knew why. If anything were to happen to her it would literally kill him. However, the thought of any other man putting his hands on her was killing him as well. He was in a no win situation. If he walked over there and did as she requested, she wins. Jason's words came back to him. *Make her never want to step out on you again.* A thought popped into his head, might as well make the game interesting.

Ty walked up behind her and allowed her to feel the reaction she wanted. Taking her small waist between his hands, he pulled her behind against him. "You want to play Kendra Issadore?" His hands roamed over the material of her dress to cup her breasts as his lips touched the back of her neck. "You laugh all day with Jason." Her hands fell to the table. "Tonight, it's the locksmith." He pushed closer to her. "Your body burns for me just as mine does for you." The friction between their bodies caused her dress to rise in the back. He positioned his manhood between her butt cheeks and almost lost his cool. "No one else will ever quench our thirst for each other--no one." He could feel her pulsating against him. Squeezing her nipples, they began to harden from his touch. "You want to play with fire?" She tried to speak. He stopped her, turning her body to face him. "Don't," his eyes warned her as he lifted her onto the table under the mirror. He dropped to his knees, placing her thighs over his shoulders, then buried his head between her thighs.

Her body jerked as his lips touched the moisture between her legs. The thin stretch of material he moved with a finger was no protection against his assault.

God, her juice was so sweet. He could stay there between her legs for the rest of his life and never quench the thirst she stirred within him. However, this was not the time for him to linger, he had a point to make. Pulling her body closer, his lips surrounded her nub as his tongue dodged in and out. His lips meeting her inner lips with a continuous vigorous motion, not giving her a second to even think about holding back any of her sweet juices from him. He could feel her body begin to vibrate from the assault and knew it was regrettably time for him to pull back as her body had just exploded.

He sat back on his heels and looked up as the glorious expression of passion showed on her face. Her head was thrown back, her body jerking, her motions vibrating through the table. Standing, he picked her up and stood her on her feet. With a finger, he put the thin thong material back in place, then smoothed her dress down. He placed the finger in his mouth and sucked it dry. He then pulled a handkerchief from his back pocket, wiped his mouth then looked at her. "Enjoy your date," he said just as Jake walked through the door.

He looked from one to the other. "Are you ready?"

"Yes, she's ready," Ty replied. He pulled her coat from the closet. He held it out for her to step into. "I wouldn't want you to catch a cold."

What in the hell happened? One minute she was pissed because he was ignoring her, and the next minute she was being deliciously eaten alive. Now he was literally pushing her out the door to another man. She stood there just staring at him in disbelief. The longer she stared the madder she became. She shoved her arms in the coat then stomped out of the condo.

Jake looked at Ty. "You good?"

Ty just turned and walked away.

Kiki and Jake rode in silence. When the elevator doors opened, Kiki stepped out, determined not to let Ty win. She was going out and was going to enjoy herself. The hell with the fact that her body was still vibrating from his touch, the feel of his tongue. Ram was leaning on the security desk, and stood as she approached. He really did clean up nicely, she thought. A vision of Ty came to her. He put his finger in his mouth and sucked every drop of her essence. Her steps slowed. *No one else will ever quench our thirst for each other--no one.* That's what he said.

"Wow. You look amazing." Ram smiled. When she didn't reply, he took her hand. "Wildcat?"

Kiki looked at him knowing she couldn't do this. It wasn't fair to him. She slowly pulled her hand away. "I can't go out with you. I'm sorry."

"Of course you can." He took her hand again and began walking towards the exit. "I've made reservations for dinner and dancing."

She pulled away. "I'm sorry Ram. I really can't go with you."

"Yes, you can," his tone was a little harsher.

Jake stepped between them. "The lady said no."

"I've made reservations." He replied.

"I'm sorry Ram," was all Kiki said as she turned and walked back to the elevator.

Jake followed her, as Ram stood in the lobby and glared at the retreating Wildcat.

It had been building all day. The stink of the green eyed monster started that morning when she was talking to Jason on the computer. He didn't like it. Then when she laughed all day with him, he didn't like it. Then she put on that damn dress, with all her legs out to see another man, that just took every ounce of his control from him. She may be out with another man, but he'd left his mark. She would be back, she had to.

He sat down in front of his computer and began to dig into the life of Roberto Garrison and the dummy corporation. He looked up every so often expecting to see her walking through the door. It was an hour later, still nothing. He walked into the familyroom to pour himself a drink when he heard the key in the door. He sat the bottle back down. In the hallway, he found Jake with Kiki in his arms. Ty reached out to take her.

"She's drunk," Jake explained as her body was exchanged.

"No I'm not, Jake, shh." She put a finger up to her lips. "Don't tell him."

"I'm not," Jake laughed. "I'm going to let you tell him."

"How did she get like this? Did he do this?"

"No," Jake replied. "She did that all by herself." Jake put her coat and purse on the table. "You two need to talk." He walked towards the door. "Don't call me tonight. I've had enough." Jake slammed the door as he walked out.

"Is Jake mad?" Kiki asked in the sweetest voice.

Ty looked down at her and all he could do was smile. The most innocent looking eyes were watching him. "He's mad at me not you."

"Me too," she pouted. "Know why?"

"Tell me why Kiki," Ty said as he carried her into the bedroom.

"Cause, I don't want to love you anymore. It hurts too much because you don't love me back and that's not fair." He sat on the bed with her in his lap as he pulled the covers back. She cried into his shoulder. She hiccuped from the crying and then said, "That's what Daddy did to my Mom and it hurt her. I can't let you hurt me like that." She threw her arms up in the air. "Daddy said one day he woke up and Mommy had saddled him with four kids and he had to get away from that. He just couldn't take it anymore." Ty laid her on the bed, then began to undress her. "He needed his freedom and he just left. Wayne was so mad. We watched as Mommy packed his bags." She sniffled, than continued. "Mommy told Daddy once he walked out of that door there was no coming back. Daddy stared at her for a minute then turned and walked out the door. I've never seen my mother cry so hard. Wayne wrapped his arms around Mommy as she just cried." Ty covered her body with her favorite jersey then laid her back onto the pillow. She looked up at him with tears running down her face. "Now, I know how she felt. You broke me just like Daddy did Mommy." She closed her eyes and fell asleep.

Ty turned out the light and looked over at her sleeping form. Those last words stung. How could he stop them both from hurting?

He was working in a more relaxed mode now. He could concentrate on the material without feeling like he had to read the same thing twice and still wasn't comprehending any of the information. The dummy corporation was formed over five years ago with a home address in upstate New York. Roberto Garrison was one of five names listed as primary owners. They were putting all of the time into Garrison because he was the one that had a connection to LaToya. Maybe they should look into some of the other names as well. The monitor on the computer buzzed, indicating a call was coming through. Ty clicked the message to see Naverone's smiling face emerge. She was dressed in an off the shoulder number tonight, with her hair hanging loosely around her shoulders.

"You stepping out tonight Naverone? Looks like you're about to hurt somebody." He smiled.

"I can't wait all my life for you, Pendleton."

"Stabbed, right in the heart." He put his hand over his heart.

"I spoke with Wendy regarding Jason Whitfield. My team can be in place as early as tomorrow. Just say the word.

"Let's get that in place. Work the details out with Wendy. What else do you have for me?"

"My resources indicate there are three people of interest active. Once it can be narrowed down we'll know if your girl is one of the assignments. If she is, you are going to need more resources than you have to apprehend him or her."

"We'll get the resources once we know all the facts."

"What's bothering you?" Naverone asked, noticing his hesitation.

"Why kidnap her? If it's LaToya, what could she gain from having Kiki kidnapped? Something's just not clicking."

"Are you certain it's the Wright woman? Could Kiki be involved in something else?"

"No." Ty shook his head. "She's a literary agent. Her life consists of reading books and making deals."

"Could it be another man, an angry woman somewhere?"

"No, Naverone. Believe me, I have thought of nothing else since Saturday. I've been over every detail of her life to the point where it's driving me crazy. Yet, I feel like I'm missing something vital and if I don't find it soon I'm going to lose her."

"Is she worth it Ty?" When he began to respond, Naverone stopped him. "Hear me out." She sat forward, then stared into the monitor. "This is the only time you are going to hear this, so here it goes." She sighed as she gathered her thoughts. "I got this thing for you. It's been there since the first time we were together. You stepped away after you met this woman. I accept that and can move on. Moving on does not diminish me caring for you as a friend. Knowing she walked away from you and you did not reopen the door for me spoke volumes. I can accept that as well. Now, you are playing at the hero game with assassins. You are an intellect Tyrone, not a fighter. You are stepping into my world and believe me, it is not the place for you. So before you sink into the abyss of the world of espionage, answer the question. Is she worth all you are going through for her?"

"I will walk through the fires of hell to protect her," he replied without hesitation.

Naverone sat back. "Well," she sighed. "You sound like a man in love Ty."

"I care deeply for her."

"You more than care." She held her hands out, displaying her body. "Hell, you're giving all this up and I ain't no slouch." She smiled.

Ty knew he had hurt Naverone when he walked away. But he had to be honest. "That is true Ms. Naverone. Those thighs alone, are enough to make a man scream."

"I don't believe this," came Kiki's angry voice. "You are sex texting from my home. First you have a woman in my house. Now you sexting some woman on my internet."

Ty looked up to see Kiki angrily stalking towards him. "You are sexting a woman in my home. I know you have lost your mind."

"Kiki." Ty stood. "That's not what's happening here. Naverone is helping...."

"Just another employee," she yelled before he could finish. "I heard that before." She picked up the vase that was on the end table next to her and hurled it in his direction. "Rules, damnit Pendleton, rules."

Tyrone ducked as the vase sailed by his head crashing into the wall. He heard Naverone laugh. "Kendra," he raised his voice.

"How in the hell are you going to disrespect me in my own home?" Before she could throw the picture frame in her hand they heard a splatter. She turned towards the window where the sound came from. When she looked back Ty was on the floor.

"Ty?" She called out as she walked over to him. Another whistle sound sailed over her head.

"Get down Kiki," Naverone yelled from the computer. When she fell to her knees she saw the blood. She screamed, "Ty."

"Close the drapes, he's shooting from across the street," Naverone shouted through the monitor.

"Ty." Kiki turned him over. He grabbed her by the waist and held her down with him. "Stay down babe. Are you hurt?" He frantically checked her over with one hand.

"No, no. It's you. You're bleeding."

He felt the sharp pain in his shoulder, and grimaced at her touch. "It's okay babe." He kissed her temple. "It's okay. Just stay down." He looked frantically around. "The shots came through the window"

"Looks that way. Naverone call the authorities."

"Already on it. Where are you hit?"

"Right shoulder."

"Is Kiki hit?"

He looked at Kiki. She shook her head, no. "She's good."

"Somebody shot through the window?" Kiki asked, still shocked from the realization.

"Apparently so."

"We're on the twentieth floor bullets don't trail upwards...do they?"

"Pulling up satellite in the area now," Naverone stated as she worked.

"The building across the street, is it condos, businesses or what?"

"Both," Kiki replied.

"A lot of help you are."

Kiki frowned up at the computer that was on the table where Ty was working. "Who in the hell are you?"

"The woman that was going to kick your ass if you had put a scratch on him."

Kiki jumped up. "Don't get your ass kicked in the process." Another shot whistled through the window.

"Hell, he's still out there," Naverone cursed. "Stay down, both of you."

Ty pulled Kiki back down and cried out from the pain.

"Oh hell." Kiki crawled over to the kitchen and pulled the hand towel from the hook. Another shot hit the island right above her head.

"Stay there Kiki," Ty yelled. He looked around and spotted the remote. Crawling on his side he reached up on the table to pull down the remote. It dropped to the floor as another shot went through his shoulder and hit his hand. "Damn." With blood streaming from his hand, he pushed the button to close the drapes. He fell backwards, looked over at Kiki, then his eyes closed.

"Ty," she screamed. She crawled over to where he was. She wrapped the towel around his hand, then pulled a pillow from the sofa to applied pressure to his shoulder.

Someone began knocking on the door. "Security. Is everyone okay in there?"

"No. Come in, but stay down," Kiki yelled. "Somebody is shooting through the window."

"Kiki what's happening with Ty?" Naverone asked.

"He's been hit again."

"Are the drapes closed all the way?"

Kiki looked around. "Yes."

"Grab the computer and put it where I can see him."

Kiki moved the computer down to the other end of the table.

"Ms. Simmons, the police are on the way."

150

"He's bleeding." She frantically continued to apply pressure.

The police came in with weapons drawn. She heard one officer call for an ambulance.

"Officer," Naverone called from the computer. "The shots came from the building across the street. The angle of the shots indicate the shooter was on the twenty-first or twenty-second floor. He's using a high powered rifle with a scope. Probably a M4."

The sight of an officer now working on Ty caused Naverone to pause for a moment. Then she continued to handle business. "I counted five shots. Send a team to the building. Don't allow anyone in the area when you locate where the shots came from. I'll be there in two hours."

"Who are you?" The officer asked.

"Rene Naverone. Secret Service."

Part Two
Pain and Pleasure

Chapter Nine

*T*he hospital was quiet for the moment, but Genesis Morgan knew that was about to change. She walked up to the receptionist in the emergency room at Mount Sinai Hospital. They knew the routine for they handled celebrities day in and day out. Flipping her case open, one side displaying her Secret Service identification, she asked, "Who's in charge here?"

A young girl with curly red hair replied, "Dr. Charles is the resident in charge tonight."

"Let's try again." She held the badge up. "Who's in charge?"

Another nurse came to the young girl's rescue. "May I help you?"

"You are?"

"Nurse Lynch."

She held the woman's eyes then nodded to her badge. "Who's in charge?"

Nurse Lynch looked closely at the badge. "I'll take a wild guess and say you are."

"That would be good. I'm Special Agent Morgan. We have a VIP that is en route. We need you to implement your security protocol level one." She looked around. "Would you contact your head of security? Have him meet me at the entrance. You are about to get hit with a whirlwind of celebrities."

Nurse Lynch watched as the slim, brown skinned woman surveyed the lobby. She was dressed in a pair of jeans, long sleeved turtleneck and spiked boots, with her hair brushed back in a ponytail that hung across her shoulder. She looked like a teenager, but her eyes let you know she was not someone you wanted to tangle with. "Special Agent Morgan, you have a call," Nurse Lynch said as she held the receiver out.

"Morgan." She listened then gave the phone back to Nurse Lynch. "Your techs are coming in with the victim. Advise the resident on duty the victim has two gunshot wounds in the shoulder, rapidly loosing blood, in an unconscious state."

"I need your security team here now," Genesis said to the young nurse.

"Kelly." Nurse Lynch turned to the redhead. "Get security down here now." She then paged Dr. Charles.

Two men dressed in uniform walked casually towards the station. Agent Morgan looked at Nurse Lynch. "You're kidding, right?"

"I'm afraid not."

Genesis pulled out her phone and pushed a button. "What's your ETA?"

"Another hour," Naverone replied.

"We're going to need some help before then."

"Anyone there with a little sense?"

Genesis looked at Nurse Lynch. "Yeah."

"Drop a few names. That might get them moving. If it doesn't ask for the Hospital Administrator."

Holding Nurse Lynch's eyes, Genesis disconnected her call. She bent over the desk. "Nurse Lynch, we may have an issue," she spoke in a low voice. "The victim coming in is Tyrone Pendleton. He happens to be the son of Miriam Davies, the singer, and the brother of Silk Davies. He also happens to be the agent for a number of other celebrities and sports figures in this area. Once his name is leaked, this place is going to erupt. As good as I am, and I think you are, we are not going to be able to contain the situation. Who do we call?"

Nurse Lynch picked up the telephone. "Code One in Emergency." She looked at Genesis. "That should take care of it." She gave Genesis a doubtful look. "Silk Davies is going to walk through that door?"

Genesis looked at her watch, and nodded. "Probably within the hour."

She turned to the guards. "Gentleman, I need you," she pointed to one man, "to secure that entrance. No one in, no one out." She looked at the second guard, ignoring the fact that the first man was looking at her as if she was crazy. "I need that exam, room secured." When neither moved, Genesis asked, "Is there a problem, Gentlemen?"

"We don't take orders from you. Hell we don't even know who you are," the younger gentleman replied.

"What's your name?"

"What's your name cutie?"

The older guard's radio clicked on. "Code One. All available personnel report to the emergency room, stat."

Before the men could move, the ambulance and several police cars pulled up at the entrance. A man in a doctor's coat, accompanied by several people in green hospital scrubs came running around the corner. The emergency doors flew open.

The next hour was a blur. The man was wheeled into an exam room, with the female that arrived with him looking on in horror. Police officers filled the area, placing officers strategically around the room immediately blocking access to the area.

Genesis jumped into action, following the instructions she had been given. "Officer." She flipped her badge. "Special Agent Morgan. It's my understanding this is the act of a possible assassin. I'm here to protect Mr. Pendleton and Ms. Simmons until backup arrives."

The officer looked the woman up and down. "You're alone?" He asked as if questioning what she could do.

This Genesis was used to, in the male dominated field she'd chosen as a profession. "Yes." Giving her another once over, he nodded his head allowing her in. "I need your two best men."

"Garcia, Harris," he called out. "Go with this lady."

Genesis walked into the area where Kendra Simmons stood. She knew the look too well. Had seen it time and time again while she was working in the field. The woman was afraid. "Ms. Simmons." Genesis flipped her badge. "I'm SSA Morgan. I've been assigned to protect you until Mr. Pendleton can resume his role."

"What?" Kiki asked only glancing in the woman's direction.

Genesis took her hand and just held it. She didn't say another word as the doctor worked.

The doctor had taken Ty to surgery to repair the damage done by the bullets. He assured Kiki that while the injuries were severe, they did not appear to be life threatening, a fractured clavicle bone and some muscle tissue damage. He would probably have a night or two in the hospital then, a six to eight week recovery period. Kiki listened, but the words did not calm her. Ty had been shot because of her. The thought wouldn't leave her. She had no idea who the woman was that was holding her hand, but she was ever so grateful that she was there.

"Kendra, what in the hell is going on?"

Kiki was so overwhelmed with emotions, she ran over to her father, and threw her arms around his waist. "They shot Ty, Daddy."

He pulled her away and held her at arm's length

"What is this all over you?"

Kiki looked down. "It's, it's Ty's blood." She was about to cry until she heard his next words.

"Is he dead?"

There was something in the way he said it that caused her to stop and stare at her father. "No Daddy, he's not."

"Then he can pay for the shattered windows and bullet ridden walls in the condo."

She took a step back. "Did you hear me Daddy? Someone shot Ty."

"That's what happens to music producers, agents or whatever he calls himself. They deal with rappers and such, who we all know deal with drugs in some kind of way. Hell, this shooting probably has to do with a drug deal gone bad." He ran a hand down his face. "It would take you to get involved with someone like that. Laura never would."

That was a slap in her face if she ever felt one. The words *go to hell* were on the tip of her tongue, when something Ty told her came to mind. *Words can be forgiven, but never forgotten. Be careful what you say in anger.* She took another step back. "Ty is none of those things. He is the most decent human being I have ever met and I love him. I believe he loves me too. Can you say the same?" He started to speak but she stopped him with a glare. "I was shot at tonight. Regardless of the reason, someone shot at me. Can you imagine for one minute that it was Laura and act like a loving father?"

"No, I can't imagine that Kendra because Laura would never be involved with anyone that deals with drugs or guns."

"But I would?" she questioned him. "Tell me one time when I gave you a reason to think so low of me. I graduated top of my class from high school, cum laude from college, then graduated in the top ten from law school, but you wouldn't know that because you weren't there for any of them."

"What are you talking about Kendra? None of that has anything to do with you having that person in my condo with people shooting up the place."

"You are right, it doesn't. It has to do with your total disregard for the family you left behind when you decided to be with your mistress and your bastard daughter."

Kenneth reached out and slapped Kiki across the face. "Don't you ever speak of your sister in that way again."

Kiki held her face, shocked at his attack. The anger in his eyes began to dissipate when he realized what he had done. He reached out to her, "Kendra, I..."

She stepped back again and calmly spoke. "You don't have to worry about it Daddy. I'll never speak of her or you again." She exhaled. "You'll have my resignation on your desk tomorrow. I'll ensure all repairs are made to the condo as soon as feasible. Or you can hire a contractor to do the repairs and send me the bill. As of this moment, I'm done trying to earn your love."

"Kendra," he pleaded.

She walked away and retook her seat. When he attempted to follow, Genesis interceded. "I think it best that you leave, sir."

Kenneth looked angrily at the woman, then back at Kiki with sorrow filled eyes. He shook his head. "I didn't mean it." Getting no response from his daughter, he turned to walk away only to find Issy standing behind him.

Her eyes burned through him. "I see you've made your decision again. Your new family over the old."

"Issy, talk to her. You know I didn't mean to hit her."

"You made that bed a long time ago Kenny. Go lay in it."

He took a step towards her, only to have Jake block him. "Now is not a good time."

Kenneth looked from Jake to Issy, then back to Jake. Slowly he stepped away. "Is that how it is Issy?"

"It is," Jake replied.

Kenneth looked at his ex-wife, then slowly walked away shaking his head.

"Kendra," her mother cried out. She rushed to her daughter and gathered her into her arms. "My baby, what happened?" She held her away and looked her over. "Are you hurt?" She ran her hands over Kiki before she could answer. Issy pulled her back into her arms and hugged her as only a mother could do.

"They shot Ty mommy, they shot him."

"I know baby, I know. Jake told me. What did the doctor say?"

"Kiki," Wendy called out as she ran over to where she was sitting. "How are you? Are you okay? How is Ty?"

Kiki looked up to see Wendy standing in front of her and the woman from the computer standing behind her. Damn Tyrone and his beautiful women.

"I'm not in the mood to fight you right now," she said to the woman.

Naverone almost smiled. In spite of herself, she was beginning to like the woman that took Ty away from her. "That's good. I would hate to kick your ass at a time like this."

Kiki almost laughed. It sounded just like something she would say.

Issy began to stand at the woman's words, but Kiki held her back.

"How are you and how is our boy doing?"

"I'm okay," Kiki replied. "He was shot twice in the shoulder. One bullet went through. They are removing the other now. The doctor indicated he should be okay after a few days in the hospital."

"What happened Rocket?" Jake asked. All ears were tuned in as she relayed the events.

"How many shots did you hear?" Genesis asked.

"Five maybe six. But I really didn't hear them. Did you?" She looked up at Naverone.

"No. Where were you standing when you threw the vase?"

160

Issy and Jake looked at each other, then back at the two women that were talking.

"About twenty twenty-five feet away."

"Which shots hit Tyrone?"

Kiki thought for a moment. "The first shot and the fourth, I think."

"Okay, that's good. Now, tell me Kendra, you were standing behind his computer, right? His back was to the window."

"Yes." Kiki sat up. "Whoever was shooting was lousy at it. They missed me by a mile every time."

Naverone and Genesis glanced at each other.

"Jake," Jason called out from the doorway with Eric in tow. "What the hell happened?"

Naverone and Genesis stepped aside as the family gathered. "The shooter wasn't aiming for Kiki." Naverone looked over Genesis' shoulder, watching the family as she spoke.

"The target was your man."

Naverone nodded. "But, he's not my man. She got him. Now, let's make sure they have their happy ever after."

Rupid A. Mann stood outside the emergency entrance, dressed in a black turtleneck sweater, black jeans and a black leather coat. Blending into the darkness was vital in his line of work. He was trained and given a license to kill ten years ago by the United States government. The pay was mediocre, but the benefits more than made up for it. Calling it patriotism would be nice, if that's what it was. The truth is, he loved the hunt. When he was a boy it was rabbits, cats, , and dogs. He didn't care. The hunt, chase, then the kill always intrigued him. Like others, he ended up in detention until he turned eighteen. Given a choice on the next stint in jail, he opted for the military.

Ah yes, the good old US military. They trained him, made him a specialist, then paid him to keep his skills sharp. One overkill and they wanted to pull him from the field to send him to sensitivity training. Hell, if he let them anywhere near his brain, they would discover just how sick he was. Discharge was the best solution. The tranquil life did not quench his thirst for the kill nor his desire to live well. He had skills. Rendering his services to those that could afford him was the American way of life.

This assignment was not his first and would not be his last. But damn if it wasn't trying his patience. He preferred to take the target out, however, he was being paid twice his going rate to inflict revenge. Revenge, a dirty little word, child's play, but what the hell, it was a job.

The hunt started with promise. He'd taken care of the first target without incident. Second target, hell he wasn't sure anyone realized he was actually a hit at this point. This third target, well, she was the cream of the crop and had proven to be the most challenging by far. The first attempt made him smile just thinking about it. Pendleton was not the nerd as he had thought. The man could handle himself quite well for someone with no military training. He almost admired the man for the way he chased him down to get his woman back. The security he put in place to protect her was above average. Hell, he left his business, not trusting anyone to do the job that only a man that was in love with a woman would do. It's sweet, if you really think about it. He had a half a million reasons not to think about it. Besides, Pendleton had to pay for interfering with his plans one too many times. To accomplish his task, he had to take

Pendleton out of the picture. Now, he should have easy access to Kendra Simmons.

Chapter Ten

*T*he sun was rising when Ty awakened from the sedatives. One arm felt like little needles were trying to cut through his skin. The other arm had a heavy weight on it. Looking to his left, he smiled at the sleeping form of Kiki lying next to him in the hospital bed. The memory of the night before came to him. He looked at his right arm. The shoulder was tight. He tried to move his fingers. It hurt like hell, but they moved.

A nurse walked in. "Good morning Mr. Pendleton."

Ty put his finger to his lips, then pointed to Kiki.

The nurse nodded. "She's been in that position crying all night. She must have fallen asleep there."

"What time is it?"

She looked at her watch as she checked his vitals. "Seven fifteen." She smiled. "Your pressure looks good. One to ten, what's your pain level?"

"Twenty."

"The doctor left a prescription for morphine."

Ty shook his head. "No drugs. Just a few aspirin to ease the discomfort."

"All right. Are you up to visitors? We have a waiting room filled with people itching to see you." She laughed. "Your mother is driving our Administrator crazy. The staff is wondering if we could keep her around. We rather enjoy seeing him jump through hoops with all the celebrities around."

"My mother is here?"

"Yes, your mother, several brothers, a few sisters, and others that claim to be distant relatives." She gave him a doubtful look.

The nurse was met with a confused look as Kiki stirred. "Give us five minutes," she moaned, "then send in his mother and brothers. Tell the others they get five minutes. No business. Just five minutes to see that he is okay." She looked up at him. "Good morning,"

Her eyes were swollen and frightened, but he couldn't have asked for a more beautiful sight. He touched her cheek. "Morning beautiful."

The kiss was meant to be just an 'I'm glad your eyes are open' kiss, but the emotions of the last week entered into both their psyches and neither wanted to stop until the other fully understood how deep their love flowed. The nurse looked on, then left the room thinking they would definitely need longer than an hour.

This is what he wants for the rest of his life, minus the pain in his shoulder and hand. Enduring that he would, if he could have this sweet sassy mouthed woman in his life.

That was it, she didn't care if he asked her to move to Australia, she had to be with him. The fear that resulted from watching him fall to the floor from the gunshots was still fresh, causing tears to flow down her cheeks. His touch as he wiped the tears away with his bandaged hand, was all the warmth she needed to ease her fears.

Breaking the kiss he held her close, his nose touching hers, and whispered, "I have a new rule." The statement had exactly the impact he wanted. Her eyes smiled up at him.

"To add to the Pendleton Rules?"

He shook his head. "No, this is the one and only rule."

She pulled back a little to really see his eyes. They reflected a serious glint. "And it is?"

"The new rule is simple. We wake up every morning in each others arms, no matter what."

A slow sensuous smile began to form on her lips as she held his gaze. She moved her leg over his thigh. "I like that rule, Pendleton."

He kissed the tip of her nose. "Do you?"

The heat began to build between her legs. The man could make her come in a hospital bed with IV's in his arm, just from his intense gaze. "I like it so much I'm tempted to mount you right here and ride you like the stallion you are."

"I love you Kendra Isadore Simmons. I don't want another day to go by without you hearing those words from me. I would walk through the fires of hell just to be able to hold you, touch you, kiss you. I don't want to spend another day with us arguing, or apart from each other. Life is too short."

What on earth was wrong with her? She had been waiting over a year to hear those words from this man and all she could do was cry. Not a sound would come out of her mouth, even when she tried, only tears would flow down her cheeks.

"Shocked you speechless, didn't I." She laughed, then sniffed, as she nodded then released a few breaths. "Me too." He kissed her temple and held her."

She exhaled and sniffled again as she squeezed him around his waist. "I love you Tyrone," she cried into his chest. "When you closed your eyes last night, I was so afraid I had lost you forever."

Ignoring the pain from her hold, he rubbed her back. "You will not lose me that easily. Shhh," he soothed her as she cried.

Kiki stood and stretched as the nurse came in to change Ty's dressing. She stepped outside the room and wasn't surprised to see Jake and Naverone sitting outside the door.

"Good morning," she said, no longer feeling threatened by Naverone, Rosa or any other woman in Ty's life. It didn't matter that Rene Naverone was dressed in a killer off the shoulder top, skinny jeans, four inch boots to die for and the prettiest French braid in her hair that Kiki had ever seen. She was dressed in a pair of jeans, sneakers and a sweater that was probably two sizes too big. She had Ty's love, that was all the confidence she needed.

"Morning," Naverone replied leaning back in the chair with her legs crossed and gun hanging from the shoulder holster.

"Rocket." Jake stood as he spoke. "How is he this morning?"

"He's in a little pain, but he's doing well. Is Wendy here?"

"Yes, she's in the waiting room with the others," Jake replied.

"Would you ask her to check Tyrone's computer? He was working on negotiations with Nick Brooks on Jason's contract."

Jake looked from her to Naverone, then back to Kiki. "You and I both know Wendy has already handled whatever Ty was working on. If you want to speak to Naverone alone all you had to do was say so. I would have left."

"Don't feel slighted Jake." Kiki punched him in the shoulder. "The fact that my mother is in New York and arrived at the hospital with you hasn't been lost in the midst of everything. We're going to talk."

Jake smiled as he walked away. "Grown folks business, Rocket. Grown folks business."

"I got your business, all right," she said to his back as a smile touched her face. She turned, exhaled then took the chair Jake had vacated.

Looking at all the activity going on at the nurse's station, she spoke. "I love Tyrone."

Naverone watched the same activity, neither looking at each other as they spoke. "I know. He loves you too."

Kiki nodded, pleased the woman knew. "Is that going to be a problem for you?"

"No more than it's been for the last eighteen months." She sat the chair down on all fours, then turned to Kiki. When Kiki looked at her, she spoke. "I'm the woman he left to be with you. If it was anything there, he would have returned when you walked away. He didn't," she shrugged her shoulder, "I had my answer."

"Okay." Kiki exhaled. "Have you been working on this case with him?"

"Tell me what you know."

"How about this? I'll tell you and Ty together."

Kiki held the woman's eyes. "I want this over so we can move forward with our life. Can you make that happen?"

"Yes."

She didn't know the woman, but she believed her. "You are as arrogant as he is, aren't you?"

"Probably more," she replied, then had the nerve to smile.

"Kendra, I want to see my son." Kiki looked up to see Miriam Davies walking down the corridor with all the grace of royalty. "I've waited long enough. Where is he?" She asked as she stopped in front of Kiki.

"He's inside." Kiki stood, then nodded towards the door.

"Look," Miriam took her hand. "He is going to Jason's home when he is released from the hospital. It's where the family is staying until this ugly mess is over with. You are coming too. Now, I don't want to fight you on this but I will if I have to," she said with a huff.

"Yes, ma'am," Kiki replied

Miriam gave her a doubtful look. "You agreed to that mighty fast Kendra."

"We need our life back Mrs. Davies. Whatever I have to do to accomplish that I will do."

Miriam gave her that Diahann Carroll smile. "Good. I'm happy you agree. Now, be a dear and tell those nurses to let Jason and Eric see their brother before they tear the hospital down."

Kiki smiled, "Yes ma'am."

"And you go with her," she said to Naverone. "I don't know who you are, but you look like you could take down anyone that tries to do her harm." She looked down. "By the way, I love those boots." She turned and walked into the room.

It was an hour later before Naverone stepped into Ty's hospital room. After the family and Wendy visited, several of his clients that were in the area stopped in just to make sure he was breathing, which allowed them to breath a little easier. Yes, they were concerned for Ty, however, they were also concerned with their finances. Each knew it was Tyrone Pendleton that kept them in the socioeconomic status they enjoyed.

As she walked in, Kiki was leaning over Ty, talking into his ear. The scene was rather intimate and at first she thought not to interrupt, but Ty looked up. "Good morning."

Kiki stood near the bed, holding his hand. He motioned for her to take a seat.

"How are you?" Naverone asked.

"Alive," Ty replied

"Much pain?" she asked as she sat in the chair next to the bed.

"Oh yeah."

She held his gaze. The words were unspoken, but she understood and so did he. "I'm okay Rene."

She exhaled, then nodded towards Kiki. "She's a tough cookie."

Ty nodded. "She's a softer you," he smiled, as he rubbed Kiki's hand. "What did you find?"

"What makes you think I found anything?"

"I know you. You were probably on the job before I came out of surgery."

She raised an eyebrow. "And you know this." She smiled. "A condo across the street had been used as a stake out. The person has been there for at least a week. Didn't leave much behind. A professional clean up job was done on the place." She sat up. "Ty, every shot except one was aimed at you. Not Kiki."

"So he's gunning for Ty now?" Kiki asked, concerned with the thought.

"It appears so."

"The police indicated they recovered several bullets from the condo and there's the one they took out of me. Can you find anything from them?"

"Possibly. I still have friends in the Service."

"Was the lady that was here last night one of them?" Kiki asked.

"Genesis Morgan, yes she is."

"She handled business last night. Is it possible to keep her on this case?"

"Agent Morgan is still active with the Service. I'll have to check on her availability."

"Is she good Naverone?"

Naverone gave him an incredulous look. "All my friends are."

Kiki had to laugh. "I really like you."

Naverone smiled. "You're growing on me."

Chapter Eleven

*T*y was released from the hospital two days later. Kiki, his mother and Jake, accompanied him on the flight from New York to Virginia. He was miserable. The only bright spot for Ty was Kiki being by his side. His right arm was in a sling, just to limit his mobility until the wound could heal. His left hand was bandaged, increasing his inability to do things for himself, such as eat, wash, or take care of his personal needs, without assistance. There are times when he had no problem with Kiki handling him, however, there was nothing sexy about having your woman assisting you to take a piss.

By the time they reached Jason's home, he was ready to take any drug that would kill the pain. With four, no make that five women arguing over him, he pleaded with his brothers to take their wives away. He loved them all, really, he did, just not at that moment.

Jason and TeKaya's home was filled with family and security. The gated suburban community consisted of four homes sitting on five-acre lots. Their home was located in the back of the community with another gate. Once through the gate there was a curving, mile long, tree lined driveway. Towards the end of the driveway, the open landscape revealed a spectacular three level white colonial, with a beautiful view of the river as its backdrop. The well manicured lawn, bordered the circular brick driveway, with a water fountain in the center.

Before the car stopped the double entry doors swung open. TeKaya and Siri rushed out, pulling the door open. "Ty." TeKaya pulled at his arm.

Ty endured the pain knowing she meant well. Siri hugged him, then kissed his cheek. "I'm so happy to see you." She then stretched her arms out to Kiki. "Are you okay?" She looked Kiki over like a mother hen.

"Yes." She returned the hug, then gently removed TeKaya's hand from Ty's arm. "He was shot in that shoulder," she explained to TeKaya.

"Oh Ty, I'm sorry."

"It's all right TeKaya." He took Kiki's hand.

"Let's get you inside," Miriam said. "Then we'll get you some food, medicine and then you're going to tell me what this mess is all about."

Jason and Eric met them at the door. "It's good to see you. Let's get you settled in," Jason said as they walked into the foyer.

Conscious of his injured hand, Kiki tried not to hold it too tight, but the moment she walked inside the house, the hold tightened. Her family was well off. Her father was the one of the partners at Crimson Publishing, her mother was a New York Times best-selling author and she was the agent to at least two NYT best sellers. Ty's condo in Atlanta was stylish, sleek and a true bachelor's pad. This home should be on 'Homes of the Rich and Famous'. She looked around thinking, they are the rich and famous. Miriam Davies, internationally known entertainer, Eric "Silk" Davies, multi Grammy winner and Jason Davies, the music producer. Yes, this was his family. She looked up at Ty as they embraced him. It was clear that they loved him and were happy to see him walk through the door. She pulled away to allow the family to fawn over him for a few minutes. Her heart smiled when his niece, Sierra walked in the room holding her arms up for Ty.

"Uncle Ty, can't pick you up this time pumpkin." Jason explained as he picked up his daughter so she could kiss Ty's cheek.

"I feel better already."

"That's what family love will do for you." Miriam smiled as she removed her coat.

"Come sit down son," She guided Ty to a chair in the family room. The room was a huge open space, with a double-sided fireplace that could also be enjoyed from the kitchen. There was a large wine colored sectional facing the fireplace that warmed the room. Another area of the room had a small table and chair set, surrounded by a variety of toys. On the far side of the room there was another sofa and chair that faced the window, overlooking the patio.

Eric and Siri sat next to each other at one end, Jason and TeKaya at another. Miriam sat in a chair near the fireplace, as Ty sat in the middle. They all turned to Kiki as if they were waiting for something. Sierra took her hand. "Come on." She said with her chubby cheeks and bouncing pigtails. "You can sit next to Uncle Ty."

"I don't want to intrude."

174

"Girl, you are family," Miriam stated. "Come take your place so I can get to the bottom of this." Kiki followed the little girl's lead, then sat next to Ty. Sierra, promptly climbed into her father's lap. "LaToya has finally showed her true colors--again." Miriam started the conversation.

"Hold on." Jason turned to Sierra, "pumpkin would you ask Gabby to prepare hot chocolate for us? Would you put some of your special marshmallows in them?"

"Yes Daddy," the five-year-old ran into the kitchen.

The adults waited until the child was gone before they continued with the conversation. "It looks that way," Ty replied as he placed his arm around Kiki's shoulder.

"If you had listened to me she would be dead by now. But, noooo, Jason had to be his father's child. I knew I should have toughened you up."

"We don't kill people mother," Jason replied as he rubbed his wife's protruding stomach.

"This is one time I think we should have," Eric stated. "She is definitely trying to kill Ty."

"Well, you can't really blame her," TeKaya smirked." All eyes turned to her. "Go back to last year and really think about all that happened."

"That's true," Siri chimed in. "You took her man, whipped her behind and now you are raising her daughter. It's a wonder she hasn't come after you yet."

TeKaya looked shocked. "That's true babe," Jason nodded. "You did do all of that."

"Okay, but she deserved it after what she was doing to you and Sierra. Besides, it was Eric that really humiliated her."

"And Kiki too." Siri nodded in agreement.

"No," Kiki chimed in. "She humiliated herself. I was only there to witness how she tried to seduce Eric."

Siri looked sideways at Eric. "She tried to seduce you? When?"

"The night she was arrested," Eric grinned. "It was fun watching her go down, though." He glanced at Kiki.

She cuddled up closer to Ty and smiled. "Yeah, I haven't had that much fun since."

"You should work for Ty," Jason smirked. "He does that kind of stuff to people all the time."

"I only have one rule in my life. Don't mess with the people I love and I won't mess with you."

"Since Kendra is one of those people now and LaToya is messing with her, are you going to take that woman out? It seems, you are my last hope in getting that woman out of our lives." Miriam eyed her son's reaction.

The air in the room tensed a little, waiting for Ty's response. He looked down at Kiki. "Do you see how she operates?"

She looked up at him. "Yeah, that was pretty smooth. Mothers do that you know." She nodded.

"Do they?"

"Yeah, I think it's taught in Mother's Love 101. You should have taken that class. Very interesting."

"All right you two." Miriam smiled. "Just go ahead and kiss one time so I'll know it's real."

"There are children in the room," Ty replied.

"Sierra sees her parents kiss all the time," Miriam replied.

"I was talking about Eric," Ty teased. "However," he reached down for Kiki's hand, "We will give you this." Kiki stood, taking his hand. "The two of us are going to retire upstairs to take a much needed nap."

"Since when did you start taking naps in the middle of the day?" Eric asked.

Ty stepped by his brothers and their wives, then looked back at them. "Since I started singing *Always and Forever*, instead of *Brick House*." They walked over to the staircase in the kitchen to laughter from his family at the private joke.

"I missed something back there didn't I?" she asked as she looked back over her shoulder to see Eric and Jason pointing at Ty, laughing.

Ty smiled as he looked down at her. "I'll tell you about it one day. In the mean time, let's give them something to talk about," he stated as he pulled her into his arms and kissed her as if they had all the time in the world.

Sierra walked over and reached in between the couple to touch Kiki's stomach.

Kiki looked down at the little girl. "What's wrong sweetie?"

The child had a confused look when she looked up. "My Daddy kissed mommy and put   a baby in her stomach."

The adults in the other room laughed harder, as Ty pulled away and stared at the child, then looked at Kiki. "Don't even think about it Tyrone Pendleton," Kiki stated. "Not until you make an honest woman out of me."

As the couple walked up the stairs, Jason turned to his mother. "Ty seems to be taking all of this well."

"I thought he would have killed someone by now." Eric shook his head. "I know I would have."

Miriam listened while the family discussed the situation, her mind still on the look in her son's eyes. Ty was always good at masking his true feelings from his brothers, but not from her. She, on the other hand knew what blood flowed through her son's veins. She knew Ty was about to cross a dark line.

(P)

The moment Kiki started her shower, Ty connected his computer, then called his office. In the sitting area of his bedroom suite, Ty and Jake began the on line conference call, giving instructions to Wendy to set up a conference call with Peace and Naverone. When the call came through, his friends found a different man. Gone was the calm exterior they knew to be Ty Pendleton. Before them was a man out for blood. "Hire the best. I want this man taken out."

"Boss, taking out the shooter will not get us the person behind the order," Peace advised.

"I don't give a damn. I want this man dead. He shot at her, in her home. She should have been safe. How in the hell can I look her in the face knowing I couldn't protect her? I want his identity in twenty-four hours, preferably with his death certificate attached."

"Peace has a lead Boss," Jake offered.

Peace retrieved the disk with the pictures taken the day he followed Tina Wright and Roberto Garrison. He placed the disk in the computer located on the media rack directly under one of four large screen monitors mounted around the room. The luxury conference room could seat anywhere from twenty-four at the table to an additional twenty in chairs sitting against the wall. The room was used for staff meetings or media conferences. Today it was the meeting place to discuss the situation concerning Ty.

On one monitor Ty, with Jake seated next to him in the library at Jason's house, waited for the pictures to load.

Another had Naverone from her office in Atlanta, and Genesis on the third from her office in New Jersey.

"Do we have ears and eyes in the Wright woman's house yet?" Genesis inquired.

"Legally we have no grounds to wire the house," Peace replied.

"Legal or not, we need ears in that house," Genesis stated. "You still have equipment Rene?"

Nodding, Naverone took notes. "It'll be done within the hour."

"Pictures up," Peace announced as he pushed the button on the remote. "Everyone have a clear view?" He asked.

All eyes turned to the monitor at the other end of the room. "These were taken two days ago here in Atlanta." A series of photos drifted across the screen. "The first stills are from Tina Wright's home, the second set from the restaurant, where this man joined them. This next set was from the visit to the correctional facility, at least as far as I could go. After leaving the facility, Garrison returned Tina to her home then met this man at the airport, where they boarded a private plane. According to the manifest, they were flying to New York."

"So they were in New York at the time of the shooting?" Jake asked.

"It appears so," Peace replied.

Ty sat forward. "Naverone, do either of them look to be someone that could take the shot?"

"Can't go by looks," she replied. "We train people everyday to blend in whereever, to get the job done."

"Is it possible to pick up when they landed in New York?" Ty asked.

"Big brother has eyes everywhere," Genesis replied. "I'll see if we can get the surveillance tapes from the airport. All I need is the flight plan and registration number of the plane. We'll track their movements from there."

"What's the turnaround time on the surveillance tapes?"

"That may take a minute Ty," Naverone then added, "The FAA and Homeland Security have to give the okay on the viewing of those tapes."

"Let me be very clear on where I stand. This has been interfering in my life for over a week. It ends now. Do whatever it takes to find out who is responsible for this. If you have contacts with the FAA reach out, get the information."

"That may cost," Genesis warned.

"I don't care about the cost," he yelled. "I do care that someone is shooting at my woman's home. Her home people. A place where she should have been safe." He exhaled, taking a moment to calm down. He ran his bandaged hand over his face, then looked into the monitor. "Look, we are missing something." Ty shook his head. "The person that took those shots had a clear path to us. He could have taken us out, yet he didn't--why? Why didn't he take out Kiki that first night? The opportunity was there. There are too many unanswered questions."

"If you truly believe this Wright woman is responsible," Genesis raised a brow, "extract the information from her."

"I've spoken with her. I didn't get much."

"I didn't say talk to her," Genesis paused. "I said extract the information. Those are two distinctly different things."

"You mean like torture?" Peace asked.

"I mean get the information by any means necessary," Genesis replied.

"Hmm, do you carry handcuffs?" He smiled.

"Contact the warden," Ty ordered. "Set up a private meeting with LaToya."

"Hold on Ty," Naverone cautioned. "We can't go into a correctional facility with the purpose of extracting information from Wright."

"Then find someone who can."

"Ty."

"Do it Naverone, or find someone that can. Call me with the details." He disconnected the call.

Turning to Jake, Ty was still trying to control his anger.

"How do you want to handle this, Boss?"

Sitting idle, waiting for the next shoe to drop was not his forté. "Put the jet on call. I'll need to fly at a moment's notice."

"Where are you going Tyrone?"

Ty looked up to see his mother standing in the doorway. The look she gave him indicated she knew what he was about to do. "Jake, will you give us a minute?'

"Sure." Jake stood to leave. "Go easy on him," he said to Miriam as he closed the door.

Miriam, with her graceful way, took a seat on the sofa across from her son. She took his bandaged hand and held it in hers. "I know where you are and I understand. You think I'm here to talk you out of whatever you plan to do. I'm not." She looked up into his eyes. "You do what you have to, to protect the woman you love. All I ask is that I not lose my son in the process. Love is a powerful emotion. If not handled with care, it can take us in so many directions. People have died in the name of love. Some have killed. I don't want you to do either." She stood, kissed him on the forehead, then just as gracefully as she entered, she left.

Ty stared at the door for a long time. The woman just never ceased to amaze him. The anger was cutting so deep he had to exert more effort to keep it contained. She saw right through him. Standing, he walked over to the huge picture window with the view of the beautiful manicured lawn, the walkway lined with shrubbery that held various colors of blooms in the spring, the octagonal shaped gazebo with the cushioned bench and the lake in the distance. The scene was tranquil and would probably calm any unsettled soul, but not his. He was troubled with the knowledge that he had not protected Kiki. Whoever this man was had penetrated the defenses he put up and gotten to her twice. Now his mother, with her infinite wisdom, had cautioned him to proceed, but to proceed with limits. To his way of thinking, there were no limits when it came to protecting the woman you love. He would take his mother's request under advisement. That's about all he could give her at this time. However, he would leave no stone unturned until he found who was behind this attempt to hurt Kiki.

Standing in the doorway between the bedroom and sitting room, Kiki watched Ty. He was so troubled. She could tell by his stance. A smile touched her heart as she observed him. Even with the arm sling, he still looked good dressed in navy blue Armani, of course. His arm with the bandaged hand leaned against the wall as he stared outside the window. His mind was working and she couldn't wait until he revealed his plan of action. Just watching him think caused her nipples to tighten, her stomach to quiver and her lips to part. He was just that sexy to her. They had wasted so much time.

She walked into the room, wrapped her arms around his waist, and placed her head between his shoulder blades. "A penny for your thoughts."

Ty smiled as his body relaxed at her touch. Funny how a simple touch from her could ease his worries. But it did not change his fear for her. "Right now, I'm thinking why do you insist on wearing that Yankees jersey."

She laughed. "You bought it for me." She kissed his back. "It's not about the jersey, it's about what's underneath it...or not." She squeezed him a little tighter.

He swung his bandaged hand around and pulled her in front of him. "Are you teasing an injured man?"

Kiki pulled away and began walking backwards. "Oops, my bad. I didn't think the injury affected all regions of your body." She reached down, pulling the bottom of the jersey up and over her head. "Can your legs work?" she asked with a grin.

Perfection, was the only word that came to his mind. His eyes roamed her body with his eyes, getting harder as he traveled south. His lips curled into a sensuous smile. "When did you do that?"

She looked down. "Oh," she grinned, "the insignia?" She looked back up at him. "I thought it would be fun to show you the impact of your branding from the other night."

He licked his lips, then took a step towards her. "When?" he asked as he removed the sling from his arm and dropped it on the floor.

She took a step back. "Yesterday."

Holding her eyes as he took another step, the suit jacket hit the floor. "Who?"

The grin turned into a huge smile as she watched him remove his tie. "My Mom's masseuse." She sat on the edge of the poster bed.

"Male or female?" He kicked his shoes off, and with a backward motion, kicked the door close.

She frowned as he stepped between her legs. "No male gets to see this. It's branded with a P, for Pendleton eyes only." The smoldering look that entered his eyes was searing her skin. She pulled his shirt from his pants, then ripped it apart, sending buttons all over the room. Her lips touched his skin right below the rib cage. The heat radiating from him could have melted the snowcaps in Alaska.

Where to start, was his dilemma. Those full kissable lips, the tempting big round chocolate nipples or the P that was neatly shaved in her pubic hair.

"Your mouth is watering," she smirked while she pushed his pants and boxers to the floor.

"My mouth is trying to decide which part of your beautiful body it wants to salute first. Your lips that I know taste like a fine wine, your nipples that roll so sweetly between my lips, or your v-jay that releases the juice that flows with love." He ran his hand through her hair to cup the back of her neck. Looking into her eyes, he asked, "Where shall I start Kendra to show you how deep my love for you flows?"

"Damn," she moaned staring up at him. She fell back on the bed, spreading her arms wide over her head. "You can start wherever you like."

The sight of her spread eagle made him hard as steel. His member jumped with anticipation. His instinct was to reach into his nightstand, but he wasn't home. The hesitation must have shown on his face. "I don't care," she whispered. "I want you inside of me now Pendleton."

He wrapped his bandaged hand around her waist, bringing her flush to the end of the bed and plunged into her. The sensation made his knees go weak. This, he thought, was heaven. They had made love before, but there was something different happening here. This was a branding of two souls. He pulled out, then surged back in, reeling at the warmth that surrounded him. Nothing existed, with her legs now wrapped around him, pulling him further into her heat. His head was spinning, rising to a place he longed for, a place that only this woman could take him. The faster he pumped into her, the closer he was to heaven. She grabbed his arm, but the pain went unnoticed as she raised her hips, allowing him to go deeper. "Kendra." He pulled her up with one arm and held her in place as he moved in and out, pulling every ounce of love she had to give from her, until he heard her scream. Only then, did he allow his senses to surrender to the myriad of emotions he was experiencing. He fell onto the bed next to her, the pain in his shoulder cried out, but nothing stopped his raging heart beats. He wanted to pull her into his arms, but his shoulder was screaming in pain. "I can't move babe," he said when his racing heart slowed. "I want to kiss you so bad right now."

Kiki could not move. Every vein in her body was singing. Nothing they had done before came close to being that sensational. Her inner lips were pulsing as if he was still inside of her. He said something, but her heart was pumping so fast she couldn't hear clearly.

"Kiki, are you all right? Did I hurt you?"

Hearing the concern in his voice, she shook her head, not realizing he could not see her. When he started to sit up, she placed her hand on his chest to stop him. "Give me a minute," she managed to say, as her heart rate began to slow down. "Oh, it is so on now."

She pulled a pillow from the bed and placed it under his head, then straddled him. "Are you ready for a ride?"

He reached out, cupping her neck and pulled her to his lips. "Be gentle with me." He grinned, then kissed her, fiercely at first, then the mood softened to a long, slow, taking his time to touch every crevice of her mouth assault that left them both breathless.

Slowly she pressed against his chest to sit up. "I promise not to hurt you...too much." She slowly eased down on him, and moaned at the feel of hot steel being engulfed by her pulsating walls. Closing her eyes, she licked her lips, then spread her legs a little wider, going down further on him. His hand gently touched the side of her face. She kissed his fingers, then took one into her mouth and began sucking it in rhythm with the movement of her body. She could feel the fire burning as he began to push up fiercely into her. His hand dropped from her mouth, joined with his other hand to cup the round globes of her behind, squeezing and pushing her over the edge of reality. Their explosion ricocheted, hitting the surface then spreading throughout their bodies.

Her drenched body fell to his chest, she could feel his heart beating. After a moment of neither moving, she began to feel the rumble of his laughter. "Damn, baby, all I asked for was a kiss."

His right hand dropped to the bed as the pain resonated through his body. His left hand continuously rubbed her behind. She joined him laughing, with their bodies still joined together. "You can have a kiss when I can move again."

Minutes ticked away with the two simply holding on to each other, allowing the world and all the craziness to stay outside the door.

"I'm going with you," she said as she began to rub her foot against the calf of his leg. "Whatever you are planning to do, I'm going with you." She felt his body tense when he exhaled.

"You can't go."

Placing her hand on his chest, she propped her chin up to look at him. His eyes looked down to meet hers. "If the last year hasn't proven anything else, it proved we are better together than apart. This person is trying to harm me. I have a constitutional right to participate in his take down."

He loved when she lawyered up on him. Fingering her cottony soft hair, he smiled. "My heart stopped when I saw that man carrying you out in a bag. When the first bullet hit me, my first thought was to throw my body over yours." His fingers stopped moving as he held her gaze. "It would kill me if anything happened to you. Make no mistake, this is going to get ugly. I will not stop until he is dead."

"You can't kill him, and you damn sure can't kill LaToya. She's Sierra's mother."

"The second amendment to the constitution states that I have the right to bear arms and use those arms for self-defense."

"It also states that you cannot inflict cruel and unusual punishment. You leaving me again would constitute cruel and unusual punishment."

He held her eyes as she did not blink or crack a smile. His thumb rubbed her eyebrow. "I'm not leaving you, Kendra, ever."

Her body contracted around him at his words. She inhaled ignoring the call of her body to move. "But you are. If you kill this person, you will cease being the damn Tyrone that I love. You will become, a man driven by remorse for taking a human's life. But worse, you will have broken the law. That's something you love even more than me." She grinned. "You know what else?"

"What?"

"You are going to become Billy-Bob's Bitch." They both laughed.

ⓟ

The morning began with Kiki's cell phone buzzing. Reaching for the night stand with one eye closed, a quick peek revealed it was her father calling, again. She hit the ignore button then turned over to the sleeping Ty. A smile formed easily on her face. He was so precious, sleeping soundly on his stomach with his arm across her waist. After placing a gentle kiss on his forehead, she slid cautiously from the bed so she would not wake him. After the evening and night of making love continuously, she knew he was tired and probably still experiencing some pain. He needed to sleep. Walking into the bathroom, she glanced around at its magnitude. She hadn't really paid much attention to her surroundings upon their arrival the day before. The last few days, with Ty in the hospital, the man shooting at them and her argument with her father had all taken a toll on her emotions. Then the quick packing and trip to Virginia, with her staying at the Davies home rather than with her family, had ruffled a few feathers on the home front, but she knew her mother understood. Wayne, however was another matter. He believed he could protect his little sister as well as Ty. However, the last thing she wanted was anyone else in the line of fire. To be honest, she felt safer with Ty, than with anyone else.

Thinking of him filled her with an indescribable feeling of completeness. They had weathered the storm and were now on their way to happy ever after, if they could shake the damn assassin. Her cell phone buzzed again. Maxine was calling. She ignored that call as well. Placing her phone on the vanity, she walked around the corner, peeking into the shower stall that was large enough for five people. There were multiple shower-heads with pressure adjustments on each. "Man, I could live in here." She smiled. Setting the adjustments, she ran into the room, grabbed her shampoo and conditioner. As she came back into the bathroom, the phone buzzed again. "What?" she answered in a tone letting the caller know she was not happy with the interruption.

"You are a selfish bitch to ignore Daddy's calls," Laura said.

"Why do you care? You have what you want...Daddy all to yourself."

"Hell, I'm ecstatic. You stepped into my turf when you came to New York."

"Then we have nothing more to say to each other."

"Wrong, you have unfinished business with Crimson Publishing."

"Oh, so he put you up to call me."

"No, Crimson is a part of my birthright. I have a vested interest in it's future. You have several projects in the works. What's your intentions?"

"To send you straight to hell without passing go."

"From the look of things you'll be going first."

Kiki hung up the call. One day she is going to stop caring one way or another about her little sister. The phone buzzed again. Looking down at the number, she pushed the ignore button as she should have done in the first place, then walked into the shower. After the shower, she twisted her hair, dressed, then went in search of the kitchen.

Walking out of the double doors into the hallway, she did not see the stairs, but she did remember the direction from which they'd walked the day before. So following her instincts, she walked down the hallway until she came to a circular hallway, with a white banister with wood grain trim leading in two directions. Looking over, she could see the downstairs foyer, a portion of the living room and family room where they'd sat yesterday, but she did not see the kitchen. Turing left, she figured the banister would eventually lead to steps descending to the lower level. Five minutes later, she still had not found the stairway, but she did hear laughter. Following the sound she came to what must be Sierra's playroom, for the little girl was crawling through a tent like object chasing a robotic puppy that was yapping and wagging his tail. The giggle of the little girl were infectious. Kiki leaned against the door and marveled at the sight and sound of a carefree happy child. Whatever Jason and TeKaya were doing, it was right, for the child was enjoying her life. Only a child surrounded by love could be this happy. Sierra emerged from the tent dressed in pj's with feet, her hair was a mess and it was clear she had crawled out of bed and come to play.

"Morning." The child stood, grabbing her play dog, ran over and smiled up at her. "Mommy said you my new auntie." She wrapped her small hand around Kiki's finger. "Want some cereal? I have to have good trition in the morning." She continued talking as she pulled Kiki along.

"Nutrition?" Kiki looked down at the child.

The big bright questioning eyes looked up at Kiki. "I'm only five. I can't say big words yet."

"Oh," Kiki smiled. "Then yes," she nodded, "you should have some trition in the morning."

"Kay." The child pulled on. "Do you have a little girl?"

"No."

"Tell Uncle Ty to give you one like Uncle Eric did for Aunt Siri."

Kiki laughed, "We'll see."

"Kay," the child replied as she easily found her way to the staircase leading to the kitchen, pulling the dog behind her.

Reaching the kitchen they found Gabby already busy with breakfast.

"Morning Ms. Gabby. Auntie Kiki is going to have trition too," the little girl explained as she climbed onto a stool at the breakfast bar after placing the dog on the surface.

"Good morning pumpkin." She kissed the child's cheek. "Where does Sparkie go?"

"Oh." Sierra took the dog off the island and placed him in the seat next to her.

"Good morning Ms. Gabby."

"Good morning Ms. Simmons. How are you this morning?"

"Kiki, please. I'm fine. I wanted to fix Ty some breakfast. Do you mind?"

"I'll be happy to prepare something. What would you like?"

"I'd kind of like to fix it for him. I'll be happy to fix you something also."

Gabby grinned. The status of the household was probably a little intimidating to someone other than family. "I don't mind at all. However, I will not tolerate anyone coming in to take over my job as the cook for this family." She walked around the island and took a seat next to Sparkie. "So we'll test what you have to offer. If it tastes better than my cooking, you have to go."

For a minute Kiki frowned, then she saw the sparkle of laughter in the woman's eyes. She smiled. "Well, I'm not one to brag, but you might be in a little trouble."

"That good are we?" Gabby teased. "In that case, grab me that cup of coffee over there and let me watch you work."

Twenty minutes later, Kiki and Gabby were talking as if they had known each other for years. On the island was a platter of bacon, sausage and hash brown potatoes, another platter with sliced melon, strawberries, and kiwi fruit, and Kiki was pilling yet another platter with homemade waffles.

Siri walked down the stairs with Heaven in her arms. "Good morning. It sure smells good in here."

"Good morning Siri." Gabby reached out for the baby.

"Morning Aunt Siri. Aunt Kiki is fixin breakfast."

Siri kissed Sierra's cheek. "Aunt Kiki is?" She smirked in Kiki's direction. "It smells good Aunt Kiki." She grinned as she pulled down a cup, filled it with water and placed it in the microwave. Opening a box on the countertop, she pulled out a tea bag as she looked at her friend. "How are you this morning, Aunt Kiki?"

Kiki placed the last waffle onto the platter then turned to Siri. "I'm fine and no waffles for you for teasing early in the morning."

Acting hurt, Siri replied, "Me, I didn't do anything Aunt Kiki." She laughed. "I bet Ty is tired from the long nap."

"Is that what they call it these days?" Gabby snickered as she played with the baby.

"Aunt Kiki is going ask Uncle Ty for a little girl," Sierra innocently added.

Gabby and Siri looked up with wide eyes at Kiki.

After closing her mouth from being shocked by the statement, Kiki looked at the two women staring at her. "That's a little girl talking," she sputtered out. Siri started to say something else, but Kiki held up her finger. "Not one word."

"What?" Siri laughed as she pulled the hot cup of tea from the microwave. "All I was going to say was I finished the manuscript."

Kiki looked at her with suspicious eyes. "Okay.....I'll take that but no more talk about babies."

"Who's talking about babies?" Miriam asked as she walked down the stairs, smiling. She looked at Siri. "Are we having another baby?"

"Not me," Siri peeked over her teacup at Kiki."

"Kendra?" Miriam eagerly smiled.

Gabby burst into laugher. "Out of the mouths of babes."

"No, Ms. Davies. Sierra started this ridiculous conversation about babies."

"I remember the statement from yesterday. However, in her defense, kissing does lead to babies Kendra."

"All day naps do too," Siri added.

Kiki picked up the tray she had prepared for Ty. "I'll be sure to let Tyrone know that."

Jake walked into the room. "Good morning Rocket. Your mother is at the gate. She wants to see you."

Kiki walked back down the one step she had taken to leave the room and the uncomfortable conversation. "Okay," she placed the platter on the island. "Is it okay to have a visitor?" She asked Mrs. Davies.

"This is your home, you don't have to ask for permission to do anything. Including making babies." Miriam turned. "I'll let your mother in."

Siri and Gabby laughed at the look on Kiki's face.

"Okay, you two," Kiki warned.

"Good morning everyone." Issy spoke, "Jake." She smiled as a look passed between them."

Kiki looked from one to the other. "Good morning Mother." She kissed her mother's cheek. "Why are you out so early?"

"To see you darling." She began taking off her coat.

Jake walked over to assist. "I'll take that for you." He smiled as she glanced back at him.

Siri and Gabby shared a knowing look, then turned back to Kiki. "You have a sitting room in your suite if you and your mother would like some privacy," Siri stated.

"I do?"

"Yes." Gabby gave the baby to Miriam. "I'll show you." Gabby picked up the tray and led the women out of the room.

Jake watched as the women walked up the stairs. He turned to find Miriam and Siri staring at him. "So that's Isadore Simmons. Interesting lady."

"Yes, she is," Jake replied then walked out of the room.

"Well." Miriam smiled. "I'm not mad at her."

Upstairs, Kiki and Issy entered the suite behind Gabby. "I'm happy you know your way around. Sierra had to show me how to get to the kitchen this morning."

"It is a big house, however, as you can see, the family stays together when needed. In Atlanta it was Eric's house. Here it's Jason's. Each family has a wing of the house. This is Mr. Pendleton's suite, which now makes it your suite." She placed the tray on the table in the hallway, then pointed to several doors, "This is your sitting room, that's your office, exercise room, second bedroom and that's the theater room over there. You know you also have a mini kitchen that is stocked with just about anything that you need. Enjoy your visit." Gabby walked off.

Issy stood there circling around, looking at the magnificence of the area. "This is your area of the house?

So this is how the other half lives." She turned to Kiki who, from the expression on her face was a little stunned. "Well," Kiki hesitated, "which door did she say was the kitchen?"

Issy looked around, then pointed. "That one I think."

Kiki picked up the tray. "Okay, let's put this in the oven to keep it warm." They opened the door and froze.

"This is a mini kitchen?" Issy asked.

Kiki walked into the kitchen, placed the tray on the breakfast bar, put her hands on her hips and just looked around. "Well, it's smaller than the one downstairs. So I guess that makes it a mini." She walked over to what she thought was the cabinet and pulled the handle. It was the refrigerator. "Would you like something cold to drink? We have, juice, soda, beer and wine."

Issy smiled and sat at the island. "Juice will be fine."

"Juice it is."

Kiki stood back and looked at the cabinets. Taking a guess, she opened another, wrong. That was plates. Pulling the next she found the glasses. Her mother began laughing.

"This is going to be your life once you marry Tyrone." Issy smiled at her daughter. "Are you ready for this?"

"I'm ready for whatever Ty is offering Mom." She sat next to Issy. "I don't care if it's not marriage. I just want to be with him."

"Sometimes love is sacrificing a part of yourself to be a part of someone else's life. Where some of us make a mistake is when we sacrifice all, like what I did with your father."

"Yeah, well, you've gotten past him."

"Not until recently." She sipped her juice. "He's been calling asking me to talk to you."

"He doesn't want to talk to me Mother. He just wants reassurances that I will not take Siri's and other authors' business with me."

"You can't be sure of that Kendra."

"Yes, Mother I can. His daughter called this morning about the same thing." She drank her juice. "So, what's going on with you and Jake?"

The pain was dull, but still there as Ty turned over in the bed. Reaching out, he found Kiki was not there. Opening his eyes, he looked around the room, still no sight of her. Sitting up, he threw his long legs over the side of the bed, looked around and smiled. All of his clothes were off the floor. His pants were folded on the chair along with his shirt, socks, and suit jacket hanging on the back of the chair. He was beginning to rub off on her. He liked that. Checking his phone, he noticed quite a few calls were missed. He called Wendy.

"Anything that needs my attention?"

"Everything is under control. When will you return?"

"I'll see you in the morning."

He disconnected the call then dialed Jason. "The office in about an hour." Afterwards, he showered, dressed and went in search of Kiki. Stepping outside the bedroom door, he began walking down the hallway when he heard voices coming from the kitchen. Turning, he walked in to find Kiki visiting with her mother. "Good morning." He kissed Issy's cheek, then kissed Kiki as if they were the only people in the room. "Morning beautiful."

She adjusted his tie. "Do you ever dress down?"

196

He unbuttoned his suit jacket. "How's that?"

"One day I'm going to get you into a pair of jeans. If nothing else, it would impress Jason Whitfield."

Ty looked as if he had just been insulted. "Jeans."

Issy laughed.

"Yes, jeans," Kiki laughed as she stood. "I have your breakfast."

"Thank you." He took a seat on the stool next to Issy. "Did I hear you guys mention Jake?"

Kiki glanced at her mother. The quick look indicated silence. "My mother mentioned my father was trying to reach me." She placed the plate in front of him after heating the food. "I have nothing to say to him."

"Never close the door on your parents. They may not always know how to show it or say it, but they are the people in the world that love you the most, with the exception of me." He said a prayer, then started eating his breakfast.

Issy smiled at her daughter who appeared to be speechless, even a bit bashful. "Now that's new."

"What?" Kiki glanced at her.

"You're blushing." Issy laughed. "You, Tyrone Pendleton, are good for my daughter." She stood. "Love her and keep her safe. Kendra, your father can be an ass, but he is still your father. Call him."

"Don't leave." Ty wiped his mouth with his napkin. "I have a meeting downstairs. Stay and visit for a while." He stood, kissed Kiki, then looked at Issy. "Jake huh? I wonder what Kenny will have to say about that." He walked out of the room smiling.

Downstairs, Jason and Eric were waiting for him in the office. The office was located in the basement of the house, next to the recording studio. The area was sound proofed, which was the reason Ty requested the meeting there. Sofas lined the walls, which were covered with platinum and gold albums, various awards, and pictures of different stars in the music industry. A large picture window looking into the studio itself, made up the north wall, a desk with a computer and various cd's on top, and Jason leaning back in a chair behind it, with his legs crossed at the ankles. "I would ask what took you so long, but I already know the answer to that."

"We both do." Eric grinned from his position on the sofa near the door, listening to music from the computer.

"Kiki's mother came by for a visit," Ty explained as he closed the door and walked over to the sofa in front of the desk.

"Hey, is something going on with her and Jake?" Jason asked.

"Not my business," Ty replied.

"If her mother is any indication," Eric sat up, "Kiki is going to be a looker as she grows older."

"You haven't met her father." Ty smirked.

"Don't like him?" Jason asked.

"No."

Jason and Eric waited for more. When none came they both laughed. "Straight to the point as always," Jason laughed.

Ty grinned then sat forward. "I need your help."

A look passed between Jason and Eric. This was new to them. It was always, always them asking Ty for help. Eric closed the computer, then sat on the edge of Jason's desk. Jason took his legs off the desk, pulled his chair up closer and they both stared at Ty.

"You have it," Eric stated.

"What's your plan?" Jason asked.

Ty stood, walked over to the window and stared into the studio. "I need you to look out for Kiki while I handle this situation."

"Without question," Jason replied.

"Are you going to Atlanta?"

"Yes." He turned to them, placed his hands in his pockets and exhaled. "I have to end this, one way or another."

"Ty, don't let your temper get the best of you," Eric cautioned.

Ty and Jason both looked at Eric not believing the statement came from him. "This from the man who wanted me to kill Roy for taking pictures of Siri."

"Hell yeah," Eric replied. "I'm still not sure he should be alive."

Jason laughed, then turned back to Ty. "You do what you have to protect Kiki. However, don't allow this person to take you from her life. You understand where I'm coming from?"

"I don't do anything half way."

The tension in the room changed. "Ty, I know how you're feeling right now," Jason started.

"No man, you don't. No one shot at TK, or Siri. This man attempted to take her. When that didn't work he tried to shoot her. No one touches what is mine and lives."

From her condo in Atlanta, Naverone sat on her chaise lounge chair, staring out of the picture window. The scene was relaxing, but she was anything but calm. As much as she hated to do it, Naverone did not see where she had a choice. Ty needed help, the kind of help that may venture on the other side of the law. Dialing the number she only used in an emergency, she wondered if Genesis was serious about extracting the information from the Wright woman. As much as she hated, torture, it may be what was needed. After this call, she would talk to Genesis.

"Are you stateside?" She asked as the telephone was answered.

"How the hell are you? I'm good, thanks for asking."

Naverone had to smile. There was no one like her friend from Quantico. "You're alive, that's all I need to know."

"What's up?" the voice on the other end of the line asked.

"I have a problem."

"Consider it fixed."

Chapter Twelve

*S*aturday was one of the most relaxing day Ty had ever had. After spending time with the family, he and Kiki retired to their suite. In his office he sat at the desk working on contracts he'd received from Wendy, while Kiki sat on the sofa with her feet up reading a manuscript. Every so often he would hear her grunt, or sigh, then laugh out loud. This last time got the best of him.

"What are you working on?"

She glanced up. "Siri's manuscript," she replied then returned to her reading, smiling as she did.

He stood, taking off his suit jacket. After placing it neatly on the back of his chair he rolled up the sleeves of his shirt, and loosened his tie. Lifting her feet with the bunny slippers TeKaya lent her, he sat and placed them across his lap.

"Listen to this," Kiki began to read.

"The only sound in the room was the roar of the fireplace with the crackling of wood burning. Neither spoke as the tension continued to build. He walked over to her. She could feel the heat rise. Was it the fire or his consuming presence that caused the temperature to rise? She didn't know. Which ever, a dribble of moisture began to form between her breasts. He removed the blanket she was wrapped in, gathered her feet between his hands and began to rub them. Yes her toes were cold, but every other part of her body was beginning to sweat from his touch. His next action caused her body to explode. He placed her big toe into his mouth and blew hot sensuous air. She may have been naive, but she knew an orgasm when she felt one."

Kiki looked up at Ty. "She has this wonderful way of writing love scenes that borders on erotic, yet she keeps them simple and sensuously funny."

"Really." Ty grinned as he removed her slippers, took her big toe into his mouth and blew on it. But he didn't stop there, he closed his lips around it, then kissed it with a pop.

Kiki's body began to yearn as she held his gaze. "Un huh." She slowly smiled at him, lowered her eyes and continued to read.

"His hands began to travel up her jean clad legs, massaging every inch of her calf along the way. The storm may have been settling on the outside, but inside her it was raging. The only light in the room was the glow from the fire that seemed to create a halo around his body. Was he as hot as he appeared to be, she wondered? Curiosity won out as she reached out to caress his cheek. The heat from the touch caused her to jerk her hand away. He caught it, brought it back to his lips, and kissed her palm. He then took each finger into his mouth, surrounding each with its warmth. All the while his eyes burned into hers.

Mesmerized, she never flinched or protested as he unbuttoned, unzipped and began to remove her wet jeans. In fact she lifted her behind to assist."

Kiki raised her hips as Ty pulled the leggings down her thighs and threw them across the room. She turned the page as his hands squeezed her behind. He stopped, waiting for her to continue. She did.

"His hands were large, his fingers long and his touch, magical. She tried to pull her fingers from his mouth, he gripped them tighter, sucking as if they were his life line to her. His hands touched the flat of her belly. The sensation sent a jolt through her body. The feeling of butterflies fluttered within. The moisture that began between her breasts now moved downward between her thighs. Why didn't she wear her sexy panties? The thought ran through her mind. Was he going to remove them too she wondered? Would he smother the flames that were now burning within? His hands moved over the white cotton material, cupping the area that was begging to be touched. He lingered, gently squeezing then releasing, then squeezing again, causing the juice to begin flowing. The motion with his lips stopped the moment his fingers touched the moisture between her thighs. His eyes caught hers. the intensity so strong her breath hitched. A finger moved the material aside then gingerly touched her. Her body jerked up as if it was a magnet to metal. His finger slid within her moisture."

Kiki squirmed as Ty's finger slid in. She closed her eyes and moaned.

"Keep reading," Ty's strained voice whispered, as his fingers moved in and out of her.

Licking her lips, she opened her eyes, while moving her body to the motion of his fingers.

"One rip with his other hand, pulled the cotton material apart. That too was thrown to the side. His eyes widened in surprise at the curly mass of hair above his fingers. He licked his lips, bent his head and replaced his fingers with his....."

The papers fell to the floor as Ty placed her legs over his shoulders then dove in head first. "Oh my," she murmured. The deeper he went, the more she cried out. "My, my, my. Oh my." She sank deeper into the sofa as he continued to royally ravish her with his tongue. "Tyrone," she moaned out. "Don't stop, don't...don't. Tyrone," she screamed out as she exploded, but he didn't stop. He pushed her top up, then ran a trail of kisses from her navel and settled between her breasts.

"I love your bed time story."

She breathlessly laughed as she pulled his shirt from his pants. "Does your shoulder hurt?"

He stopped and frowned up at her. He wiped his face with his hand. "I'm making some monster moves here and you're asking about my shoulder."

She grinned up at him. "Yeah, I wanted to know before I throw your ass on the floor and take what you are teasing me with."

"The hell with the shoulder." He rolled over, carrying her with him to the floor. Held his hands above his head and grinned. "Take me baby."

Sunday morning Ty entered his office in Atlanta for a meeting that Naverone insisted they have. He was surprised to see his office was at full staff. There was usually a skeleton staff on the weekends, unless there was an event planned, which wasn't the case.

"Hey Boss," Wendy spoke as she looked up at Ty, then kissed his cheek. "It's good to have you back in the office. Your nine o'clock, and some are waiting in your office.

"Thank you, Wendy."

"Oh, before you go in, Nicholas Brooks asked if you would call him when you have a few minutes."

Give me about thirty minutes, then get him on the line for me," Ty replied then opened the door to his office.

They were met with yet another surprise. Two women standing at the door became alert the moment Ty and the Towers entered the room. Naverone was there with three other women. The weapon holstered at her side looked out of place on the woman who was dressed in a form fitting tunic dress. Genesis stood next to the sofa with her hands folded across her chest.

"Good morning Ty," Naverone spoke from her seat on the sofa. "Peace, Jake."

"Damn," was the appreciative response that came from Peace.

"Amen to that," Jake replied.

Ty ignored the comments as he approached the women.

"You care to tell me what this is about," he said to Naverone. The innocent, wide eyed look on the woman who was sitting in the chair in front of his desk was enticing to say the least. However, none of them fooled him. The women were dangerous. Jake and Peace stood behind Ty

"If you are insisting on confronting this man, you need to be protected."

He looked around the room. "And, these women are supposed to be my protection?" He raised an eyebrow.

"Most men make their mistake by underestimating the power of a woman."

"True dat," one of the women replied sitting on the windowsill looking out at the backdrop of downtown Atlanta.

Peace chuckled. Genesis, pulled an object from her belt, clicked a button and a whip snapped at his foot.

Not many things surprised Ty. The whip shocked the hell out of him. If it weren't for the fact that he was a master at concealing his thoughts, he would have jumped out of the way of the whip.

"I would have stung you, but I think you would have liked it too much," Genesis, retracted the whip and placed the device back on her belt.

"Damn," Jake laughed as he watched the blood drain from Peace's face.

"So you are the Towers," one of the other women huffed. "Thought you would be bigger," Karess Parker, a red-bone with her hair slicked back into a ponytail, wearing an off the shoulder long sleeve top that proudly displayed her voluptuous breasts, a black mini-skirt and spiked boots that traveled up her solid thick thighs, stated then went back to reading from her reader.

The Towers glanced at each other as if they were offended.

"My partners," Naverone announced. "You've met Genesis," she nodded towards the woman. "She has a mean whip," she smirked. Pointing she stated, "Karess Parker," who was sitting in the corner looking out the window, waved without turning around. "Raven Junee," a petite woman, with her hair also in a ponytail, sat in the seat in front of Ty, looking as innocent as a child, in a dress that showed her muscular thighs, which he was sure could be lethal. Looking at them you could have easily mistaken them for the eighties girl group En Vogue. Each was as beautiful as they were dangerous.

"Allow me to share their credentials. Raven Junee, an abused child who took her father's life at the age of fourteen, juvenile detention until eighteen, at which time she joined the Marine Corps, from there, Special Services. Her specialty, martial arts. She can kill with her bare hands, or her thighs, your choice. Genesis Morgan, attended Howard University and received a Master's in Business Management. Joined the Army, excelled in weaponry. Weapon of choice, the whip. Has been known to disarm a man from fifty feet away, Her specialty, however, is extracting information from those unwilling to share. Karess Parker, a member of the Cherokee tribe, joined the Army after high school. Received the Purple Heart for single handedly rescuing a troop of six from enemy hands while serving in Afghanistan. Specialty, precision with a knife, spear, bow and arrow or any sharp item. And, you know me. Secret Service Agent. Assigned to the First Family after graduating from MIT, recruited by the FBI. Trained at Quantico. One of the best sharp shooters in the world.

Ty nodded towards Jake, "Tower One" then he nodded towards Peace, "Tower Two." He inhaled then sighed. "The earlier demonstration was cute," he said to Genesis. "Make no mistake, with a nod of my head, either of the Towers could have disarmed you." Ty looked at each as he spoke. "If you think you and your partners can handle this job The Pendleton Agency would like to hire you. Each of you will receive fifty thousand dollars for your services. A hundred thousand to get you started. The balance will be paid once this is over."

"What exactly is this and what makes you think our services are available?" Raven asked with an arched eyebrow and arms folded across her breasts."

"We don't charge friends," Naverone stated.

Genesis quickly walked up beside her. "Um my sister, don't turn down the funds," she whispered then sat back down.

"This is business," Ty stated. "I want and expect results."

"We'll take the job," Naverone replied. "With a provision."

"What's the provision?"

Naverone looked back at Ty. "If you are satisfied with our services, we have a proposition for a business venture we would like you to consider."

Ty, nodded to Naverone. He had an idea of what the venture was about. "Welcome to the Pendleton Agency."

"What exactly are we protecting you from?" Karess asked from her seat, never raising her head from the reader.

"Man's nemesis from the beginning of time--a woman." Ty replied. "Naverone will brief you on your assignment. Failure is not an acceptable result. If you will excuse me, I have a conference call coming through."

Jake looked straight ahead as he watched the women walk out. He then looked at Ty. "You know we could not have disarmed Naverone."

"I damn sure was not going to grab that whip," Peace laughed.

Ty turned to look up at them. "They don't know that."

"He just left? Without me?"

"Yes," Jason said for the third time. "Kiki, he has to handle this without worrying if you are safe."

The look of disbelief was very evident on her face. "He promised he wouldn't leave me." Tears began to form in her eyes.

"He didn't leave you sweetie." Siri rubbed Kiki's shoulder.

"No," TeKaya added in. "You are with us. Where you are safe. If anything were to happen to you, I'm afraid Tyrone will never open his heart again." She took Kiki's hand in hers and bent down. "Sweetie, he loves you so much, he was afraid he could not say no to you if you asked to go with him."

Jason walked over and grabbed his wife under her arms. "Baby, please don't do this again. You can barely put your shoes on. Bending down is not something you should be doing."

Eric walked over and took the area in front of Kiki that TeKaya had vacated. "Kiki," he sighed. "I know better than anyone in this room how you are feeling. When Siri left me, I thought my world had ended. Then when I got her back, the mess with LaToya happened. You were there for me. Please allow me to be here for you now." He pushed his locks back over his shoulder. "Ty would have taken you, if he was certain there was no danger. He's not and until he finds this man, he can't be with you the way he desperately wants to be. Please let him handle this so the two of you can finally be together. I promise once all of this is over, I'll write the song you will dance to at your wedding."

"Ha," she cried out as she wiped a tear from her cheek and stood. "I'm going back upstairs."

"I'll go with you," Siri offered.

"No," she said. "I need to be alone for a little while."

"Okay," Siri replied. "Will you come down and have Sunday dinner with us?"

"Sure," Kiki turned and walked out of the room. As she entered the suite, her cell phone was on the nightstand near the bed where she'd left it. She couldn't shake the felling that something was going to happen now that she and Ty were separated. They needed to stay together. She fell face down across the bed. The cell buzzed and vibrated against the stand again. Reaching over she grabbed the phone, rolled over and just held it over her heart. "Put on your big girl panties," she said to herself. "He's going to be safe," she sighed.

Looking at her phone, she noticed there were a number of messages, three from Ty explaining why he was not taking her calls. It was the third one that made her smile. It had silly balloons, roses and a happy face and said, "I promise to suck every toe on your body when I come home."

She exhaled, then looked at the other messages. All from her father. The last one indicated he was in Richmond for the day and wanted to talk. He specifically asked that she come alone, stating he did not want Ty or anyone to interfere in their conversation.

"Hmm." She remembered Ty indicated she should open the door of communication with her father. "I'll give it a try." She looked at her watch. She'd discuss the idea of meeting him at dinner.

"No," Jason exclaimed.

"Absolutely not," Eric added.

"Well, why not?" Miriam asked. "She could take one of the security guys with her."

"No," Jason said again.

"Absolutely not," Eric echoed again. "You are not leaving these grounds under any circumstances."

"Honey," Siri spoke as she fed Heaven. "Kiki promised to take me shopping for some natural hair products."

"Yeah," TeKaya chimed in, "And she promised to take me to the store with the fancy boots."

Jason and Eric stared at their wives. "You don't use natural hair products," Eric stated.

"And you can't wear boots right now," Jason frowned.

"None of that matters," Miriam replied. "The girls just want to go shopping. There is safety in numbers."

Jason shook his head, as Eric sat back and sighed. Neither wanted to say no to their wife.

"Ladies." Kiki smiled, "Thank you, but none of those things are true."

TeKaya sighed, "You know you ruined a perfectly good lie there."

Siri and Miriam laughed. "Well, you know we have your back."

Kiki smiled, "Thank you all for trying. Jason and Eric, I'm sorry I put you in this position." She pushed her chair back, "Would you excuse me, please?"

"Of course," Miriam replied.

Siri said, once Kiki left the room, "I don't understand why she can't go see her father. Would you stop me from going to see my mother? No, you wouldn't."

"I think it was kind of you to ask," Miriam stated as she turned to her sons. "Jason." She folded her hands under her chin and just stared at her oldest son.

"Mother, if anything happens, Ty is going to kill me."

"Us," Eric added.

"What would Ty do if he was here?"

"Take her himself," Jason replied.

"Then one of you must take her," Miriam replied.

Jason dropped his napkin on the table and slid his chair back.

TeKaya stood and kissed her husband. "I'll keep your food warm for you."

"Thank you babe," he said then left the room.

"Thank you for this Jason," Kiki said as they pulled through the gate. "I really could have met my father alone. I am capable of taking care of myself."

"I know you are and so does Ty." Jason turned from the driveway. "However, things are a little different right now. I think you know that." Jason looked at the profile of the woman that had finally knocked Ty to his knees. She was a natural beauty. "He loves you, you know."

The car lit up with the smile she gave him. "I know now."

"So, where are we meeting your father?"

Before she could answer, the car swung towards the curb. "Whoa." The motion of the car pushed her into the car door. "You okay over there?" When he did not reply, she grabbed his arm. His head fell back against the seat. "Jason," she yelled as something stung her neck. Then there was blackness.

Siri walked into the nursery and placed Heaven in her crib. Before reaching over to turn on the light, she noticed a weird light outside on the road. At first she thought it was nothing, but when it did not continue down the road, she walked across the hall. "Eric."

"Yeah babe."

"Look at this." She pointed to the window in the baby's room. He reached to turn the light on and she stopped him. "No, don't turn that on. Look out the window."

Seeing the concern on her face, he walked over to the window and looked out. "What is it?"

"I don't know, but it's not supposed to be there."

He pulled his cell from his pocket, then called security.

They stood in the window and watched as one of the security men drove out the gate and stopped where the light was on the road. Watching in the darkness, they couldn't see much from the window. When Eric's cell phone chimed, he dropped his head. Then he noticed the security team in motion and knew something wasn't right. "Stay here with Heaven." He ran from the room.

He ran out the door, but was stopped before he could get out of the gate. "Mr. Davies, I need you back inside the house."

"Get the hell out of my way."

"Mr. Davies, please sir. Back inside the house."

"Eric?" TeKaya called from the door in a questioning voice.

"TK." He turned to her more composed. "Let's go back into the house."

"What's going on Eric?" Concern was etched in her voice. "Where's Jason?"

Eric looked over her shoulder to see Miriam and Siri. "Where are the children?"

"Gabby has them in the play room," Siri replied.

"Eric?" Miriam held her son's eyes.

"I'll find out. Please, everybody stay in the house." He closed the door, then ran back to the gate. Sirens could be heard in the background. One of the security men followed him. As he got closer to the scene, Jason's car came into view. "Jason." He ran full speed to towards the car.

"He's alive Mr. Davies," another man said as he saw the frantic look on Eric's face.

"What happened? Was it an accident?"

"No." The man held up what appeared to be a dot inside a plastic bag. "Someone shot him with this."

"What in the hell is that?"

"A tranquilizer dot."

Confusion was on every person's face, until fear gripped Eric. He ran to the passenger side of the SUV. "Where's Kiki?"

Chapter Thirteen

*J*ake disconnected the call then motioned for Peace to follow. He ran into the office where Ty sat behind his desk.

Ty looked up to see Jake and Peace as his cell phone buzzed. His heart dropped the moment he saw the call was from Eric. He stood and began walking towards the door. "What happened?"

"She's gone Ty."

He froze. "What do you mean she's gone?"

The lethal sound of his voice prompted Peace into action. He pulled out his cell. "Trent, emergency flight to Virginia."

Jake held the door open as Ty ran through.

Hearing the commotion, Wendy pushed the button to open the private elevator. As the men ran out she could see the fear in Ty's eyes. She glanced up at Jake. There was no reassurance there.

(P)

Two hours later Tyrone walked through the doors of his family's home. Eric braced himself for the onslaught he knew was coming. Miriam stood next to her son ready to keep the two from throwing blows as she had done so many times before. They were both surprised.

He kissed his mother on the cheek. "Jason is going to be fine. The tranquilizer used was a mild one called Benzoniazepine. It will wear off soon. He'll have a headache, nothing more. He turned to Eric as they walked towards the family room. "Tell me what you know."

"Kiki asked to meet with her father."

"In New York?" Ty asked as he took a seat on the sofa.

"No, here." Eric sat in the chair across from him near the fireplace.

"Where?"

"I don't know. She told Jason."

"Jake contact Issy. Peace call Naverone, have her to get Kenneth Simmons' phone records."

"She said it was a text message," Miriam added as she took a seat next to Ty.

Ty glanced at Peace. "I'm on it Boss."

"Who spotted the car?"

"Siri did when she was putting Heaven to bed."

"Where is she?"

"Upstairs, why?"

"I need to ask her some questions."

"She didn't see anything," Eric replied.

"You don't know what she saw," Ty snapped back. He took a second to calm his nerves. "Any little thing can be a lead in a situation of this nature. Would you ask Siri to come down?" Eric hesitated. "Please," Ty insisted.

Eric stared at his brother. "Do not interrogate my wife."

"I'll treat her as gently as you protected Kiki." He held his brother's glare.

Eric softened. He had failed Ty and he knew it. "I'll get her."

Miriam waited until Eric was out of the room. She took Ty's hand. He pulled away, stood, then walked over to the fireplace. "I don't want to be consoled Mother."

"What you want and need are two different things." She walked over to him. "Your brothers did as you asked. Jason is in the hospital because of your request."

"At least we know where he is. Can we say the same for Kiki?"

"That's not fair Tyrone. Your brothers did all they could to protect her."

"Did they Mother? Here's what I know. Siri and TeKaya have not been past that gate since this ordeal began. Why was Kendra?" He sighed. "I don't blame them Mother. I was the one that brought her here. It was me that left her here. Your concern is unfounded. I blame myself, not your sons."

Miriam's jaw tightened. "You are my son as well, Tyrone. I know you are upset as you should be."

"Mother, upset does not begin to describe what I'm feeling at this moment."

"Boss." Jake stepped into the room, "Issy and Rocket's brothers are on their way over. She will contact Kenneth, but she is sure he is in New York and has not been in contact with Rocket."

Ty stood from the fireplace. "Then who sent the text message?" He turned to Peace.

"Naverone is MIA. Genesis is checking the records." Peace walked over to him. "His cell location confirms Ms. Simmons statement. He is in New York. At least his cell phone is."

"It may not have come directly from his phone," Jake stated. "It's possible to make the text or call appear to come from a recognized number, when it doesn't. Hackers do it all the time."

"Track those records Jake. Whoever sent that message orchestrated this string of events." The police walked in the door with one of the security men. "Anything?" Ty asked.

Shaking his head, the officer stated, "Nothing. Not a trace of anything. Not one foot step leading to or away from the vehicle. Her cell phone and identification were found in the passenger seat of the vehicle. Whoever took Ms. Simmons is a pro. They left no trail, no forensic evidence, no fingerprints or DNA that we could find."

Ty closed his eyes. Time was slipping away and he had nothing to lead him to Kendra. "I should not have left her." He dropped his head then walked over to the window. The lights in the wooded area near the scene were bright as if it was daylight. "I want the area searched inch by inch, something has to be there."

"My team couldn't find anything," the officer scratched his head. "I'll leave a team in place to assist the agent. They may have better luck."

"What agent?" Ty turned back to ask.

"I don't know her name, but she's been on sight for about twenty minutes now." The officer looked at the concerned faces around the room. "We'll keep looking until we find her." The officer and security guard walked out the door.

Ty nodded at Peace. "See who's out there."

"I'll check it out, Boss."

"Ty," Siri called from the staircase, where Eric stood behind her. "Any word yet?"

"Nothing." He walked over and kissed her temple. "Can you tell me what you saw?"

"Not much, I'm afraid. Jason and Kiki had not been gone five minutes when I took Heaven upstairs."

"What made you notice the light?"

"We're in the back of the subdivision. The only light we normally see is from the cross street before we turn in. Only cars coming or going from this house would be in that area. When the light did not continue down the road I knew something wasn't right. That's when I called Eric."

"I called security immediately after that," Eric added.

"Whoever it was, knew she would be leaving the house." Ty said more to himself than anyone else.

"Who knew she was here?" Miriam asked. "Did you tell anyone you were bringing her here?"

Ty stared at his mother thinking. They hadn't told anyone where they were going except family. He picked up his coat from the sofa to put it on. "I'm going to check out the scene." He walked out the door, stopped on the front porch and exhaled. No one except family knew where they were. Her father only knew she was in Richmond, he did not know an address. Issy, Jake, Peace, Wendy, Naverone and his family knew. Is it possible family is involved? He walked down the steps toward the gate. The first incident in New York, how did the man get into a secure building? How did he know which condo she lived in? The front desk did not give out that information. Who would have access to that information? The questions continued to plaque him as he walked to the site.

Before he reached the gate, a vehicle pulled through, then stopped near him. Issy stepped out first. "Tyrone, has there been any word?" Her voice trembled as she asked.

Ty hugged her, then grimly smiled, shaking his head. "Nothing yet."

Wayne, who was driving, got out of the vehicle, swung connecting to Ty's jaw, then yelled as he fell to the ground. "You were supposed to protect my sister."

Ty rubbed his jaw, as Peace ran through the gate, then Eric and Jake from the house. "Get off my brother." Eric swung, hitting Wayne in the jaw.

Peace grabbed Eric as Jake stepped to Wayne. "Step the hell off."

"Jake," Issy stepped between him and her son.

He looked down at Issy, then back up to Wayne. "Step off."

Eric extended a hand down to Ty to help him from the ground as officers ran through the gate.

"We got this," Peace stopped them. "Family situation." The officers slowly retreated.

Ty walked over to Wayne. "Is it out of your system? You don't want to kick my ass anymore then I wanted to for allowing this to happen. Get it out of your system now. So I can go find Kendra."

"All the guards, secured facility and your money didn't protect her," Wayne yelled as he pushed Ty in the chest.

"Stop," Ty demanded as he saw Peace move towards them, then he stood up to Wayne "I'm not going to fight you Wayne. You have every right to be pissed."

"I don't need your approval. You with your suits and money strutting around like you own the world." He pushed Ty again in the chest. Ty stepped back. "I tried to tell her you wasn't worth the damn tears she cried for over a year. The same tears I had to endure from my mother over a no good ass man."

"Wayne." Issy stepped forward, but Jake held her back.

"Let them get it out Issy."

"I am not your father." Ty gritted through clenched teeth.

"I'm her family. It was my job to protect her." He yelled, "You're nothing but a worthless piece of crap just like Kenneth."

The blow that connected to Wayne's mouth knocked him to the ground. Ty reached down and pulled him up by his leather jacket lapel. "I am not... your father. What he did to your mother was not your fault. I would never do that to Kendra." He released his jacket, then stood over him. "I love your sister, therefore, I'm not going to kick your ass. If you ever compare me to your father again, I'm going to forget you are family." He turned, walking through the small group of people, through the gate towards the scene.

"I was wondering how long it was going to take you to get here?" Ty looked up to see Naverone walking towards him. "Walk with me." She turned him and walked in a different direction. "This is above my pay grade." She pulled out a plastic bag. "Look over my shoulder." He did as she instructed. "The tree bark to your left has scuff marks on it. The person has been perched in that tree, to keep any evidence from the ground where they know police officers will be looking." She held up the bag. "There are serial numbers on the dot. I'm willing to bet the $100,000 you gave us this is military issued. This is above my pay grade."

"This guy works for the government?" He shook his head. "Why?"

"I have no idea. This is what I know. She's not dead. This person had every opportunity to kill. He wanted her alive. Still, the question is why?"

"Bring him in."

"Who?"

"Roberto Garrison. Find him and bring him to me."

"Ty, this is not the Garrison guy."

"It may not be, but he damn sure knows who has her and why. I'm tired of wondering when the next shoe is going to drop. I want her back. Now."

Naverone watched as he walked away.

"Good afternoon Mr. Pendleton." The woman said as Ty looked up from his computer on his desk. "Nice of you to take the time to see me."

"Boss, I tried to stop her," Jake explained.

"Oh, there is no stopping me when I have my mind set on something." The woman waved Jake off. "Ask my Dad. He's been trying to stop me from doing things all my life."

Ty stared at the scene taking place in front of him. He had no idea who the woman was or what on earth she and Jake were talking about. What he did know was he had to figure out where this professional hit man had taken Kiki and if she is still alive. Angry with the scene, Ty stood. "Excuse me. The drama needs to be outside that door."

"The drama is what's going on in your life." The woman with the black wavy hair, petite, killer body, and beautiful expressive brown eyes declared as she walked towards him. "Man, I have been through some drama, believe me, but this crap you are involved in is madness, just madness."

"Boss, you want me to take her out?"

"CIA trumps security Jake Newman. But you can close the door behind you when you leave."

Ty stared at the woman. "I'll take care of it Jake." He never took his eyes from the woman. "Who are you and what do you think you know about my life?"

"Think, ha, I know more about you than you know about yourself. Allow me to prove it. You are Tyrone Sylvester Pendleton. Born August tenth, you know the year, to Loretta Pendleton and a father you never knew whose name is Sylvester Dawson, adopted by Phillip and Miriam Davies at the age of twelve, when you were abandoned by your mother. Attended Martin Luther King high school graduating with honors, BA from Morehouse College then on to Florida State University where you received a joint degree in Law and Business. Prepared a few creative contracts for some very prominent professional athletes and voila, here you are. A fine brother with a booming business, powerful connections, a family that loves you and people in high places."

"I don't know who you are. So whatever you are selling I'm not in the mood. Now, if you would excuse me I believe you know where the door is."

"And I thought you were the smart one. From what I was told you could recognize bull a mile away. Losing the woman you love to her assassin must be messing with your mind. I would leave you in your misery, but I promised Naverone I would help you out. Besides, the man you are looking for is an enemy of the United States and I have a sworn duty to protect this country against all enemies, foreign or domestic."

The statement stopped Ty in his tracks. "What?"

"You heard me and I don't repeat myself. It appears you have caught the attention of someone who is on our radar. And when I say our, I am referring to the CIA, Central Intelligence Agency. He's an international assassin named Rupid A. Mann, also known as RAM." She pulled a device from her pocket, then showed him a picture. "Look familiar?" The picture took the wind from him. "I thought that would get your attention." She pushed another button. "RAM is a dangerous man. I don't doubt your ability to handle most situations. I've seen you in action. This one is different. You're thinking with your heart and not your head."

"You say that because you know me so well?"

"I know Kiki Simmons is missing and you feel as if you failed her. You may not want to take me seriously, but you have no choice."

Ty sat down in the chair, dejected. "I gave her my word that I would protect her."

"I know." No one said anything for a moment. "You still can. The man that has her is the third most skilled assassin in the world. You are an agent. You do not have the skills to stop him."

"Whoever he is, get him here."

"Just like a man to be a chauvinist. It never occurred to you that the best could be a female."

"It doesn't matter if it's a male or female. If he or she can get Kiki back then that's who I want."

"He is out of the country on Presidential orders. But I can get you the second best."

Quickly standing, he ordered. "Get him here."

"Her, get her here," she gritted through her teeth.

"Her damn it, her," he yelled.

Monique Day smiled. "You're looking at her."

He gave her a doubtful look. "You."

She shook her head. "Why do men find it so hard to accept help from a woman?"

"I don't have trouble working with women. My concern is I don't know you."

"You don't need to know me. What you need to know is that I'm damn good at what I do."

"And that is?"

"I kill people and I'm damn good at it." She leaned across the desk and stared at him. "Can you handle that?"

"Where do we start?"

She smiled. "Atlanta."

Chapter Fourteen

*"I'*m not a part of this, whatever it is Ty. I swear this to you on my life."

"How did you meet him?"

"I'm in jail. How in the hell do you think I met him?"

Monique looked at Ty expecting a reaction or something that would stop her from proceeding with her actions. When she received no response, she grabbed LaToya by her hair and slammed her face into the table. "The time for cuteness has passed. We need answers. Who introduced you to Roberto Garrison, when, where and how? Anything else and I start pulling your hair out strand by strand."

LaToya struggled to escape the woman's hold, but the grip was too tight and there wasn't even room to wiggle. Monique continued to apply pressure until LaToya stopped

226

struggling. She released LaToya, then sat on the table next to her. "Are you ready to answer questions?"

LaToya angrily pulled her hair away from the woman.

"Strand by strand," Monique repeated.

"We met here during a visit."

"Who introduced you?" Ty asked.

"Bertha, Bertha Michaels."

"How does she know him?"

"Cousin."

"On whose side?"

"How in the hell am I supposed to know?" Monique reached out, grabbed a handfull of hair. "I don't know." LaToya jerked away.

Ty glared at her, not sure if he believed her or not. "Do you have a phone number for him?" She nodded. "Call him."

"No," Monique stood. "We can get the number." She now glared at Monique. "I don't trust her. I want her on ice until this is over with." LaToya began to protest. Monique turned from her and looked at Ty. "If we find she is an innocent bystander in all of this, we'll find a way to compensate her. However," she glared back at LaToya, "if I determine she had any part in this. I'm charging her."

"You can't do that. You can't put me in isolation for no reason."

The warden looked at Monique and nodded in agreement. "She's right. There's been no violation. I have no reason to isolate her."

"Put her in there for her own protection."

The look in Ty's eyes frightened her. "What in the hell is going on?" LaToya asked. "I haven't done anything. Why are you doing this Ty?" She was desperate now and would give anything not to be placed in isolation. "What do you want? What are you looking for?" She struggled to pull away from the corrections officer that was pulling her from the room.

Ty put up his hand to stop the officer. "LaToya, how did you know Kiki was in New York?"

"What?" she asked relieved to be out of the officer's grasp.

"How did you know Kiki was in New York?"

She was rubbing her arm where the officer had been pulling her. "Roberto told me she had moved to New York to be near her father."

"Why did he tell you that?"

"I don't know," she replied testily. "He was always telling me things about her."

Ty looked up at the officer and nodded his head. "What things and why was Kiki the topic of conversation?"

LaToya looked around at the faces. All of them were turned, waiting for her next words. They needed something from her. Damn if she knew what, but they needed some information she had. What in the hell had she and Roberto talked about? She was now trying to recall their conversations. "Well, it wasn't all about that Kiki woman. We mostly talked about the situation with Eric."

"Sit down Latoya," Monique said as she pulled a small device from her pocket and placed it on the table.

LaToya hesitated, giving all of them a suspicious eye, then she complied with the request. "Okay."

"Tell us what you talked about," Monique requested.

They all listened as LaToya talked about her conversations with Roberto for about an hour. They stepped out of the room, leaving the corrections officer with LaToya.

The warden asked Ty how did he want to proceed with LaToya. "Do you still want her in isolation?"

"We can't take the chance of her tipping off Roberto or Tina," Monique said to Ty.

"Put her in for her own protection. Make it somewhere nice."

"Nice?" The warden's brow rose.

"Yes," Ty sighed. "If what she said is true, she was a pawn in all of this, not the aggressor." He began walking away with Monique. "What could this Roberto character have against Kiki?"

"Maybe nothing at all. You would be surprised how little it takes to manipulate people into doing what you want."

"Money is a powerful motivator." Ty's cell phone buzzed.

"Give me something."

"How about Roberto Garrison," Naverone smiled.

"You have him?"

"Will in about an hour. I'll call you with the details."

He hung up the cell. "We're going to have an opportunity to ask him in about an hour."

"Let's go," Monique said as her cell buzzed. "What do you have?" Monique listened, "I'll be there in two hours. Have a final destination for me by then." She turned to Ty. "Change of plans. I have a lead I need to follow."

"Where to?"

"You are going to meet with Naverone. Allow them to do their job. Kendra's life could depend on it."

"You think I'll get squeamish?"

"I do."

"Then you have no idea what I'm capable of." He pulled off determined to get what he needed from Roberto by any means necessary.

Roberto Garrison, entered the gates of an estate located in Fulton County. The lavish grounds, with waterfalls, swimming pools and a guest house were only a few indicators that the security on the property was going to be a challenge, but not impenetrable.

As the gate closed, Naverone and her team observed the grounds from the black SUV parked a few yards away from the entrance. "Pull up the schematics on the place," Naverone instructed.

Karess pulled up her computer to obtain the requested information, as Genesis made her assessment. "Eight, nine million dollar estate. We're probably looking at one or two guards, a dog or two, security system and a panic room."

"But we can get in?" Naverone asked.

"Oh yeah," Genesis nodded.

"What's the probability that the man we just saw in the club owns this house?" Raven asked. "Low is my take. So, who is the owner?"

The interior of the SUV was silent as they waited patiently for the answer to their questions. "The Garrison Corporation owns this property, several in New York, New Jersey, California, Texas and The Cayman Islands. The house in question has a security system, codes being sent to your cell. The master bedroom is on the first floor, however, there are two bedrooms located in each wing of

230

the house." Karess looked up. "The best entrance into the house would be by invitation."

"I don't foresee that happening."

"Oh I don't know, Genesis," Karess dialed a number on her cell. "Anything is possible." She held the phone to he ear. "Hello Bobby. It's KK are we still on or what?" She winked at Raven who sat next to her in the back seat. "Is it okay if I bring a friend?"

Roberto Garrison couldn't believe his luck. The shorty with the long legs was on her way with her friend. Doing the old lady wasn't terrible, her prison bound daughter compensated for it on her knees, but he was ready to get his freak on. The two Black beauties from the club was a good way to end his weekend in Atlanta. It was back to New York in the morning. Hanging in the club was his celebration. He'd proved his worth to his uncle. Hell, it wasn't a difficult assignment. Get the information on Kendra Simmons, then pass it on. Why, he had no idea and didn't care. He got to live in the mansion while in Atlanta and had an opportunity to move up in the organization. Why not leave the city with a good bang.

"Nice place you have here Bobby." Karess walked in dressed in a red off the shoulder, body-hugging dress that stopped mid-thigh, and black leather spiked boots. A black clutch bag finished her ensemble that was meant to entice. Her hair hung loose around her shoulders. Raven, dressed in a black, one shoulder mini, with her thigh high boots walked up to Bobby. Looking him up and down, she put her hands on her hips. "You get him, I get the two friends."

"I think we can handle all three," Karess walked over to one of the two men standing near the door, then licked her lips. Looking towards the other man leaning against the wall, she smiled. "Actually, I think we are one man short of making this a real party. You don't have anymore friends around, Bobby?"

Bobby smirked. "Don't need no more. It's going to take both of you to handle me." He rubbed his chest where his shirt was open, checking Raven out in much the same way she did him.

Karess winked at the man standing at the door. "He promised me a party. Is he worth my time?"

"You're packing like that blue eyes?" Raven ran her hand down the front of Bobby's pants until she reached his penis. She squeezed gently. "Not bad. How about yours?"

Karess looked at the man, raising an eyebrow, "Are you game?"

"I'm game, if he's not," the man leaning against the wall smiled.

Her eyes brightened as she walked sensuously toward the man. "You it is then," she ran here hands inside his jacket, down to his waist, then to his penis. She winked at Raven. "His is bigger."

Both women closed their hands, squeezing so hard neither man could do anything more than squeal.

The man at the door, yelled, "What the hell?" then reached into his jacket to pull out his weapon. A swooshing sound echoed through the air and snapped against his hand, causing him to drop the weapon. The whip retracted, then snapped out again this time wrapping around the man's neck.

Naverone followed behind Genesis from the kitchen area of the house. "Ladies," Raven and Karess released the men, watching as they dropped to the floor.

Naverone stopped near the doorway where the two guards were on their knees. "Gentlemen, your services are no longer needed." She inserted a needle into the neck of the man against the wall, as Genesis did the same with the man at the door. Dropping the needle into a plastic bag which she then held out to Genesis and waited for her to dispose of her needle as well. She dropped the bag inside a tube, then placed it in her pocket. She slowly walked over. "Roberto Garrison." She stopped in front of the man who was on his knees still holding his jewels cupped in his hand. She held his chin up, and looked down into his beet red face. "We have to talk."

Raven pulled Roberto to his feet. "Let's go player."

His footsteps echoed across the foyer of the house as if it was the walk of doom. He opened the door to the left as instructed to find, Peace and Naverone's team with Roberto Garrison. There was a single chair near the door facing the desk where Roberto Garrison sat.

Ty flipped his calf length trench coat back, took a seat, then crossed his legs. He glared up at the man trying to read him. How much fortitude did he have? He would give him fifteen minutes to give him what he needed, after that, he could not be held responsible for any actions by the team. "Good evening Mr. Garrison. My name is Tyrone Pendleton. You have been involved in a conspiracy against either me or someone I love deeply, Kendra Simmons. She is missing. Was taken from our family home last night. By the time the twenty-fourth hour ticks my plan is to have her back. You are going to help me do that."

"Go to hell," Roberto spit out.

"All right," Ty smiled, then looked at Genesis. "Your specialty is extracting information. Is it not?"

"It is," Genesis stepped forward grinning.

"Extract."

Genesis licked her lips, with anticipation. "Mr. Garrison," she walked slowly in front of him. "I want Ms. Simmons' location and the name of the man that took her."

"I have no idea what you are talking about, but I do know this. You're a dead man when my people find out about this."

"Who's going to tell them?" Karess pulled a metal object from her pocket, then pushed a button, extending a six inch blade. She tossed it, landing it in the back of the chair next to his ear. "You will be missing a tongue."

"Let's try again," Ty said as Karess walked over to remove the blade. "The name of the man, Roberto." Ty glanced at his watch. "Time doesn't appear to be on your side."

"I don't know." Fear was clearly in his cry. "I swear I don't know."

"Tell me what you do know," Ty asked as calmly as he could.

"Look man, I don't know who you are, but I can pay you whatever you want to let me go."

"I'll let you go and it will not cost you a dime, only a name. Please....don't make me ask again."

Frantic now, Roberto, looked at the women in the room. "I don't know a name, I swear I don't. All I was told was to get information from the woman and report back. That's all I know man. I swear that's all I know."

"Who and why?" Genesis snapped the whip across his shoulder and the man cried out in pain.

"It doesn't work like that. You do what you are told and do not ask questions at my level."

"Roberto, I'm not a dentist. I grow tried of attempting to extract information from you." He nodded at Genesis.

"What's more important to you Mr. Garrison, your hearing or touch?" Genesis snapped the whip across his knuckles, then walked towards him. "I could begin with plucking your finger nails, or simply cut off an ear." Pulling a handkerchief from her pocket she tossed it.

Karess caught it, pressed her blade against his ear and held the handkerchief below it.

Roberto's eyes grew wide as the color drained completely from his already pale face. The man fell forward in the chair.

"No, he didn't." Raven began to laugh. "He fainted."

Genesis shook her head. "Weak."

"I guess he was a lover, not a fighter," Karess laughed.

Peace shook his head. "Boss, what do we do now?"

"Wake him up and begin again."

Twenty minutes later Ty had a portion of the information he needed. According to Roberto, he was sent a plane ticket and instructions to receive final payment on a stopover at Richmond International Airport. He instructed Naverone to keep Roberto secure until Kiki was found, then let him go. On his jet, he placed a call to Monique. "Garrison led us back to Richmond. I'm on my way."

"This is where we need to be. Big brother watching us has its advantages. Using face recognition, we placed Ram renting a vehicle here." She advised. "When he steps out of whatever building he's in, we should get a hit on his location."

Chapter Fifteen

*I*t was a jail cell, that she was certain of. Opening her eyes did nothing, for there was total blackness. She closed her eyes again, trying to adjust to the darkness. This time when she opened them, she could make out a few outlines of poles. No, she blinked again, not poles, bars. "What the hell?" The realization cut deep. All the things she had done in her life, this was not where she wanted to die. No, she was not going to die. Ty wasn't going to let her. Not now, just when he has accepted his love for her. God would not be that cruel. A tear slipped down her cheek. "Please God, don't do this to him. He doesn't deserve that kind of pain. I don't want to be the one to cause him any pain." She went to wipe the tears away and found her hands were bound above her head. Looking up, it was not handcuffs that were tied to the old pipe, it appeared to be some type of thick plastic. She pulled, testing the stability. There was no give. A little rust from the pipe dropped but that was it.

Looking around, her eyes seemed to adjust a little better. It was definitely a jail cell. A very old one, but a jail cell all the same. The pipe she was bound to was connected to a sink. Turning, she found the cold surface she was leaning against was the base of a toilet, which explained the stench she was smelling. Then she saw several mousetraps with mice in them. She hurriedly pulled her feet up under her. "God what have I done to bring me to this?"

The place was cold and musty. The leather jacket and jeans was not enough to protect her against the temperature. With no window to the outside, she had no idea if it was day or night. It was after six and dark when they left the house. "Jason," she cried out as the memories of what occurred flashed through her mind. If he was hit with the same thing she was, then he wasn't dead, she didn't think. Was he there somewhere with her? "Jason," she called out again, then listened. Nothing. She closed her eyes, said a quick prayer for his safety. Stretching out her legs she found her muscles were not fully functional, for her movements were slow. She stopped with one leg mid air, she heard something. Holding perfectly still, she heard it again. It was footsteps. Ty, she thought. She listened more intently. No, that's not Ty. It was the walk of a woman in heels. Something in the sound of the walk caused her not to call out. The steps stopped, she heard a click and the lights came on, then the steps started again. As the steps drew nearer, the more menacing they sounded. From the floor up she saw the tan, suede platform boots, with three inch heels, the black tights, tan coat tied at the waist, the matching gloves being pulled from her hands, then finally, the curly hair that hung around her shoulders.

Shock was the first emotion that seized her, then it was instant anger. "Laura," she yanked her hands, "I'm going to kick your ass if you don't let me out of here right now."

Laura stood there in the doorway of the cell, removing her gloves as if it was the most natural thing in the world to be doing.

"Right now, Laura," Kiki yelled, yanking on the pipe.

"Well, hello Kiki." Laura smiled as she looked around. "I see you are exactly where you should be, amongst filth. I think it was thoughtful of him to put a few rat traps in to keep them away until I had a chance to visit." She looked around. "I have to say, I like what you've done with the place."

"Let me go Laura."

"Why would I let you out if I know you are going to kick my ass? That does not make sense. And after all the planning and money I've paid to put you here."

"You," Kiki could not believe what she had heard. "You had me kidnapped, not once but twice." Her eyes grew wide. "You had Ty shot. I know I'm going to kick your ass. You are crazy. I always knew you had a few marbles missing, but this is beyond what I even thought."

"Crazy." She kicked Kiki in the face. Blood oozed from her lip. Laura laughed. "You have no idea how long I've waited to do that. God, that felt good."

Stunned, Kiki wiped her face against her bound hands. "Taking sibling rivalry to a new level don't you think?"

"Oh, you haven't seen anything yet." She stooped down and grinned, I have something special planned for you."

Kiki had on flat boots, but she thought one good turn deserved another. She kicked Laura in the face, knocking her backwards to the floor. "You never were too bright," she grinned as she watched Laura pick herself off the ground.

Laura reached into her pocket and pulled out a gun. Kiki pulled her legs up, turned her face and ducked towards the pipe as much as she could.

"What, the great Kiki don't have anything to say now? Don't worry," she put the gun away as Kiki peeked up. "I'm not going to be the one to kill you. I'm here because I wanted you to know why you are going to die. My favorite part is you knowing it was me that planned it." She laughed. "Oh, you helped, or at least one of your authors did. I was reading one of the manuscripts you threw into the 'No Way in Hell' pile. While reading it, all I could imagine was you being the victim of the plot. So I began a plot of my own. First, I had to set up a fall guy, or girl in this case. Who better than LaToya Wright? Everybody hates her for what she did to Silk Davies and his wife. That part was easy. Next I needed details. So I hired a man to seduce LaToya into giving him the details that only she would know. Here's the wonderful part, he has no idea who hired him. If your Ty finds him, and I'm sure he will, it still will not lead to me. After I got all the information, I hired a hit man and gave him specific instructions on how I wanted my revenge dished out."

"Revenge, for what?" Kiki asked. "If anyone should seek revenge, it should be me. It was you who ruined my family."

"It was you," she screamed. "His precious Kendra that he cried for when he thought my mother wasn't looking." She kicked her then stood over her, snarling as if she was about to attack. "It was you he always worried about. You, not the boys, no, it was his little girl that he prayed would one day understand and forgive him. As if being with us was a sin." She stood up, pushed her hair back, then straightened her shoulders. "Once you are gone, I will have Daddy to myself." She smiled. "After all, I am the pretty one." Her lips curled with a frown, "He never understood this ethnic look you carry as if you were the Queen of the Nile. That was the one thing I always had over you." A distant look came into her eyes as she smiled. "The look, and style he prefers. That's why he left your mother and turned to mine. My mother understood what a man like my daddy needed and so do I." She turned her back on Kiki. "We were doing fine until you came to New York and ruined everything." She shook her head, then turned back to Kiki. "Did you know the week before you came, Daddy said he was going to show me the ropes of the company so he could retire?" She nodded her head up and down. "Yep, he was going to turn Crimson over to me." She frowned down at Kiki. "Then you came," she snarled then kicked her again. "All of a sudden you were in line to take over Crimson as if I never existed. It didn't matter that you never had one nice thing to say to him, and all I gave him was love, it was you, his Kendra that was the apple of his eye. Well," she sighed, then smiled. "That ends today," she said in a strange perky voice, as she began to put her gloves back on. "Oh he will mourn you for a while. No worries though. I'll be there to console him. Then things will be as they should. Daddy, Mother and me." She walked to the cell door opening. Turning back she smiled. "Don't worry now. It will be quick. I don't want you to suffer. I just want you gone. Bye bye now."

Kiki heard the footsteps retreating, with menacing laughter that followed. The light went out and again she was plunged into darkness. Now she could admit to herself that she was afraid, pissed and hurt. The tears flowed. She was sure Laura had cracked one of her ribs. "Oh God, Laura." Her own sister was the one behind all of this. "Daddy." For the first time in twenty years she was afraid for her Daddy. Laura had lost touch with reality. If she was capable of doing this, what would be next. She shouldn't care, after the way he treated Mom. "Oh God, Mommy." Tears welled up in her eyes again. "Give her the strength to handle this. Help her to find real love. She deserves it." She sniffed, thinking her brothers would be there to help her mother. Maybe even Jake. She still did not know how she felt about Jake and her mom, but if he would be there for her, then so be it. It's not like she could do anything about it. "Why God? Why? Was I that bad of a person for this to be happening? Yes, I burned up Laura's dolls, tore up her certificates and award book, and oh yeah, I was the one that cut her hair while she was asleep. But I was only twelve and the law forgives anything that happens before the age of eighteen."

She laughed at the notion. "I know that was weak." She sighed. "Lord, if you could find a way to forgive me for any wrong I've done against anyone. I may not have attended church every Sunday, but you have and always will be in my heart. And Lord, one more thing, bless Tyrone's heart in a way to let him know you are there. That's it Lord. Let your will be done."

She leaned her head against the pipe, thinking she should have asked forgiveness for blaming LaToya for all of this. It was never about her, Silk or Ty. "Ty," she cried. He was out there looking for her in the wrong direction. "Please God, make sure he knows how much I love him. Don't allow this to turn him bitter again." She sniffed. "Naverone will love him when I'm gone." She thought about that for a moment because she'd wanted to spend her life with him. But if she couldn't, she did not want him to be alone. "Yes, okay, she can have him. Just don't leave him to live his life alone."

Leaning back against the commode, her side hurt, her face hurt and her heart was breaking for Ty, a thought came to her. She had to find that manuscript Laura was talking about. If this is any indication, it's going to be a bestseller. She laughed as tears streamed down her face.

Ram decided he did not like the sister after she kicked Wildcat's face. The woman was bound and defenseless. That was the act of a coward. Wildcat would have never stooped so low. He watched her on the monitor from his hotel room. The video equipment was put there as his protection. If he ever went down, this video recording would be his get out of jail card. If they had enough money to hire him, they would have enough to buy a district attorney.

He continued to watch Kiki as she talked to God. He had to smile at her confession. The more he was around her the more he liked her. If it were up to him, he would let her go. According to her performance, the sister had lost touch with reality. Those are usually the people who hire him. Then there was that thing called integrity, that caused him to complete the job he was hired for regardless of his disdain for his boss.

Stepping out into the cold, Ram inhaled. There was nothing like the fresh air, when the adrenaline was flowing. It was time for the kill. He had to admit as he climbed into his SUV, this was an intriguing assignment. The sister had planned things to a T. Even down to eliminating her fellow conspirator when he arrived for final payment.

$\textcircled{P}$

He parked his vehicle near the James River in downtown Richmond then walked the canal towards Spring Street. Most people that lived in the area did not remember that the Corrections Department once had a prison located on the very site a beautiful office building now occupied. It was affectionately called The State Pen. He thought it was appropriate to use the site for Wildcat's demise since her authors lived or died by her red pen. He smirked at the irony. It was the best he could do in a pinch. This was supposed to take place in New York where there were plenty of deserted buildings. Richmond was rebuilding, growing by leaps and bounds. There were other places he could have used, but this suited his needs well. He walked under the bridge, then easily slipped into the darkness of the trees that hid the entrance to a tunnel that led to the cells used for solitary confinement for the worst offenders before The Pen was demolished. He had learned about the tunnel from his grandfather who helped construct the area, back in the nineteen hundreds. Only those who worked the area knew of the tunnels existence, for it was the way they allowed prisoners to escape for a few hours, for a price of course.

Steps led down to a door that opened to the cells that still existed below. Looking around, it was a shame he was going to have to blow the place up. It was secluded, near the river and a major highway for easy escape if needed. However, the woman insisted on having a moment with Kiki, so he had to disclose the location, leaving him no choice but to destroy the place.

Clicking on the light switch, he wondered how Wildcat was going to feel when she saw it was him. Would she immediately know, he was a part of this scheme from the beginning? Would she be hurt, upset, angry? "Angry," he smiled.

Monique peeked up as the monitors, at the FBI field office located on Parham Road in Richmond, began to flash. The satellite picked up a location on RAM. "Pull up that location," she instructed the Technician.

"Crowne Plaza on East Canal Street," he replied.

Monique grabbed her coat, "Send his movements to my phone." The two technicians watched the woman dressed in a black turtleneck, jeans and boots, as she walked to the door. "Stop looking at my ass and send me the intel." The techs turned back and did as they were instructed.

Jumping into a black jeep, she pushed a button on the console to activate the communication system. "Have you landed?"

"Just touched down."

"Meet me at the Crowne Plaza Hotel on Canal Street."

"I know the place."

Ty put the hotel in his phone to get directions. "You know the area better than I do," he said to Peace. "You drive."

"Where to Boss?" Peace asked as they climbed into the vehicle.

"Here's the address."

Fifteen minutes later they were at the hotel walking down the steps into the lobby. Looking around at the elegantly designed lobby for any signs of Monique was fruitless. This was not the type of hotel where you would see people hanging around in the lobby, there was only a couple waiting for their driver to pick them up. Ty noticed the platinum pass the man was holding in his hand. Once shown to the driver, he will take you wherever you wanted to go. It was unlimited access to the city, he had used it often.

Ty walked over to the Receptionist desk and spoke to the gentleman dressed in a black suit, white shirt, and thin black tie. "I'm looking for a woman that may have come in within the last twenty minutes. Short, wavy hair..."

"Whew," the man shook his head appreciatively, "The one in all black. She's speaking with my manager. Follow me."

They followed him to a door that was partially open. "She's been giving him hell for about ten minutes now." The man smirked, then returned to his station.

"You have one minute before I fill your lobby with FBI Agents. How do think your guests will like that? Give me the damn key."

"Excuse me," Tyrone interceded. "Hello Jerome."

"Mr. Pendleton," said Jerome, an older Caucasian man, dressed as elegantly as the hotel he manager. "Please forgive me. I'm assisting this young lady. I will be with you in one moment."

"I'm with the young lady." Ty shook the man's hand.

Jerome looked at Monique then back to Ty. "How may I assist you sir?"

Tyrone looked to Monique. "We need access to a room?" he questioned

"Yes, Ram is staying in this hotel. I've explained the situation to...," she hesitated, "Jerome, who is insisting on a warrant, which I've explained we don't have time for."

Ty nodded. "Jerome, I personally take full responsibility for any mishaps and I would personally appreciate your cooperation."

"In that case sir," he reached into his pocket and pulled out a key card.

"You had it in your pocket the whole time," Monique fussed.

Ty pulled her out the office. "Thank you Jerome. Is the man in his room?"

"No sir. Harold indicated he left roughly twenty minutes ago."

"Thank you Jerome," Ty walked pulling Monique with him with the gentle touch of his hand on her lower back. "Do you raise hell with everyone you meet?"

"Only with bull headed men," she replied as they stepped into the elevator.

When they reached the room, Monique stopped them from entering. "Step away from the door." She turned to Peace. "Lift me up."

After looking at her strangely, he shrugged his shoulders, then lifted her by the waist. She ran her hand over the doorframe. "Okay." When he put her down she examined the side of the frame until she found what she was looking for located close to the floor. She looked up at them. "Motion detector. If activated, it would send him a message that someone has entered the room," she said as she knelt down and pulled a small black case from her pocket. "This will deactivate it without sending a message." She placed a small thin object, not larger than a dime on it, then stood. Using the card she opened the door, but did not enter the room. "Stay until I give you the all clear."

Ty and Peace looked at each other, questioningly.

From the case she pulled out an object that looked like a pen, pushed the top and a small light appeared. When the top of the pin flashed, she stepped back, twisted the pen, and the top stopped flashing. "Okay, we should be clear." Ty and Peace hesitated. When she walked in, they followed.

"Do I want to know..."

"No." She stopped Ty's question as she stood looking around the room. The room was spotless. The only things indicating someone was occupying the room were a black tote bag on the bed and a pair of binoculars on the table near the window. A chair was facing the window as if someone was doing surveillance. "Don't touch anything." She instructed.

"There's nothing to touch," Peace stated as he looked around.

"Why are we here?" Ty asked.

"This is Ram's room."

"How do you know for sure?"

Monique laughed, shaking her head. "Well, if the detector on the door didn't convince you, the small explosive I detonated was conclusive enough for me."

Peace frantically looked around. "What explosive?"

"Not important," Monique replied as she pushed a button on the tote bag. A drawer popped out. She looked up at and smiled at a confused Ty. "Pay dirt." She pushed a release button and the top popped up.

"I'll be damn." Peace walked over. "It's a computer."

"No, that's too simple of a term. This is an operatives lifeline," Monique replied as she pulled out her cell phone and pushed a button. "I need a bypass on a computer," she said into the phone.

"You've been off the grid Spicy. Where are you?"

"Ned, you're not my father. How many times do I have to have this discussion with you?"

"Spicy?" Ty raised an eyebrow.

"Don't ask."

"Who's with you?" Ned, her handler asked.

"Tyrone Pendleton, agent to the super rich and famous entertainers."

"Oh, don't know the name."

"You will."

"Password, Killer One." Monique laughed. "Yeah, Absolute will get a kick out of that, after he kills him."

"I may have to beat him to that one," Monique replied as she keyed in the password. The computer powered up. "I'm connecting you. Take what you can from the hard drive while I search for what I need."

"How much time do I have?"

"Five minutes tops."

"Hook me up."

Monique took a small drive, placed it into the computer and a solid green light came on. "Now, what do you have for me?" She did a quick scan of the items on the desktop. The last one loaded was a video. She clicked it on.

"There's Kendra." Ty bent down to get a closer look. At first he closed his eyes to the sight of her on the floor between a toilet and a sink, tied to a rusted pipe. It took a moment for him to control his emotions.

"Are those rats around her on the floor?" Peace asked.

Monique looked over her shoulders at him as if she wanted to kill him. Peace realized his mistake and took a step back.

"She's going to be pissed if anything crawls in her hair," Ty commented.

Monique smiled inwardly at his composure and resolve. "Ned, stop what you are working on. Take a look at this video and tell me where it's located."

"Somebody just walked in." Ty looked closer.

"It's a female." Monique looked closer. "From the angle of the camera, you can't see who she is."

"Laura," they heard Kiki call out.

"Laura, oh hell."

"Who's Laura?" Peace asked.

"Her sister," Monique replied as she continued to watch the video.

Ty jumped up when Laura kicked Kiki in the face. "Where is this?"

"Damn," Monique exclaimed. "I hate a coward."

"There you go Rocket," Peace yelled when Kiki kicked the woman in the face.

"Got the location," Ned announced. "Based on your signal you're less than five minutes away."

"Where is it," Ty demanded.

"It's the basement of one of our underground secure facilities at the corner of Spring Street and Belvedere.

"What is it used for Ned," Monique asked as she, started to close down the video.

"Don't turn it off," Ty yelled. "Let it play out."

Monique understood he needed to see the outcome. "Ned?"

"It's a location we use when we want to interrogate without police interruption. The basement has not been used for years. Any operative who was active in the area would know about its existence."

"Send me the schematics."

"Will do and take one step further." The video froze, then returned without Laura in the pictures. "I tapped into the camera at the location. This is all live, people."

They looked at the monitor to see Kiki, now with blood on her face, her head leaning against the pipe. "Kendra," Ty sighed.

As they watched a light came on. "He's there." Monique sprang up. "Send this feed to my phone and get me those schematics." She ran from the room, with Ty and Peace behind her.

"On its way." Ned replied. "I'll monitor from here."

"Sweep my last location for any explosives." They ran out the side door of the hotel and jumped into her jeep. She pulled off with Peace still climbing into the back seat.

Pushing a button on the console the video feed was live. She pushed another button. "Ned, how many ways into the facility?"

"Two. There's an apartment on the corner of Spring Street. I'm sending the code to your phone. The closet in the hallway is an elevator that will take you down to the top level of the facility. In the basement, they will not detect your entry. The other entrance is under the bridge by the Canal. I'm showing the detectors have been disabled there."

"That's how he's getting in," Monique said as she pulled up to the location. "Stay here," she said to Ty.

"You've lost your damn mind," he said as he pulled out his Glock, checked the magazine, then pushed it back into place.

"The man is a professional. They will have my ass if something happened to you in there."

"He broke the damn rule," Tyrone yelled as he hit the dashboard. "He broke the rule," he repeated.

"What damn rule? What are you talking about Pendleton?"

Ty sighed and ran a hand down his face. This wasn't the time to lose his composure. He turned back to Monique. "He touched what is mine. He has to die." He opened the door and stepped out.

"Boss?" Peace called out.

"Get the car ready."

"Hold up." Monique stepped out of the jeep. "This isn't a regular vehicle. He hit a wrong button and this city will... well let's not think about that." She turned to Peace. "Key in the ignition, don't touch anything else," she emphasized, nothing. She turned to Ty and they ran across the street.

Chapter Sixteen

*"H*ello Wildcat."

Kiki hadn't turned to see who was coming when the lights came on. She knew it wasn't Ty. Anyone else, she didn't care to see. When she heard the voice, she slowly turned and looked at the entrance of the cell. Recognition was instant and all she could do was shake her head and turn away.

"I think you owe me a little more than that, Wildcat. After all, you stood me up."

"Go to hell."

"A fighter to the end," he laughed. "You are a woman after my heart."

"You don't have a heart if you are working with Laura."

"I can understand your feelings. I don't like her too much either."

"Then why are you doing this?"

"She paid me." He shrugged as if that was reason enough.

"What is a person's life worth these days?"

"An average person, not much. You, a hundred grand."

"Huh, she short changed you." Kiki adjusted her position and looked at him. "Ty would have paid you a cool million to keep me alive."

"You're right. That man loves you. Hell he took several bullets for you. Now that's love."

The elevator stopped and swished open. Monique held the doors open and listened. "Where is he, Ned?"

"North end of the building one floor below your location. One of you take the steps to the right and come up the corridor behind him. The other take the corridor above him and take the steps at the end. Come up on the side of the cell they're in."

"Got it." She looked at Ty, and pointed for him to take the steps, while she walked above. "I'm light on my feet, you got this swagger thing going, with the swinging duster, dressed in Armani. You remind me of that damn Absolute," she mumbled as she walked down the corridor.

Ty had no idea what or who she was talking about and didn't care at this moment. All he wanted was Kendra alive. With his Glock in his hand, he ran down the steps. Not caring if he was heard or not.

"He's been detected," Ned said into the earpiece Monique was wearing.

"That's what I was hoping for. Keep him alive Ned."

"Got you. Be careful Spicy"

Suddenly Ram stopped talking and listened. He tilted his head. "I think you have a visitor. Now who do you suppose that could be? He stepped out of the cell doorway and looked down the corridor to see Ty walking towards him as if it was the most natural thing for him to be there. "Somehow I knew it would come to this," Ram laughed. "From the moment we met in the stairwell, I knew you were going to be a thorn in my side."

Ty continued to walk towards him. "Game recognizes game."

"Ty," he heard Kiki call out. He couldn't respond. Never give the enemy the upper hand.

Ram laughed. "Two different leagues my brother."

"You didn't do your homework, Rupid." He watched Ram take the battle stance.

"Now see, you're trying to piss me off by calling me that."

"Always know your enemy better than you know yourself." Ty saw him flinch at his words.

"You're giving me words of wisdom."

"Lessons learned," Ty replied as he read the fear in Ram's eyes. "Where does the truth lie?"

Ram glared at Ty harder. "In the eyes."

Ty pulled his Glock up. "What's the rule Rupid?"

Ram snickered. "So you're Sly's son. Damn."

"What's the rule?" Ty demanded as he continued to advance without cover.

"Get down there Spicy," Ned yelled. "He's going to kill him."

"Rules are made to be broken," Ram replied.

Ty watched the subtle movement of Ram's right hand. He fired one shot, hitting the hand. "I've got an itchy finger."

"Warning man, warning. The rules call for a warning before shooting."

"There's only one rule that applies here. You touch what's mine and you die."

Before Ty could pull the trigger, Ram's body jerked forward as his eyes widened in surprise. He watched as the man fell to his knees, revealing Monique behind him. Ram fell forward, face down on the cement floor.

An angry Ty lowered his gun and glared at Monique. "Why in the hell did you do that?"

Monique bent over, pulled her knife out and wiped it clean. "I have a license to kill, you don't."

Ty stepped into the cell and leaned against the opening. "Why can't you ever do what I ask?"

"You left me," Kiki cried.

Ty walked over and bent down next to her and gently kissed her lips. "I'm sorry."

"Don't kiss me. I'm funky, from pissing on myself. I haven't brushed my teeth in hours if not days. My side and my lip hurt." She whimpered. "What took you so long?"

"Spicy, somethings been activated at the lower entrance. Check his pocket for a detonator.

Monique, yelled at Ty as she searched Ram's pockets. "We've got to get her out of here."

Ty checked the plastic bonding around her hand. "We need something to cut this with."

Monique pulled a small device from Ram's pocket. It was blinking. She walked into the cell and held it up to the camera. "Ned, can you deactivate it?"

"Can you hold it closer to the camera?"

"Tyrone, hold me up."

"Short women," Ty lifted her by the waist.

"Got it," Ned said. "You work on getting out of there."

Monique reached into her back pocket as Ty sat her down. Something resembling a nail file was pulled out. "Cover her face," she told Ty.

The area was small and cramped that they were working in. He pulled his coat off and covered Kiki's face. Monique held the device against the plastic. A spark flashed and began cutting into the restraints. Kiki's hands fell to the floor when the cable split.

"Um, Spicy, you got to move," Ned said into the earpiece. "The lower entrance is compromised, and I don't know how long you have to get out. Use the apartment entrance to get out.

Ty wrapped his coat around Kiki and carried her out in his arms. He heard her intake of breath from the movement. "I'm sorry, Kendra." He kissed her temple.

"Follow me." Monique stepped over Ram and ran up the steps. "Ned, send a cleaning crew."

"Not until we deactivate the device."

"You can handle that little thing," Monique said as she quickly moved down the corridor.

"Get to the elevator," Ned encouraged. Monique began to run. Ty followed suit. "It'll protect you from the impact in five, four, three, two..."

The elevator door closed with Monique, Ty and Kiki inside as the building rocked. The car shook, as it ascended upwards. It stopped with a jolt and the doors swished opened. They stepped off the elevator and the door closed and disappeared. They walked out of the closet to find Sylvester Dawson sitting on the sofa in the apartment with his legs crossed. "What took you so long?" He asked his son.

Ty shook his head. "Pops, Kendra. Kendra my father, CIA operative Sly Dawson."

Sly stood and walked over to the woman in Ty's arms. "You are a natural beauty."

Kiki looked from Sly to Ty. "Are you going to look like that when you get older?"

"Are you going to be around when I get older?"

"Don't answer a question with a question, Pendleton."

Monique looked at the man in the suit. "They're going to be at that for a while." She walked around Sly. "So you're the mentor."

Sly stood there smiling at the couple. He was at peace now. This woman would not desert Tyrone the way his mother had. "Miriam did a good job," he said to his son.

Ty stopped talking to Kiki and looked up at his father. "Until the next time." He walked over to the door.

Monique turned to help Ty with the door. "So Sly, are you going to teach me...." Her question trailed off as she realized she was talking to an empty room. "Where in the hell did you go?"

Ty held Kiki closer to his heart as he smiled knowing, he had the woman he loved back in his arms and a father that would be looking out for them from whereever he may be.

Chapter Seventeen

Monique escorted the physician to the elevator that was connected to Ty's suite. Until they apprehended Laura Simmons, she did not want anyone to know Kendra had been found. From the hallway she answered Ned's call. "Has her location been verified?"

"Not yet. We're tracking the GPS in her cell phone," he replied. "Once she turns it on, we will lock in on her location."

"We need to make that happen sooner than later." Monique stopped in the hallway. "Did you send the message to her father?"

"He's en route."

"Where's the mother?"

"She's at the hotel. Do you think she's involved?"

Monique shook her head. "I don't think so. But crazy can be genetic. Keep an eye on her."

"Sly is MIA. Any idea where he may be?"

Monique looked out the window at the figure in the garden talking to Miriam Davies. "Haven't seen the man." She disconnected the call as she walked into the sitting area of Ty's bedroom. There she found Jason on the sofa with TeKaya's feet in his lap along with Eric and Siri, sitting together on the chaise lounge. "Is there a reason why you all are here?"

"We live here," Jason replied. "Who are you?"

Monique smiled. "If I tell you, I'll have to kill you and I don't think Ty would like that. Excuse me," she walked by with four sets of eyes staring at her. Ty was sitting in a chair next to the bed with his legs stretched out and crossed at the ankles. "Ty, the doctor said her ribs are bruised, not cracked or broken. The medication is only to ease some of the discomfort. You don't have to watch her."

He never looked back at Monique as she spoke, his eyes stayed on Kiki. "While I was bathing her, she never looked into my eyes. For some reason she's ashamed of the way I found her."

"I wouldn't worry about that. She's going to be pissed when she sees what you did to her hair."

Ty looked back at Monique, then looked at Kiki, and burst out laughing. She had fallen asleep during her bath, so he dried her off with a heated towel, applied lotion on her body and put her under the comforter. He knew she was very particular about her hair, so he tried to do what he saw her do each night. His twists did not look like hers now that he was paying closer attention. They were sticking up all over her head and going in different directions.

Gabby walked into the sitting area as laughter filled the room. She looked at the astonished look on the occupant's faces. "What are they laughing at?"

"We don't know," TeKaya said. "Jason and Eric are too afraid to go into the room.

"Afraid?" Gabby looked at the two brothers. "Of what?"

"Ty's kind of pissed at us," Jason replied.

"Oh nonsense." She walked by them and entered the room. She looked over to the bed where Kiki was asleep and her mouth dropped open. Tyrone looked over his shoulder at her and burst out laughing again at the expression on her face. "What have you done to that child's hair?"

Monique was on the floor laughing as Jason, Eric and Siri entered the room. "What is it?" TeKaya who was too large to get up quickly asked.

Jason and Eric looked at each other. Jason pulled out his cell phone and took several pictures. "We got him now."

"Gabby would you please fix her hair?"

"My Lord," Gabby declared as she walked into the bathroom and returned with a comb. Sitting on the side of the bed, she began untangling the contraptions Tyrone called twists. "Tyrone, Mr. Simmons has arrived." She frowned as she worked on Kiki's hair. "From the sound of things I think you'd better go down."

Ty sobered, then stood. Turning, he saw Jason and Eric in the doorway, with a look of uncertainty on their faces. The last words he'd had with Eric were rough. At the time he meant every word. But he knew they would not intentionally place Kiki's life in danger. They both stepped back when he walked towards them.

"Now Ty," Siri spoke. "I love you, but I'm going to take you out if you touch Eric."

"Yeah, me too," TeKaya said as she struggled to get up off the sofa. "If you touch Jason."

Ty walked by his brothers and helped TeKaya up. "What was that again?"

"You're not funny." TeKaya smiled at him, then kissed his cheek.

He looked at his brothers. "No one except the people here and my father know Kiki is back. It has to stay that way. Will you protect her while I'm gone?"

"Of course we will," Jason replied as Eric nodded in agreement. They would not make the same mistake twice. As Ty and Monique walked out of the room, Eric tilted his head with a questioning glance at Jason. "Father?"

Kenneth was ushered into the family room. His family was there waiting on word from the police or Ty. It was difficult for Kenneth to look his boys in the eyes. Martin and Garland had kept the lines of communication open, but Wayne hated his guts. He understood that they had lost respect for him that day in New York when they discovered his other family. Truth is, so had he. If he could change any moment in his life, that would be it. "Any word on Kendra?"

"What do you care?" Wayne barked, "You have another daughter."

"Watch your tone, I'm still your father.

"No disrespect Dad," Garland said from the chair near the fireplace, "but you haven't been our father in 20 years."

Kenneth looked at Issy, "Why is everyone here? Why aren't you at our home?"

Issy stood from the chair where she was sitting in and glared at him. "We," she said, "don't have a home. You destroyed that when you decided to have an affair and a bastard child."

"I know you are angry Issy, but don't take it out on Laura. She's innocent in all of this."

"Then we'll take it out on you," Wayne snarled. "Are you innocent too?"

"This isn't about me son. This is about Kendra. Where is Pendleton and why are we letting him run things? She's my daughter."

"Look around Kenny," Issy groaned. "He has the means to locate her. We don't."

"We have money."

"No, Kenny," Issy put her hands on her hips and stepped in front of him. "You cleaned out the bank account when you decided to stay with your family in New York. I've been rebuilding every since."

"What did you expect me to do Issy? You divorced me and tried to take everything, including the publishing company," Kenneth yelled.

"You had a bastard child during our marriage. You're damn right I divorced you."

"Don't call my daughter a bastard."

"You're defending her to me," Issy's temper flared more. "Look up the definition in the dictionary Kenny," she emphasized the name. "Your wife was a whore, who had a child outside of wedlock. That makes the child a bastard." She turned her back on him.

"Don't you walk away from me," he reached out to grab her arm when Jake came out of nowhere, yanked him by the throat then pushed him against the wall. "Don't ever touch what is mine."

"Let him go," Ty calmly instructed. "Jake," he said again as he touched the angry man on his shoulder. "Let him go."

Jake slowly released Kenneth, who immediately grabbed his throat, then looked from Issy to Jake. "Issy?"

Issy walked back over to the chair. "You heard what the man said. Don't touch what's his."

Wayne looked from his mother, to Jake then to his father, then released the air he was holding in. "I ain't even mad at that," he smirked at his father, then looked at Ty. "When did you get here? Anything on Kendra?"

"Why don't we all take a seat."

"I don't want a damn seat," Kenneth exclaimed. "Where is my daughter?"

"Mr. Simmons, I'm about two minutes away from resuming what Jake started a moment ago. Please, have a seat."

"Ty?" Issy looked up, fearful. Jake walked over, took her hand and waited for Ty to speak.

"Monique would you?"

"Sure." Monique walked over, put the drive into the television monitor, then gave the remote to Ty.

"Garland, would you let your father have your seat?" Ty asked.

"Okay," Garland replied wondering what was about to happen. He walked over to stand next to Martin and Wayne who had his hand on his mother's shoulder.

"Mr. Simmons, I don't like you," Ty said. "I am truly sorry to do this. However, you would not believe me if told you. I have to show you."

"Show me what?" A frustrated Kenneth continued to rub his throat.

Ty pushed the play button. Ned had shortened the feed to just the pertinent part.

They all watched as the light came up and Kiki came into view. A gasp could be heard around the room.

"Kendra." Issy cried.

"It's a woman," Wayne whispered, as he bent to get a closer looked.

Ty watched as Kenneth sat up and listened. That was when the blood began to drain from his face.

"Oh hell no she didn't kick my sister in the face. Who in the hell is it?" Garland stood ready to battle.

While others were watching the picture, Ty turned to Issy. She was listening to the conversation. She inhaled when Kiki kicked the woman in her face. She knew. The boys cheered at the act, then the room grew quiet as Ty paused the video.

No one said anything. No one moved until Naverone walked into the room with Peace. Suddenly all hell broke lose as Wayne grabbed Kenneth out of the chair. "Did you do this?"

Peace and Jake pulled Wayne off of Kenneth. He fell back into the chair shell-shocked.

Issy walked in front of Kenneth. The look on his face told her everything she needed to know. She looked up at Ty, fearful. "Play the rest."

Ty pushed play to show the video where Laura pulled her gun out on Kiki. Everyone held their breath, until Laura turned and walked out. The video ended.

A tear dropped down Issy's face. "Where's my daughter Ty?"

Ty turned to Jake. "Take Issy up to my suite."

Naverone, Monique and Peace stood next to the Simmons boys as Ty sat next to Kenneth. "I can't imagine what you are thinking at this moment. What I'm about to ask you to do is extremely difficult. However, I implore you to think of the consequences if you don't."

Kenneth turned to him still shocked.

"Nod if you understand what I'm saying." Kenneth nodded. "Good. I want you to call you daughter. Can you do that?"

He shook his head, "I can't." He ran his hand down his face. "I can't."

"Mr. Simmons," Monique spoke. "I'm a trained CIA agent, Naverone is with the Secret Service. If either of us goes after her, we will kill her."

Kenneth stared at her, disbelief clearly on his face.

"If they don't," Ty spoke calmly, "I will."

"Where's Kendra?"

"You are not going anywhere near her until Laura is apprehended." Ty looked at his watch. "Mr. Simmons I understand this may be a difficult decision for you. It isn't for me. You have one minute to make that call."

Kenneth pulled out his cell phone and dialed a number.

Monique touched her earpiece as she listened to Ned. "He's calling his wife's cell," she relayed to Ty.

Naverone pulled her Magnum and held it to Kenneth's head. "Choose your words very carefully Mr. Simmons.

"Whoa," Martin stepped back. He looked from Naverone to Ty. "You can't let her do this."

"Garland and Martin, leave the room," Wayne instructed, as he walked around to face his father. "Not many men get a second chance. Last time you chose Laura over Kiki. Look at the outcome."

"What's it going to be this time Dad?" Garland asked.

"Max," he said as he held Ty's stare. "It's not good." He hesitated. "Is Laura back?"

Ⓟ

Kenneth walked into the hotel suite with Ty, Monique and the police. Max walked into the sitting area and knew immediately something was wrong. "Kenneth?" She touched his face.

Laura came running out of one of the bedrooms right into her father's arms. "Daddy, I'm so sorry about Kiki," she cried, as she hugged him tightly.

Kenneth, took her arms and gently held her away from him. He looked down at her "Laura," tears began to roll down his face. "Kendra is alive."

He watched as she looked up at him. She then looked over to see Ty, and the others standing in the room. She shook her head and began laughing. "So now what Daddy? Are you going to allow these people to take me away?"

"What?" A shocked Maxine asked, as she pulled her daughter behind her. "What's going on here?"

"Tell her Daddy," Laura laughed, "Tell her what's happening Daddy."

Maxine looked at Laura. "What is wrong with you?"

"More than you would ever be able to comprehend Mother." Laura turned to walk back into the bedroom.

"Don't do that." Monique walked over to her.

Laura looked her up and down, then backhanded her across the face.

Before anyone could take a step, Monique punched Laura in the face, knocking her out. Maxine screamed, then ran over to her daughter who was sprawled out on the floor. "One of you should have whipped her ass as at some point." She motioned to one of the officers to handcuff

Laura. "But no, you were too busy feeling guilty for how she was conceived." She stopped in front of Kenneth. "Did it ever occur to you to attempt to bring the two families together? Of course not, you were too busy thinking about yourself."

"Mr. Simmons." Ty stepped over. "I will not let Laura be held accountable for your sins. There is a facility that will help Laura. I will see to it that she gets the best psychiatric care possible. You, however, will have to answer for your sins."

The officers picked Laura up off the floor. "Kenneth do something," Maxine cried out.

Kenneth fell into the chair retreating into his own world.

Ty turned to a distraught Maxine. "She needs help Max. Get her a good attorney. We'll work together to get her the help she needs." He looked at Kenneth. "You should get a good attorney too." He rubbed her arm and walked out of the hotel room with the officers and Monique.

Maxine stared at the closed door for a long time after the police left with Laura. She'd turned her back on her family to have a life with Kenneth and Laura. Now her baby was gone. All she had left was Kenneth. She turned and looked at him. How pathetic. She walked into the bedroom Laura was occupying then came back out. A dejected Kenneth had not moved when she returned. "I fell in love with you the first time you walked into Crimson," she said as she looked at the floor. "I knew you were married and it was wrong," she laughed, "but you were so brilliant, handsome and charming. God you were charming. It wasn't until later that I realized Issy made you the man you were. When you left her, the man I thought I loved disappeared." She stopped laughing and shook her head.

"Call it stupidity, but one day I thought you would come to love me. It never happened. I knew and Laura knew it too. She was all I had and you let them take her from me." Kenneth never looked up as a single gunshot echoed through the air.

Epilogue

*T*he last two months were a whirlwind of activity for Ty and Kiki. First, a decision had to be made on where they were going to live. Before that decision could be made, her employment had to be determined. After everything that happened, she could not continue with Crimson. With the battle for Crimson Publishing in divorce court with Kenneth and Maxine, there was no telling who was going to end up heading it. Ty didn't care where they lived as long as they were together. He could run his business from anywhere. Since the decision was hers, she chose to live in Virginia, with a second home in Atlanta.

Looking into the mirror at her new image, Kiki exhaled. "Do you think he will like it Mom?"

Issy smiled at her daughter through the mirror. "Ty kissed you when you were funky and dirty. He couldn't care less about all of this." She motioned with her hands at all the clothes Kiki had thrown on the bed preparing for the first family dinner in their new home.

"Would you say that if you were dressing for a date with Jake?"

"Moot point. Jack prefers me with my clothes off."

Kiki covered her ears. "TMI Mommy, TMI." They laughed. Kiki turned from the mirror to face her mother. "Daddy asked about you again."

"No need. That ship sailed with Laura."

"Have you been to see her at the hospital?"

"No," Issy shook her head. "I think you are the one person that can help her heal. Kenneth did some serious damage with his selfishness. After our divorce, he should have made sure Laura had a relationship with her half-brothers and you."

"Well, he's paying the price for his deeds."

Issy laughed. "I could not believe it when Ty told me where Maxine shot him. Karma is a bitch."

Kiki laughed with her. "I'm just thankful he went back to that room."

"I always new Maxine had balls when it came to work, but with Kenny she was weak. I think shooting him in the balls was the best therapy she could have given herself. Hell I should have tried it."

"It's good Monique had friends in the right places, or Max could be in jail right along with Laura."

The two sighed, each with their own thoughts about that night. "You know, I love your father. But I could never be with a man I don't respect. I hope he finds happiness."

"What about you Mommy? Is your happiness with Jake?"

"For the moment, he's doing just fine."

"He's just a few years older than Wayne and you're fifty something," she laughed.

"And everything we use works the same whether I'm fifty something or thirty something."

"Excuse me," Kiki smiled as she stood.

"So, the Rosa woman found this house for you and Ty?" Issy sent a questioning glance at her daughter.

"Yes." she sighed. "I've come to the realization that Ty will always have beautiful women around him, Naverone and her troop, Wendy, Rosa, and now Monique. The only one that matters to him is me. He has proven that."

"Yes, well he definitely has a type."

"What do you mean a type?"

"Every last one of them can kick your ass and that's saying something."

"Let one of them look at him wrong and I'll be the one kicking their azzes." They looked at each other and laughed. "Well, I might think twice about Monique. She looks dangerous."

"I wonder if she's single." She stood to join her daughter, "Wayne needs a woman like her to keep his temper in check."

Kiki began walking out of the room. "I don't mean any harm, but I don't want to see Monique again for a very long time. When she's around that means someone is in danger. I've had enough of that for a lifetime." Looking down at her attire, she asked again. "You think Ty will like this?"

Issy walked beside her daughter shaking her head. "With that outfit on I doubt we will make it out of this house."

Walking down the stairs of her new home Kiki looked down to see the knowing expressions on the faces of TeKaya and Siri. "I knew it would work," a now slimmer TeKaya smiled brightly, as she took pictures of her creation.

"Ty is going to lose his cool." Siri began to laugh. "You are not going to make it out of this house in that outfit."

"That's the same thing I told her," Issy walked past the ladies into the partially furnished family room. She stopped and looked around. "How do I get to the theater room?"

"Through the kitchen, into the hallway on the right," Kiki replied. "I still don't know why we need such a big house."

"It's really not that big," TeKaya said as she checked the pictures on her camera.

"You don't call a house with a ballroom, theater, indoor basketball court and swimming pool, with two kitchens and five bedrooms large?" Siri asked.

TK, looked up from her camera. "See how large you think it is when Ty has his clients over for a party."

"Who's supposed to clean this monster is my concern."

Siri walked towards the spacious kitchen and took a seat at the island. "That you don't have to worry about. If Ty doesn't clean it himself, he will hire a staff that will."

Jason, Eric, Wayne, Martin, Garland, Peace and Jake walked into the kitchen from the hallway that Issy had taken. They stopped when they saw Kiki.

"Whoa," Jake exclaimed. "Oh hell, we are not eating tonight."

"Correction," Eric walked over to Siri laughing. "Ty's not eating tonight, at least not food anyway." Siri smiled up at her husband.

Jason walked over to TK and kissed her. "Ty is going to get his freak on tonight."

"Hey," Wayne yelled. "That's my sister you are talking about." He turned to Kiki. "You need to go back upstairs and put some clothes on."

Garland snickered. "When she goes back upstairs, those clothes are coming off."

"I know that's right." Martin held out his fist, to give Garland a pound.

"I thought y'all were in the theater room watching the game," Kiki said as she ignored her brothers.

"We were, until your mother came into the room and declared it off limits." Jason replied.

"Why?" Kiki asked.

"I have no idea," he replied.

"Where's Ty?" Miriam asked as she walked into the kitchen.

"In his office meeting with Nick Brooks," Kiki replied.

She glanced at her watch. "That meeting should have been over with an hour ago." She started to walk away, then stopped. "Where's the office?"

"On the other side of the living room." Kiki pointed back to where they had come walked from.

"I think this will do," Nick Brooks said as he reviewed the document in his hand. "The merger of Pendleton & Brooks agencies is official."

Ty sat behind his desk in his office. "We agree for now that I remain the primary agent for Jason Whitfield, Jarrett Bryson and Justin Hylton."

"They are your clients." Nick nodded. I don't have an issue with that. The arrangement with Rene Naverone. She will select the location, handle contractors and hire staffing for this exclusive club?"

"Yes, we are silent partners in that venture," Ty explained. "I believe in the long run it's going to be one of the best moves we make. Think about our clientele. Don't you think it's better that we supply them with entertainment, rather than have them patronizing someone else's establishment? This way we can at least control the outcome before it hits the media. "

"The concept is great. The name Enticement concerns me."

Ty laughed. "Wait until you meet the women that will be running it. You'll understand."

Miriam knocked on the partially open door. "Excuse me. Tyrone are you wrapping up?"

The look on her face indicated it was not a question. Nick smiled. "I know that look." He stood, closed his computer, then extended his hand. "I look forward to working with you."

Ty took his new partner's hand. "Same here. I'll walk you out."

"No need," Nick said as he walked towards the door. "It was nice meeting you Ms. Davies. My mother loves you, my father adores you."

"Thank you Nicholas. Be sure to tell both of them hello."

"I will. Have a good day."

Miriam closed the door behind Nick as he walked out of the room. "Five minutes before we get this show going." She took the seat Nick had vacated. "First, your father."

"Mother, you don't have to explain."

"Sit down. Yes I do." Miriam crossed her legs as she waited for Ty to sit. "I don't have to tell you his occupation is dangerous. For that reason, he came to me when your mother decided it was too much for her and asked me if I would take care of you. Well, as Jason's friend you were already a part of our family when he came to us. Pierre and I didn't even think about it, we said yes. Sly asked that we not tell you about his life for safety reasons."

"I know," Ty replied.

"Here's what you don't know. He was the one that took your mother to safety with a new identity and a new life. He loved her enough to let her go." She squirmed a little in the seat before she continued. "I don't want you to be upset with me because I've kept this from you all this time. So, I'm asking for your forgiveness."

Miriam Davies, to his knowledge, had never asked anyone for anything in her life. "You think I'm upset with you?"

"Yes," she replied as dignified as she could.

He stood, walked around to the chair she was sitting in and kissed her on the cheek. "I'm not." Miriam was too stunned to reply, as she looked him up and down. "Don't say a word. Not one word."

"Oh my," she finally laughed out.

"Where is everyone?"

She stood and circled around him smiling. "In the kitchen."

"Is dinner ready?"

She stood there smiling as she took in her son. "I suppose." Her smile disappeared, "You're not doing this in the kitchen."

"No, get everyone into the dining room. I'll be there in a minute."

She walked towards the door looking back. "I have just the right song for this." She began laughing as she walked out of the door.

Ty took the cell phone from his pocket and sent a text message. "Thank you." He then pulled volume three of one of his law review books from the bookshelf and waited for the opening to a small room to appear. Stepping inside, he placed the cell phone on its stand, next to the secured computer on the desk. He smiled at the picture of his mother and father then walked back out of the room.

The document he had prepared for the parole board on LaToya's behalf lay on his desk. Now, all he had to do was get though the next ten minutes and his life would be as it should. He prayed.

"Okay everyone, into the dining room." Miriam walked through the kitchen with her phone in her hand.

"Where's Ty," Kiki asked.

She took Kiki's hand as they walked into the elegantly set dining room, with a serving staff of four standing off to the side. "He's coming."

"This is beautiful," Issy said as she marveled at the table that could easily seat twelve.

"You sit here dear." Miriam, pointed to one end of the table. "You should take a picture of this TeKaya for Kiki.

"I'll get my camera." She ran back to the kitchen as everyone else took their seats.

Suddenly, the song Brick house by the Commodores began to play. After a few beats, Jason and Eric looked at each other and burst out into laughter.

Kiki along with everyone else in the room turned to them wondering what in the hell was going on. Kiki looked behind her as shock gripped her. She slowly stood as Ty, with TeKaya and her camera behind him, walked towards her looking like a God stepping off the cover of Men's Weekly magazine. The swagger with those bowlegs of his was more intense as he approached her dressed in a Yankee jersey tucked inside of a pair of jeans. He was always sexy, this put him over the top. "Damn, you look good in those jeans."

"For he's a brick house," Eric and Jason began singing. "Mighty, mighty, just letting it all hang out." They laughed.

His steps slowed as he focused on the vision known as Kiki, dressed simply in a Yankees thigh high jersey, with a black belt around her waist and thigh high boots that met the end of the jersey. A thought ran through his mind. Shaking it off, he had to concentrate on this moment. Before her, he pulled out a box and opened it.

The solitaire diamond in a platinum setting was brilliant, in the velvet box. The family stared in awe as he bent down on one knee. "Kendra Isadore Simmons would you do me the honor of becoming my wife?"

Kiki stood there shocked, unable to speak as tears came to her eyes. Seconds ticked away as she stared at him. The women in the room discretely dabbed at tears as they watched the couple. Kiki wiped a tear aside. "I can't believe you have on jeans."

Every person in the family room roared with laughter. Miriam and Issy shook their heads at their children. "You got to love them," Miriam laughed.

Ty, was serious. All the laughter in the room did not stop him from sweating. The fact that she loved him and he loved her did not ease his apprehension. She could say no and walk away. Her tear fell on the thumb of the hand that was holding the 1.2 million dollar diamond. He looked at the wet spot on his thumb. It seemed to seep into his skin, travel through his veins and touch his heart, for at that moment all his doubts disappeared.

"Yes."

Taking the ring from the box, he looked around for a place to sit it, as Wayne took it from his hand. Ty thanked him with a nod. He placed the ring on Kiki's finger. Wrapping his arms around her waist, he buried his face in her stomach. His thoughts were right. Without looking back, he put her over his shoulder and stood. "Enjoy your dinner," he said as he walked out of the room. Kiki began laughing uncontrollably.

Upstairs in their bedroom, he dropped her on the bed with a bounce. "You can't man handle me like that Pendleton just because I agreed to marry you."

"Another one of your rules," Ty asked as he pulled his shirt off. "I have a rule for you."

"What's that?" She smiled brightly up at him.

"You can't walk around the house with no under panties with people here."

She sat up on her elbows and laughed. "Haven't you learned yet, there are no rules in love."

He bent to step out of his jeans, and grew hard as steel looking at her legs in those boots. "I have a new rule, no more rules." He threw the jeans aside then ran his hands up her thighs. "Well there is one. No one touches what's mine."

"Is that so?" She pulled the end of the jersey up and stripped out of it, revealing a smooth, chocolate body, with one distinctive mark. "My sentiments, exactly."

Kneeling on the edge of the bed, she was breath taking with nothing on but her thigh high boots. Pride exploded in him. She had given him the ultimate tribute. The P that was once carved in her pubic hair was now a permanent tattoo. He dropped to his knees, gathered her hips in his hands pulling her close and kissed the P.

The look on his face was priceless. "Looks like the Pendleton rule is now in effect," she laughed.

He looked up at her and said one word. "Mine."

CPSIA information can be obtained
at www.ICGtesting.com
Printed in the USA
LVHW051710130120
643457LV00014B/1104/P

9 780980 106688